For my mom and dad, whose love for each other
is stronger than the toughest metal.

ACKNOWLEDGEMENTS

Husband; this one was hard, thanks for being my cheerleader through it all.

Mom, Dad, Mel and Chris, this one is about love, and you all do it incredibly well.

Deb, I have a jar of tears waiting on a shelf for you. I don't think I would've made it through this without you constantly poking fun at me.

Kimberly, you're in a class all your own. Thanks for seeing me through this one.

Nina; it's time to make your own magic.

Jessica, there was a lot of breathing in to a paper bag over this one. You're irreplaceable. I hope you get that.

Shannon you made the outsides so pretty on this one, like you do every single time.

Teeny, you make things look so easy, when really they're pretty darn difficult.

Sarah, thank you for listening and for being so awesome. You're amazing and I'm so glad I have you.

Hustlers, you're made of magic. You have no idea how much you helped me through this one.

Beaver Babes, you make every day better. Thank you for taking a chance on me.

To my Backdoor Babes; Tara, Meghan, Deb and Katherine, you're my constants. I'm so glad I know all of you.

Melanie, you're a special human. I'm glad you're in my world.

Pams, Filets, my Nap girls; 101'ers, my Holiday's and Indies,

Tijan, Susi, Deb, Erika, Katherine, Shalu, Kellie, Ruth, Julia, Melissa, Sarah, Kelly—you keep me sane. Well, sane-ish. Thank you for being my friends, my colleagues, my supporters, my teachers, my cheerleaders and my soft places to land.

My WC crew; you know who you are. Thank you for being with me on this journey. I'm honored to have had all these years with you.

It really is amazing to be part of the indie community. Thank you for embracing me, and for being so incredibly supportive, even when I take you on a different journey.

To all the amazing bloggers and readers who keep traveling this road with me, thank you for letting me change gears and try new things.

This one really is for my Originals. You're the reason I wrote this book. Thank you for your kindness over the years and your dedication. I won't forget where I started.

PROLOGUE

CHRIS

Hot, wet suction and a discordant chilly tickle across my stomach pulled me from sleep. It took a few seconds to figure out what was going on.

"Sorry I woke you."

Sarah, who I'd been seeing for the past six months, followed her insincere statement with the return of her mouth to my very awake cock.

The rest of me took a little longer to shake off the haze.

"Time is it?" I reached out in the dark to touch some part of her. I met damp hair. She must've come directly from the shower.

"Late." She licked up the shaft, making me groan.

The clock on the nightstand told me it was three a.m., in glowing red numbers. Sarah's late arrival wasn't unusual. She worked long hours as a waitress at a strip club just outside the Chicago Loop. Middle-of-the-night visits were sometimes all we could manage. "Don't you have an early class?"

She popped off, but her lips moved against the head as she spoke. "You're worried about what time my class is right now?"

I hooked my hands under her arms and pulled her up, then flipped her over.

"I wasn't done," she complained.

"I think that's my new favorite alarm clock."

Sarah parted her legs so I could fit myself between them. She was so, so naked. I kissed along her neck; her skin was shower-warm and damp. She'd used my body wash, but her hair smelled like the shampoo she kept in my apartment for nights like these—mint and rosemary.

Sarah linked her legs behind my back and smoothed her hands down my arms, over the ink she couldn't see in the dark. She made an impatient noise when I brushed my lips over hers but ignored her invitation for tongue.

"Kiss me." She nipped at my bottom lip.

"You don't want me to rinse with mouthwash? I think I have mints in the nightstand."

She gripped the back of my neck, her fingernails digging in as she fused her mouth to mine. I guess she didn't care about sleep breath.

Sarah was rarely aggressive when it came to sex. She liked things soft and easy most of the time, and she got off on the teasing almost as much as the actual fucking. But not tonight—or this morning, as it were.

She shifted against me, lining everything up. I was still half foggy from being woken by a blow job.

I pulled back, which wasn't easy with the way she was latched on to my neck and my tongue. "Take it easy, sugar."

"I missed you." Her fingers danced across my cheek. "I want you."

"You got me. I'm right here."

Sarah couldn't seem to decide what she wanted to do with her hands. They were in my hair, down my back, grabbing my ass as she lifted her hips and I slid low. She was ready with the condom before I could protest again and slow us down.

I stopped fighting what she wanted. It'd been a week since we'd seen each other. If she didn't have to leave too early in the morning, we could have a slower second round.

When she pushed on my chest, I rolled to the side and lay down beside her. Sarah's wet hair swept across my neck as she straddled my hips. It was too dark to see the soft, delicate features of her face as she rolled on the condom and took me inside. She braced her palms on my chest as she rode me, swiveling her hips, grinding hard until she came. She was nearly silent, emitting only the faintest moans, barely audible over the sound of the fan running in the corner of my room. I knew she was coming only by the way her rhythm faltered and her nails dug into my skin.

Once she had what she needed, she let me take over. I moved her onto her back, rolling my hips without urgency. My eyes had adjusted to the lack of light. The blackout shades kept the glow of the streetlights outside and residents of the neighboring apartment building from seeing things they shouldn't.

"Give me your mouth, baby," I murmured in her ear.

Her nose brushed across my cheek, lips following the same trail until I caught her mouth with mine again. I stroked against her tongue and she arched, arms and legs wrapped tightly around me again. I followed the long, toned line of her left thigh until I reached her knee. Pulling it higher, I tucked her leg against my ribs so I could go deeper without changing the tempo.

"Chris." Sarah's whimper was followed by a shudder. Her fingertips dragged soft down the side of my face, close to our touching lips.

"You coming again?"

She nodded and pressed her face into my neck, her soft moan muffled by my skin. It didn't take me long to come after that.

Afterward, Sarah snuggled into my side and stayed there, which was also unusual. Typically I'd get a couple minutes of closeness out of her, and then she'd complain about being hot and move away. But not tonight. She kept her head on my chest and traced the lines of my sleeve until I fell asleep.

I woke a few hours later to the feel of fingers tickling my arm. I turned to find Sarah lying on her side, her pale blond hair fanned out across the pillow. She snatched her hand away and pressed her knuckles to her mouth. Her sea blue eyes were red rimmed, like she needed more sleep. She closed them and inched closer, her whole body pressing against me before her lips connected with the ink on my shoulder.

I pushed unruly blond away from her forehead, then traced the heart shape of her face. Sarah nuzzled her cheek against my arm for a few seconds, a shuddery sigh warming my skin.

"You got time for some morning lovin'?" I rasped, my voice less awake than the rest of me, just like it had been last night, or much earlier this morning.

"I need the bathroom." She rolled away and threw off the covers. The room was still mostly dark, but I could make out her willowy silhouette as she tiptoed across the room, naked, and slipped out the bedroom door.

I checked the time. It was only seven. She had to be exhausted, but I assumed her going to the bathroom meant morning sex was on the menu. Priorities and all.

Except when she returned ten minutes later, she was fully dressed. Her white blouse was crisp and buttoned almost to her throat. She'd pulled her long hair up into a bun, the style too severe for her pretty face.

I folded an arm behind my head. "Not getting back into bed with me?"

She traced the edge of the footboard, her head bowed. "I can't. I have class."

"Wanna come give me a kiss goodbye?"

Her voice was a whisper I had to strain to hear. "I think we need to take a break."

I hit the light on the nightstand so I could see her better. "What kinda break you talking about?"

"My internship starts soon. I'll be working a lot of hours. At both jobs. I'm exhausted, and I think something's got to give." Her voice wavered, as if she were on the verge of tears.

The conversation wasn't unexpected. Of course I'd be the something she was ready to give up. I'd known this day was coming, eventually, since the moment she'd agreed to go out with me. Still, I stared at her for a few long seconds, trying to see the motivation that pushed her to this decision now.

Maybe she'd finally realized she was too good for me—that

she was out of my league and could find someone better, someone who could give her the things I couldn't. Sarah deserved a nice life with a pretty house and a fancy car she didn't have to worry about. I wasn't that guy.

For her, it seemed I was mostly a middle-of-the-night booty call, which was ironic because for years I'd been the one to pull that move. I guess it was about time I experienced it from the other side.

"You want to call it quits?" I asked.

She lifted one slight shoulder, still tracing imaginary lines on the footboard.

"So last night was the goodbye fuck and the see-you-later blow job?" That would definitely explain the aggression.

"We barely see each other." She swiped at her eye with her pinkie before she lifted her head, but her gaze didn't quite meet mine. "It's not going to get better once I start my internship."

As much as I didn't want to admit it, she had a point. We'd been treading water for months now; it was only a matter of time before we sank. "You're right. It probably won't."

"I'm sorry, Chris. I need to stay focused on school. Maybe after it's over, when things settle down again..."

"Yeah. I don't know about that." I had my doubts that Sarah would want to keep doing this with me once she'd had a break. One of the guys in her program would jump all over her being single, and she'd see me for the mistake I'd been all along. Sarah and I weren't meant to be permanent, and this was exactly the reminder I needed. "You gotta do you, sugar."

She bowed her head, fingers fluttering up to cover her eyes. Her back expanded in a deep inhale. On the exhale she dropped her hands and squared her shoulders, but her next statement still came out a question. "I'll leave your key on the counter."

"Sure. If that's what you want to do."

She gave one final nod before she left.

The emptiness was a lot bigger than I'd expected it to be.

ONE

CHRIS

Two weeks later

Inked Armor was humming today, and not just with the sound of tattoo machines. Waiting clients sat in the chairs by the windows, leafing through ink magazines and chatting with the person they'd brought along for the ride. College girls colluded at the body jewelry case, deciding what kind of piercing would have the most benefits.

In the five years since we'd opened the shop, it had never been this busy. And ultimately that was a good thing, though my business partner, Hayden Stryker, probably joined me in wishing it was strictly due to our mind-blowing skills and artistry. Instead, a few months back we'd gleaned quite a bit of unintentional media attention.

Hayden had been seventeen when his parents were murdered. He'd been the one to find them shot in their own bedroom when he came home three hours after curfew. But he'd never known why they were killed, or who killed them. Then after seven years, last winter Hayden had finally—and rather publicly—gotten the answers he was looking for.

The trial hadn't lasted long, thank Christ, but I was still trying to get my head around its aftermath.

I'd met Hayden not long before his parents died. Over the years he'd become my family, and his pain was mine. He'd been into piercings more than ink when we were first introduced, so I hadn't gotten to know him until Damen—the guy who ran Art Addicts, the shop where I'd worked at the time—took him on as an apprentice. While the shop had been legit, Damen had also had some criminal leanings, including a drugs-and-prostitution ring he ran at The Dollhouse, a local strip club. But we'd needed the opportunity and the steady pay, so we kept our heads down. But time had given us perspective we hadn't had then. My choices had been limited, and my focus had been on survival. Damen had taken me in when I had nowhere else to go.

Anyway, along with the horror of reliving it all and the sheer emotional overload of finally understanding what had happened, the trial and its media coverage had yielded Inked Armor a schedule booked solid with appointments made months in advance.

Recently, a local pro hockey player and some of his teammates had come in for tattoos, so it was even crazier that day. Not that I could complain. Much. Our paychecks were nicely padded, and Inked Armor had earned some serious recognition in the tattooing community. After all the shit we'd dealt with, it was good to have some positive outcomes.

The door tinkled with the arrival of a group of girls who headed straight for the jewelry counter. Lisa, the shop piercer and bookkeeper sometimes had to schedule the piercings a couple of days in advance depending on how busy we were.

My client, Eric, watched them swarm the jewelry case. "Does it ever slow down in here?"

"Not lately. You know how it is. We've been booked pretty solid with summer coming." This time of year was always busy—people wanting to add art they could display during shorts and T-shirt weather—but this far surpassed that.

"Oh I get it. I would've been in here a month ago if I could've gotten an appointment."

"Lisa's already scheduled your next two sessions, so we just have to make sure the dates work for you."

"I'll make 'em work if I have to."

I'd overbooked today, leaving me no time between clients.

When this session was over, the next one would take me to closing. The less free time I had these days, the better.

My phone buzzed in my pants, and my automatic response was to check the apartments across the street since my hands were busy with the needles.

From Inked Armor's front window I had a perfect view of the converted house across the street, which boasted a café and bookshop at street level and two apartments on the second floor. Sarah lived in the one on the right. I hadn't seen her up close since she'd left my apartment two weeks ago. Her exit from my bed and my life continued to leave a much bigger void than I'd expected.

Prior to fourteen mornings ago, a buzz in my pants had usually meant a message from Sarah. And often I'd see her silhouette in the window, especially if she was waiting for me to drop by when I had a break between clients.

As I looked there now, the curtain in her window fluttered with movement, though if it was Sarah, she clearly didn't want to be seen. That had been happening a lot lately—for the past two weeks, to be more specific. But the messages I'd sent her remained unanswered, so I had my doubts this latest text was her looking to talk, unless she'd changed her mind about me recently.

The apartment window to the left of hers remained dark, the blinds pulled shut. The space was currently unrented. Hayden's girlfriend, Tenley, used to live there, but she'd moved into his house. Hayden had hung up his bachelor balls shortly after he met her, and they'd settled into domesticated stability. They even had a cat, which he'd named after Tee. I made fun of him often, and he didn't give a shit.

I doubted Tee's old apartment would remain vacant for long, considering the prime location near DePaul University. Some student would take it over soon. I'd entertained moving there myself before me and Sarah went on the outs. It would be totally convenient for work. But now that would make things even more awkward. Besides, rent was cheap where I lived, and moving my shit would be a pain in the ass. At least those were the excuses I went with.

I turned back to the art I was outlining, pausing before I started a new line of ink. "You need a break or anything? Water?"

"Nah, I'm good to keep going."

In the four hours he'd been here I'd only stopped once. When the design was complete, it would span his entire back. Today we were finishing the basic outline and some of the minor detail. I loved working on the Celtic designs. The intricacy and the detail allowed me to get lost in the art for hours. Except not right now, because I couldn't seem to manage my divided attention, and that was because of Sarah.

I wasn't sure why this was such a big deal for me. I was used to not getting what I wanted. Over the years it had been a pretty common occurrence. Anything remotely good in my life was fairly fleeting, and Sarah was a master's student in a business program. Her tuition cost more than my yearly salary, based on the research I'd done. Her starting wage after she graduated would likely be double what I made in any given year, even one as good as this.

I'd met Sarah at The Dollhouse, back before it had been shut down. She'd only ever been a waitress there, never up on the stage or pulled into the darker side of the industry. But even serving drinks was no picnic since most of those assholes couldn't keep their hands or their comments to themselves. It was almost as bad as getting naked and swinging from a pole.

The Sanctuary—Sarah's current place of employment— boasted an elite staff and a classy vibe, but its polished veneer was just that: a false face. It might've seemed better than The Dollhouse, but I had a feeling underneath the clean exterior was a dark and dirty interior Sarah wasn't talking to me about.

And it hadn't ever been anything I'd pushed to hear. Encouraging her to talk about it had meant she might feel like asking me questions about my own history, and that wasn't a place I'd wanted to go with her. We'd kept things pretty light, our protective walls firmly in place, which was probably why we lasted as long as we did.

I'd always figured if there was a real issue, she'd say something.

But maybe I'd been wrong about that, just like I'd been wrong about predicting the end of this thing we'd had going.

Anyway, Sarah's work wardrobe might currently consist of skimpy dresses, but she'd soon be trashing those for the kind of buttoned-up outfit she'd been wearing that morning two weeks ago. This was just another sign that Sarah and I were on different paths, moving in opposite directions. My uniform wasn't going to change; I'd still be wearing jeans and a T-shirt bearing the Inked Armor logo a few years from now.

I swiped at the ink with a damp cloth, wiping the site clean to make sure the lines were clear before I continued. "We're getting close. Another ten and you can check it out."

Eric rolled his neck. He had to be stiff from sitting in the same position for so long. "Looking forward to it."

I glanced briefly at the girls who had relocated to couches while they filled out body-piercing paperwork. They looked like college students. One of them gave me a flirty smile, which I returned before refocusing on the ink. I was glad I was too busy to be chatted up, considering where my mind was these days.

I hadn't been under any illusion that what Sarah and I had was going to turn serious. Except based on the way I was dealing with her exit, it kind of had anyway. At least on my end. I'd gotten used to her nearly daily messages. I'd enjoyed the mornings I woke up with her in my bed.

And I'd wondered what it would be like if that turned into *every* morning. Which was fucking stupid. Because deep down I knew I was a temporary fixture in her life. I was the second-hand sofa college students bought, trashed for a while, and later traded in for a nicer one.

Sarah was destined to upgrade.

The thing was, since she'd broken things off, she'd also stopped talking to some of our mutual friends. She and Lisa had been close, but Lisa said her texts and phone calls to Sarah had gone mostly unanswered over the past two weeks. I couldn't decide whether it was Sarah feeling weird about talking to Lisa since I worked with her, or more than that. My gut told me it was the latter.

The more I thought about it—obsessed, really—the more I questioned whether Sarah's reason for walking was honestly her internship, or if there had been something else going on. The way it went down hadn't sat right with me. The lack of warning was part of the problem. There'd been no awkward lead up, no signs things were about to take a shit, and I was usually pretty good at predicting when the bottom was going to fall out.

I dipped the needle into black ink and touched up a few lines.

I hoped Sarah's silence would end eventually, particularly where Lisa was concerned. Just because we weren't middle-of-the-night fucking any more didn't mean she had to cut all ties with the people she'd gotten close to. And honestly, Lisa was just as concerned as I was about Sarah's sudden silence.

Lisa had once worked at The Dollhouse too, and her past experiences, combined with what had come out about the inner workings of those places during the recent trial, were good reason to worry.

I put the finishing touches on the outline and set down my tattoo machine. "All right, man, that's it. Wanna take a look?"

"Fucking right." He sat up stiffly, stretching his arms over his head. I followed him to the three-way mirror, my stomach tightening a little while I waited for his approval.

He clapped me on the shoulder. "This is unreal. Thanks, man."

Hayden came over to check it out while I was dressing the tattoo and reviewing aftercare. Then we checked the dates on Eric's next two sessions before he left happy, and probably sore.

I still had a few minutes before my next client, so I checked my messages. There were two. Neither was from Sarah.

These were from Candy, a chick I used to date long before Sarah and I started warming each other's beds. I doubted it was a coincidence that she'd started messaging me this week, wanting to get together for a drink.

It was pretty clear she had ulterior motives, so I'd put her off, saying I was busy, but her persistence was wearing me down—though not because I wanted, or needed, a hook up. I didn't. And especially not with her. Still, over the past few days, Candy's messages had grown progressively more insistent. Her most recent informed me that she had some information I might want. It was hard not to wonder who or what it pertained to.

Things with Candy hadn't ended well. I'd met her while she was working at The Dollhouse, and she'd been in the same position as Sarah and Lisa—just serving drinks, not getting up on stage. But the slope was slippery, and Candy found the money to be a lot better when she was taking her clothes off and grinding on the pole.

Then she started hitting the back rooms after sets for private dances. It didn't take long to turn into fucking. Between that and the drugs I'd been working hard to stay away from, I couldn't deal, so I bailed.

Normally I wouldn't even entertain the idea of seeing her, for all of the previously mentioned reasons—but Candy now worked at The Sanctuary with Sarah. I could only guess what the information might be, and that was driving me crazy. Since I wasn't going to get anything out of Sarah directly, it might not hurt to go in through the back door.

Candy had been pissed when I started seeing Sarah, to the point that she'd made life miserable for her at the club—although Sarah had downplayed it, as she was prone to doing. I suspected that if I agreed to see Candy, she'd rub it in Sarah's face. It wasn't the nicest way to go about things, and I wasn't one to play games, but any reaction right now was better than no reaction at all. If I could piss Sarah off enough, maybe she'd talk to me. Shady and shitty, but I needed some answers, and I wanted to make sure she was okay.

I needed to keep tabs on her until she was out of that place for good. We might not be meant for the long haul, but I didn't want her pulled down into a lifestyle that could turn her into another Candy.

I stared at Candy's messages for a few more seconds before I hit her back. Once I did, my phone beeped right away, asking if tomorrow would work. Before I replied, I scrolled through my messages from Sarah. Or mostly my messages to Sarah, because the last one I'd gotten from her was the night before she broke it off, telling me how she couldn't wait to fight me for sheets.

I typed out a message to Candy and hit send. Her reply was the kind I used to like getting from Sarah, with all the heart and smiley face emoticons. I had a hard time believing Candy's was sincere, though.

Lisa's arm came around my shoulder, her lavender hair tickling my cheek. Lisa was small, narrow lines filled out by *Alice in Wonderland* dresses and combat boots. Her hair was always some pale rainbow shade. "Your next appointment's in fifteen. You need to set up."

She snatched my phone before I could shut it down and jumped out of reach when I grabbed for it.

"What're you doing?" I snapped.

"What am I doing? What're you doing?" She held up my phone, pointing to the contact. "We need to talk."

"I gotta set up."

Lisa dug her nails into my arm and pulled me out of my chair. I could've argued, but then I'd draw more attention our way. Hayden or Jamie—the other artist in the shop and Lisa's fiancé—might notice and want to know what was going on. Neither would approve of me spending time with Candy.

I followed her to the storage room. She pushed me inside and closed the door. "Seriously, Chris? *Candy?*"

"It's not what you think."

She crossed her arms over her chest. "So you're not going for coffee tomorrow morning. I read that wrong?" Lisa knew Candy only too well, having worked with her and been around us when Candy and I were dating.

"I'm trying to get information. Sarah won't talk to me."

"There are better ways to do that than through Candy."

"Really? 'Cause I'm all outta options right now."

"Just call her."

I slapped my own forehead. "Why didn't I think of that?"

Lisa gave me one of her looks.

"I've even left messages. She won't respond. The only thing I haven't done is go to her work, and that's not happening, 'cause I'm not real interested in revisiting my juvie days, and I have a feeling that's what's going down if I go there."

"And you think Candy's going to tell you what's going on? When Sarah finds out she's going to freak."

I moved the rolls of paper towels so they were lined up straight. Usually that was Hayden's habit, but I needed to do something with my hands.

"Enough that she'll talk to me?"

"That's your motivation? Push Sarah's buttons? That could backfire on you pretty bad."

"Candy says she has information I might want."

"Candy's a manipulative bitch."

"I know, but something's not right."

"You don't think Sarah's dancing, do you?"

"I don't fucking know. It's a logical conclusion, isn't it? One second she's all excited about a sleepover, comes over and rides me like I'm a goddamn theme park, and the next morning she tells me we can't see each other any more. Then she pretty much stops talking to all of us."

Lisa fiddled with the piercing above her lip. "I invited her to hang out with me and Tenley later this week."

"What? Why didn't you tell me?" Jesus. I hated how pissed off I sounded. "Wait. Let me guess; she didn't want me to know."

"Honestly, I called her last night and managed to get her on the phone. I seriously didn't think she was going to say yes, but she did. I'm crossing my fingers she doesn't bail." She put a hand on my forearm. "I won't hide things from you. If she shares something I think you need to know, I'll tell you, even if it's something you won't want to hear."

I tapped the space between my eyes. I was gonna have one hell of a headache by the end of the day. "If she's on the pole, it's a good thing she ended things, 'cause I'm not going down that road again."

"But you'll go out for coffee with Candy?"

"It's not the same. I'm only seeing her to get information." I changed the subject. My relationship with Candy wasn't a favorite topic, and I wanted details from Lisa. "What are you doing with Sarah?"

"We're getting together with Tenley. Girl's night kind of thing. It took a lot of persuading to get her to agree. She feels awkward."

"She said that?"

"Not in so many words."

"Right." It felt like a kick in the balls that Sarah would make time for Tee and Lisa, but when it came to quitting me, she'd delivered a one-paragraph monologue, and then cut out.

My phone buzzed again with another message from Candy. She wanted me to pick her up in the morning. I let her know I'd meet her there since I had a few errands to run. I knew how Candy worked. If I came to get her, she'd want me to come up to her apartment, and that would lead to situations I wasn't interested in entertaining.

I didn't think I was at risk of getting involved with her again, but sometimes the head on my shoulders didn't work all that well. I'd give myself all the help I could.

TWO

CHRIS

The next morning I met Candy at a diner a few blocks from my apartment. I was late, having debated canceling. I'd tried messaging Sarah last night, to see if she would respond, but as usual, I got nothing.

Candy was already sitting at a table for two in the back of the dingy diner. She held a coffee cup with a chip in the handle and smiled when she saw me. She stood, revealing a pair of old jeans and a tight, worn top. She'd rounded out the look with stripper heels. I guess to dress it up. She looked a lot like her outfit—older, worn out. I wondered if she saw the same when she looked at me.

"Hey. I'm so glad this worked." Her smile was warm but strained as she wrapped her arms around my waist.

I was over six feet, and she was maybe five-five, so the top of her head barely brushed my chin, even with the heels.

She was thin, maybe a little thinner than I remembered, or maybe I'd just been used to Sarah's longer, willowy frame. Candy smelled like stale cigarettes and perfume. She clearly hadn't given up her vices.

"It's good to see you," I said, sort of meaning it as I slid into the chair across from her.

"You look great." Her smile was almost shy.

I didn't buy it. Her job was acting. She'd never been shy with me. Coy? Sure. Devious? Definitely. But not shy.

Sarah, on the other hand, could pull off shy and mean it. She'd been full of angry fire when I'd first asked her out, basically telling me to fuck off. When she'd finally agreed, she'd been this sweet, sexy, shy girl who wore jeans and oversized shirts, and insisted we go to a juice bar because, as she'd told me, there was no way she was drinking alcohol with me.

I hadn't argued, just glad she'd finally agreed to a date. And I'd been hooked after one evening. Which was exactly why I now sat here, across from a woman who had never understood why I wasn't okay with her screwing other guys for money when she was supposed to be with me.

"You look good, too," I finally said, realizing I hadn't responded to her compliment.

Now that I was sitting down and could have a closer look, she didn't look good at all. Her blond hair had been bleached until it was almost white, like Sarah's, though Sarah's was naturally pale. Candy had also added extensions, but they weren't quite the same color, so it was obvious the longer hair wasn't hers. Dark liner accentuated the circles under her eyes.

I flipped over my coffee mug as the waitress came by. She filled it and topped off Candy's.

"You hungry?" she asked. "Want something to eat?"

Candy shook her head, eyeing the waitress who was eyeing me.

"You sure? I'm gonna eat something." I looked to the waitress. "You got any specials?"

She listed a few options, including an omelet and eggs Benedict. I doubted the eggs Benny here would be any good, so I opted for bacon and eggs. Candy ordered the same with little persuasion.

Sitting across from her brought back all my memories of The Dollhouse and the people who came with it. She'd been a witness at the trial, but her testimony hadn't carried much weight, considering all the narcotics she'd tested positive for. I wasn't sure she'd been able to give those up, judging from the look of her.

I started with basic conversation to fill the silence. "How's work?"

"Same old, same old, just with a different club and a different stage." She dumped two packets of sugar into her cup. "How 'bout you?"

"Keeping busy."

"I heard Inked Armor is doing real good. I should come in and get some work done or something."

"We're making appointments for a few months out now. The summer is pretty much booked solid."

"Wow. That's good. That's great."

"You doing okay these days? Outside of work?" I asked.

Candy shrugged. "Sure. I moved a few months back. Got an apartment without a roommate."

"That's good." Fuck. This was painful.

"Yeah. You remember Trina, right?"

I thought Hayden had hooked up with her a couple of times. Back before Tee, of course. I nodded.

"She was always stealing my money and stuff. This is better. I think my new place is close to yours."

"Oh yeah, where abouts?" I wondered how much more chitchat I had to endure before I could ask her questions about Sarah.

"Near Ashland and Roosevelt. It's decent. Got a balcony and everything."

"That's great. Sounds real nice." That was definitely close to me. Probably closer than I'd like.

"It is. You still living in the same apartment?"

"Yeah. For now. I've been thinking about moving closer to Inked Armor," I lied.

"Oh. That's too bad." She looked down at the empty packet of sugar she had rolled and unrolled. Her expression was all contrived innocence when she asked, "Doesn't Sarah live close to Inked Armor?"

"Yeah. Across the street." I rearranged my knife and fork, waiting.

"I guess that's convenient," she muttered.

"It was."

"Was?" Her eyes went wide with fake shock.

It took a lot not to sigh at how obvious she was being. "We're not seeing each other anymore."

She touched my hand. "I'm sorry. I know you liked her."

I pulled away and took a sip of my coffee. It tasted burned and shitty. Nothing like the coffee from Serendipity, Hayden's aunt's little shop across the street from Inked Armor. "Yeah, well, some things just don't work out."

"Well, I can't say I'm surprised. It was only a matter of time." She flipped her hair over her shoulder.

I set my coffee down. "What was only a matter of time?"

"We all cave at some point, Chris."

"What're you talking about?" The waitress came by with our food, putting the conversation on hold. Candy got busy with her silverware, keeping her eyes averted.

"Candy?"

She glanced up. "Huh?"

"Wanna answer that question?"

She bit the corner of a piece of buttered toast. The restless tap of her foot made the table jiggle. "You broke it off with her, right?"

I pushed my plate away and leaned back in my chair, having caught her in a lie. "I thought you were surprised about that."

"There were some rumors. You can never be sure what's true and what's not."

"So that's why I'm here? So you can get confirmation on whether I'm still fucking Sarah?"

"Is that all it was? Were you just fucking her, Chris? Seemed like a lot more than that."

Candy was playing games like she always did. That was another reason things never worked between us. She liked the drama.

"What does it even matter? Just answer the question. What do you mean we all cave?"

Candy knew me well enough to back off. This time she gave me a straightish answer. "I figured it was like what happened with you and me. You couldn't deal with her job being what it is."

"Sarah's job and yours are not the same. She serves people

drinks. You fuck people for money. It was the lying and the getting into bed with me smelling like someone else's dick that was our problem."

Candy gave me a hard look. "Jesus, Chris, you're a damn hypocrite. I seem to remember you spending time in the back rooms with an awful lot of girls when I first met you, and I know for a fact you weren't just getting private lap dances."

I looked around the busy, noisy restaurant. The couple beside us had definitely overheard, based on their shocked expressions. They turned away quickly, eyes on their food instead of us.

I could imagine what they saw: the strung-out stripper and the tatted-up loser in worn jeans and beat-up shoes. We were a perfect pair, a few steps away from the bottom of the barrel. If it had been Sarah sitting across from me, ivory skinned and effortlessly beautiful in her blouses and dress pants, people would've wondered how the hell I'd managed to trick her into being with me. Even I'd wondered on more than one occasion, and felt guilty about pursuing her. For now I wanted to be the one to take care of her until she ended up with someone worthy of her.

I lowered my voice. "When I was with you, I was only with *you*."

"Aren't you the hero," she bit back.

"Not even a little bit. But serving drinks to assholes and fucking them isn't the same thing, and you know it."

I was beginning to regret this breakfast. Rehashing all the shit between us wasn't what I needed. It made me question whether I should want to keep my place in Sarah's life, even if it was just to make sure she wasn't making worse decisions than sleeping with me. My past wasn't pretty, and nothing I did to make my future better would ever erase the things I'd done. If Sarah and I did get back together, I'd still shield her from who I'd been before Hayden brought me into Inked Armor and saved me from a life of poverty and debauchery—or more of that than I'd already had. I'd rotated through a lot of the girls at The Dollhouse for the same reason I think Sarah finally went out with me—being with me was often a better option than the perceived alternative.

Candy poked at an egg with her toast until the yolk broke and bright yellow ran out the side. "I've never been good at saying no to the drugs, and you know how Damen was, always ready to provide for the right price."

"The Sanctuary's better though, right?"

Candy laughed. "At first it was. Right after The Dollhouse got shut down everyone was playing straight, but it's been a while. People get lax. Xander's good at keeping up a clean front."

I scrubbed a hand over my face. Xander was the manager and majority owner of The Sanctuary. Sarah couldn't stand him, and neither could I. I wasn't allowed in the club when she was working, because according to Xander, it impacted her ability to do her job. He wasn't wrong.

"So The Sanctuary's as bad as The Dollhouse was?" I asked, pushing for more information.

"The money's better, so that's something."

She was still playing her game.

Balling up my napkin, I tossed it on the table. "This was a bad idea."

Candy grabbed my hand before I could get up. "I didn't mean to make you upset. Look, Chris, I just figured maybe you ended things with Sarah 'cause of whatever deals she's been making with Xander."

Now she had my attention. "Deals?"

I didn't want to think about the kinds of things those girls did for that asshole.

"Explain, please."

"Maybe *deals* is the wrong word. It's just gossip, so I don't know what's true, but she was serving left stage a couple of weeks ago. I guess it was right around the same time you stopped seeing her. I figured one had to do with the other."

"Left stage, huh? Just like The Dollhouse?"

Candy gave me a piteous look. "It never changes, Chris."

The roll in my stomach had become a heave. The unspoken rule was that the girls dancing or serving closest to the private rooms off to the left, hidden by the tables at the back of the club, were available for additional services. For the right amount of money, and often the right type of drug, anything could be bought.

Back when I'd been apprenticing with Damen at Art Addicts, I'd had privileges at The Dollhouse. I'd had a free pass to whatever and whoever I wanted, whenever I wanted. It was pretty fucking twisted how that place worked.

I'd also lived in a house Damen had set up, and some of the girls rented rooms from him. It was cheap, and there hadn't been a lot of boundaries. I'd been seventeen and surrounded by sin. My perceived innocence had been something a lot of the girls wanted to hold on to. I'd been someone to try to save, or to corrupt, depending on the person.

Then as I got older, I'd remained the preferred option because even though emotions weren't involved, I was always safe. I was always good to whoever I was with, and the girls knew that.

Candy had been a waitress back then, not yet tainted by the lifestyle she now found herself caught in. I'd decided I wanted her, and I gave up everyone else so I could be with just her. But I couldn't give her what Damen could: numbness and lots of extra money to pay for her nightly chemical lobotomy.

I didn't want to believe Sarah had fallen into that trap. She was strong willed, smart, and she'd managed to stay off the pole so far. But I also knew Xander had been pushing her to get up on the stage. That had been my main concern about her staying there, and I'd used Candy's downward spiral as an example of how quickly things could change. But Sarah had assured me she was only staying until she finished school. Still, no matter her bigger plans, once she stepped over that line, it would be impossible to come back. Sitting across from Candy, I could see exactly how right I'd been about that.

The lines weren't blurred at that point; they were erased.

I didn't want to ask the question, but I had to, because I needed the answer more than I needed the illusion. "Has she been in the private rooms?"

Candy shook her head. She'd started ripping up her napkin. "I don't know about that."

"You don't know or you don't want to say?"

"I honestly don't know. I figured if you stopped seeing her, there had to be some good reason, especially with how Xander treats her different than the other girls who waitress."

"Different how?" I pressed.

"I don't know how to explain it."

"Well, try, please." My patience was thinning. All the worst possible scenarios ran through my head, and each ended with Sarah being screwed by someone other than me, possibly her asshole boss. If I'd been under any misapprehension about my feelings for Sarah, there was no denying it now. I'd managed to fall for a woman I didn't deserve, but wanted to.

I wanted to commit murder at the thought of Xander or anyone else's hands on Sarah. I wanted to chop her boss's fingers off and shove them up his ass. Which was exceedingly violent, even for me.

"Oh God," Candy whispered.

"What?"

"You're in love with her."

"What're you talking about?"

"You love her." Her brown eyes, colored blue with contacts, went wide and watery. "What is it about her? Why didn't you ever feel like that about me?"

"Shit, Candy, I don't know. I was young. It was years ago." I gestured between us. "A lot has changed. How I feel about Sarah isn't relevant, and you're skirting the question. How is Xander different with her?"

"He's—" Candy poked at her yolk some more with her toast, watching as the yellow liquid seeped into her hash browns. "Protective," she finally said.

"Protective how?"

"It's no secret he wants her on the stage. Of all the girls, she's the one he's been pushing the most. I think he puts up with crap from her that he wouldn't from other girls 'cause he knows she'd bring in mad bank. Like, she gets bitchy with him, and usually that would land a girl on left stage to teach her a lesson 'cause those guys get all righteous and touchy, even before they put money out. But he hasn't done that with Sarah—until that one time two weeks ago. I don't know. It seems like something's going on. Maybe he's finally getting to her."

I leaned back in my chair, observing Candy's mannerisms. I couldn't decide on her motive. "Why are you telling me this?"

"I just thought you should know." She stuffed a forkful of egg into her mouth.

"So you're trying to be nice?"

She shrugged and covered her mouth with her hand instead of swallowing before she answered. "I figured it would be good information to have, in case you decided you wanted to get back together with her."

"She's the one who broke it off," I said, setting her straight. "I'm pretty sure she's not interested in changing that, so that's not likely."

She dropped her hand. "Oh. I didn't know."

"Well, you and Sarah aren't exactly friendly with each other, right?" I checked the time on my phone. I still had a while before my first appointment, but I was pretty much done here. "I gotta head to the shop."

"But you haven't eaten anything." Candy gestured to my untouched plate.

"I don't have much of an appetite right now."

Candy put her hand on my arm. "I didn't mean to upset you."

"What did you think was going to happen when you told me the chick I've been seeing is probably screwing other people for money?"

"It's just rumors, Chris."

"So why bother telling me at all? Unless there's more you're not saying."

Candy bowed her head so I couldn't see her expression. It was hard to know how much of this was an act.

"Has Sarah gotten into the drugs?" I asked.

Sarah worked insane hours that she had to balance with school. It wasn't much of a leap for her to pop uppers to manage her exhaustion. I knew she'd been worried about the demands of her internship and her job.

"Maybe? I don't know. They're kinda hard to avoid."

This conversation was turning into a circle jerk. When the waitress passed us again, I asked for the check.

"Can we get takeout boxes?" Candy asked.

I was about to say I didn't need one, but that would be a waste, even if cold eggs were a poor excuse for a meal. As a kid there often hadn't been enough food at my house, either because we hadn't had the money, or because my mom hadn't had time to get to the store. Often it was both. As a result, I tried not to be wasteful.

Candy finished her eggs before the waitress returned with boxes and the bill. I passed her the containers and pulled out my wallet.

"You don't have to get this." She didn't make a move for her purse.

"It's on me."

She gave me a small smile. "Thanks. I caught some trouble with Xander last week and he's cut my shifts back."

"What kind of trouble?" I tossed a couple of bills on the table, covering the check and leaving a decent tip.

"I did something I shouldn't have behind his back. He's just trying to teach me a lesson like he does. Ain't nothing I haven't learned before." She sounded bitter. Candy transferred the remnants of her toast and hash browns into the Styrofoam container. Then she did the same with mine.

We left the restaurant. The morning was warming up, promising to turn into a nice day. Outside the dimly lit diner, Candy looked even more worn out, the shadows under her eyes accented by her heavy makeup.

"Still on a bike?" Candy observed when I stopped at the Kawasaki and picked up my helmet.

"Yup. Where's your ride?" I glanced down the street.

Candy dropped her head, kicking at a stone close to her toe. "My wheels got confiscated."

"Confiscated? You get a DUI or something?"

"No. Nothing like that."

"You park in a bad spot?"

"Xander was leasing me a car, but when I pissed him off, he took it back. It's gonna take a bit to earn it again."

Jesus. She sounded like a scolded kid who'd had her Xbox taken away. "What the hell is he leasing you a car for?"

"Perks for bringing in big bank."

"For fuck's sake, Candy. What does earning it back entail?"

"Nothing you wanna hear about."

I scratched the back of my neck. "You should get outta there."

Candy regarded me sadly. "I shoulda gotten out of there when I had something worth getting out for."

"You gotta get out for you, not any other reason."

"Maybe if I had you again, I'd be able to get clean and get a real job." She brushed my knuckles with her fingers.

I stuffed my hands in my pockets. "That's not gonna happen."

"Because you're in love with Sarah."

"Because we've already been down that road, and I'm not willing to go there again."

"I know. I'm sorry. I shouldn't have said that." Her remorse seemed genuine.

"I gotta get going; I've got a full day booked. You need a ride?"

"It's okay. I can walk."

"It's kinda a long way, isn't it?" If she lived anywhere close to me, she'd be looking at half a dozen blocks. She wasn't wearing shoes meant for that kind of distance. I had to wonder where she'd come from to pick this diner, but I wasn't about to ask. The answer was probably another thing I didn't want to know anything about.

"I'll be fine."

I passed her Sarah's helmet. As much as I regretted this meeting with her, it wasn't her fault she'd ended up the way she had. Part of the reason Candy and I had worked at all was that we both came from shitty homes where the options were limited. She just didn't have the strength or will to change any more.

Sarah's upbringing hadn't been a whole lot better than mine, from the little she'd told me: single parent, poverty, a lot of moving around. But she'd made better choices, done things to make her future brighter, apart from her current job, anyway.

It had been a long time since Candy had been on the back of my bike. Her arms around my waist felt foreign and wrong. I was glad it was a short trip to her apartment. She wasn't wrong about the location; she was only a few blocks away from my place. Her neighborhood was a slight upgrade from mine, and the building seemed secure, which was a good thing.

In Candy's line of work, she could never be too careful. Those guys who frequented the club weren't the most upstanding members of society, especially the ones who partook in the private-room opportunities.

I pulled up in front of her building and cut the engine, flipping up my visor. It was a relief when she wasn't touching me anymore. She took off her helmet, and I reattached it to the back of the seat.

"Thanks a lot for agreeing to see me." Candy fluffed out her hair self-consciously and gave me a shy smile. "Do you want to come up and see my place?"

"I gotta go to work."

"Right. Of course. Maybe another time?"

"I don't think that's a good idea."

"Not even for old-time's sake? It's okay if you still have feelings for Sarah. You could even pretend I'm her."

I sighed. "Christ, Candy. Why would you want me to use you like that?"

Her shoulders caved, and she hid behind her hair. "I'm sorry. That was stupid. It's just... You were always really good to me, even when I wasn't good to you."

With that she turned and walked up the cracked sidewalk. I waited until she'd disappeared inside the building before I flipped down my visor and gunned the engine. I wanted to get as far away from that part of my past as I could.

Maybe it was a good thing Sarah had walked away from me. Maybe I should leave her alone. But I wouldn't, not if The Sanctuary was as bad as Candy had said and Sarah might be getting dragged into things she couldn't get out of.

It wasn't that she couldn't take care of herself. She'd been doing that for years, as far as I knew. It was that once a guy like Xander found a weakness, any weakness, he'd exploit it until he broke her. I'd seen it done to Candy. I'd seen people try to take Lisa down the same road. If Jamie and Hayden and I hadn't been there, she might've ended up like Candy. I wouldn't let that happen to Sarah.

I parked around the back of Inked Armor and poked my head in the shop to see if anyone wanted coffee. After I took orders, I ran across the street, glancing up briefly at Sarah's apartment. I couldn't see any movement in the windows, but that didn't mean she wasn't there.

I passed through the bookstore connected to the café to say hi to Hayden's Aunt Cassie, who owned the place. Her smile was warm as she looked up from the book she was cataloging.

"Chris! How are you?" She came out from behind the cash register to hug me.

"I'm all right. How 'bout you?"

"Good, good. Busy." She gestured to the pile of books. "But that's never a bad thing, is it?"

"Nope. You get someone to rent Tee's old apartment yet?"

Cassie rolled her eyes. "My highly motivated husband wants to redo the floors and put in air, but he's going to have to hire someone, especially since he can't ask Hayden for help."

"Yeah, we're way too busy at the shop these days. Hayden's already cranky about not getting enough time with Tee. I don't think I can deal with him if he's going through full-on Tenley withdrawal."

Cassie laughed. "He doesn't do moderation well."

"Not even a little."

"How're things with Sarah? I haven't seen much of her lately."

I tapped the counter and gave her a half-smile. "Me either. We're not hanging out anymore."

"Oh, no. I'm so sorry. What happened?"

I looked at the floor. "She realized I wasn't any good for her, I guess."

"Did she say that to you?"

Cassie's anger almost made me smile. "No, but it's pretty accurate. I don't really think I'm good for anyone, so it's probably better this way."

"I can't say I agree with that. You've been a good friend to Hayden for a lot of years, and Lisa and Jamie."

I traced the cover of one of her books. "I don't know about that. Hayden's pretty much carried me since he got his shit together."

"That's what friends do, though, don't they? You carry each other when it's needed." She put a hand over mine. "I know the trial was hard on you, Chris. You were all kids when his parents died, and you barely even knew each other. You never could've known."

Her small, sad smile made my heart ache. While Hayden had lost his parents, Cassie had lost her only sister. There had been a gap in their ages, like with me and my sister, but they'd been close. After his parents died, Hayden had gone to live with Cassie and her husband, Nate, for a few months. But he'd already been out of control by that point, blaming himself for their deaths and unable to deal with the horror he'd witnessed in finding them dead.

"It's hard, you know? To find out someone I trusted and shouldn't have pretty much ruined my friend's life."

"Hayden's life isn't ruined."

"Yeah, but he'll never be the same, and neither will you."

Cassie nodded slowly. "No, we won't, and neither will you. But if there's anything we do know, it's that people survive trauma and learn how to move on. Hayden and Tenley are the perfect example of that, aren't they?"

"I guess."

About a year and a half ago, Tenley had lost her entire family, including her fiancé, in a plane crash. They'd been on their way to a destination wedding when turbulence and human error took them down. Tee had been the one to insist on the island wedding. She'd been one of thirteen survivors, but she hadn't escaped unscathed. Her back had been badly burned, and she'd suffered several broken bones. She still had a slight limp.

"There's no guessing, Chris. If Hayden and Tenley hadn't suffered the way they did, they might never have found each other. And although their losses are tragic, I don't think there are two people more suited to each other, and that's *because* of how much they've struggled."

"It sucks that they had to lose so much to find each other, you know?"

"I do. I also know that they both blamed themselves for a long time. You don't need to take on Hayden's guilt now that he's not carrying it anymore."

"Are you sure Nate's the therapist and not you?" I asked, trying to alleviate the heavy turn of our conversation. Cassie made good points, but it was hard not to take on the guilt when that's what I was used to doing.

Cassie flicked my arm. "Hayden said the same thing yesterday."

"Maybe you two need to stop reading all these deep philosophy books and get into something lighter."

My phone beeped, signaling that I had fifteen minutes before my first appointment. "I gotta go."

"Of course. I hope things work out with you and Sarah. I think you're better for each other than you realize."

"Yeah. Maybe. See you later, Cass."

I left her to her books and crossed through to the café to place my coffee order. Cassie wasn't much older than me, but she had a real motherly vibe about her, always taking care of people. Ever since we opened Inked Armor we'd celebrated all our major holidays with her and Nate. They were the kind of family I'd always wanted and never really had.

On the way back to Inked Armor, coffees in hand, I looked up at Sarah's apartment window again, out of compulsion. Now more than ever I wanted to talk to her. The flutter of curtain indicated I wasn't the only one with a voyeurism problem.

I sighed and went in to the shop. I had ten minutes before my first client would arrive. No time to drop by Sarah's apartment for answers to the new, unpleasant questions I had.

I'd set out my folder with the artwork last night, so all I needed was to hit the back room for a few supplies. I found Hayden in there gathering his own.

"Hey, man. How's it goin'?"

I grabbed a few pairs of gloves. "S'all right."

He cocked a brow. "Yeah?"

I nodded and scanned the shelves, mentally reviewing anything else I might need.

"Lisa said you went out with Candy this morning."

I rubbed the back of my neck. Of course Lisa would tell Hayden. Nothing was a secret in here. "It wasn't anything."

"If you say so."

"I'm not getting back on that ride."

He gave me a look. "So what was the point of seeing her? To piss Sarah off?"

"No."

"No?"

"Not really. Candy said she had some information."

Hayden's eyebrow rose. "About Sarah?"

"Yeah."

"So did she?"

"She did."

"And you believe her?"

The door tinkled, likely with the arrival of a client.

"Honestly, I have no fucking clue. I don't know if Candy's playing me or trying to make drama since she's pretty fucking good at that, or if whatever rumors going around have some truth to them. But she says Sarah was serving left stage a couple of weeks ago, and that The Sanctuary is as bad as The Dollhouse was."

"Motherfuck. That's not good news."

"Yeah. That's what I said."

Hayden poked at the corner of his lip with his tongue, where his viper bites used to be. He'd gotten rid of them before the trial. With a suit on, he now looked like he should be part of the corporate world, not running a tattoo studio. Aside from the lick of vine running up the side of his neck, anyway. "I don't know that I'd trust much of what comes out of Candy's mouth."

"Pretty sure there's a lot of jizz involved there."

Hayden rolled his eyes. "That girl always was a train wreck."

"We all were back then."

He nodded.

Lisa poked her head in the door. "Hey, your ten-thirty's here, Hayden."

"Thanks. I'll be right out." Hayden grabbed another roll of paper towels.

"Everything go okay this morning?" Lisa asked me.

"That's questionable."

"Questionable how?"

"I have more questions than answers at this point. I'll fill you in after my first session."

She pointed at me. "I'm holding you to that." The door chimed again. "That one's probably yours."

"She'll be devastated if Sarah's on the pole," Hayden murmured after she left us alone again.

So would I. "It's hard enough that Sarah's working with all those girls she used to hang around with."

"Can you imagine what would've happened if Jamie hadn't gotten her out of The Dollhouse?" Hayden asked.

"I try not to think about that." Without Jamie to save Lisa from herself, all three of us would probably have ended up face down in a ditch after an overdose.

Lisa's time at The Dollhouse hadn't been good for her. She

wasn't made for that life, and it took a lot out of her emotionally. She'd coped with drugs, and Damen had been more than willing to provide them in exchange for special services. She'd been barely eighteen and vulnerable. She'd grown up in the system, and though I didn't have details, I knew a lot of bad things had happened to her. Kids didn't get taken away from their parents unless the adults were doing damage to them that couldn't be repaired—what's worse, sometimes they didn't even get out then. I was pretty sure my teachers had known there was something going down in my house when I was a kid, but no one ever did anything to stop it. I'd figured it was better me getting the beats than my mom and sister.

"Tenley's got the girls coming over tomorrow night for some chick thing, and Sarah's supposed to be there," Hayden added on his way out. "Me and Jamie were going to go for beers if you want to come with. We can make an excuse to stop by my place, and maybe you can talk to her. Figure out if what Candy's saying is bullshit or not."

"I don't know if talking to her is going to change anything."

"You can't know if you don't try. Lisa said she talked to Sarah again last night, and she asked about you. If she didn't give a shit, she wouldn't ask. Sometimes people make decisions before they think them through."

Maybe that was the case with Sarah. Then again, maybe not.

I finished with my last client after ten. Long days with little down time had become the norm. Back when there used to be an hour between appointments, and light nights in the middle of the week, it was easy to get things done around the shop. But with our growing popularity, we were all tired by the end of the day, and none of us— not even Hayden the neat freak—was enthusiastic about cleaning up.

Jamie was in the storage room checking supplies, and Lisa sat in the back, finishing up end-of-day paperwork. As promised, I'd filled her in on my breakfast with Candy, and she hadn't been happy about the details, or lack of them.

After I set up for my first session in the morning, I dropped into my chair and closed my eyes. Staying busy had kept me from thinking about my conversation with Candy this morning, but now I could fixate on it all I wanted.

"You doing okay?" Hayden asked.

"Bagged." I answered without opening my eyes.

"You're worried, huh?"

I nodded. "I don't want to be right about this one. I don't want what Candy said to be anywhere close to true."

"I know, man. Maybe it's just Candy being Candy, making things sound a lot worse than they are."

Hayden's phone went off, saving me from more depressing discussion. After he began to speak, I could tell it was Tenley, AKA kitten. I tuned out their domestic conversation and picked up my phone to check my messages. I sighed. Sarah might be creeping me from her window, but she still wasn't answering my texts. My sister, on the other hand, had left a voicemail and two texts.

Ivy was nineteen and a little better than eight years my junior. We shared the same mom, but had different dads. Mom's choice number one had been a real loser. I didn't have a single memory of him. Probably because he left when I was two, so there wasn't much to remember. John, Ivy's dad, was his replacement. He wasn't much of a step up. Like me and my mom, he was uneducated. I'd lucked out with a skill set that had proved to be useful, but from what I could see, John was missing that, along with the motivation to do anything good for anyone but himself.

I still wasn't all that clear on John's current job, and Ivy hadn't been much help. From what I understood he was pulling long-haul deliveries for some private company, which meant he'd be gone for a good week or two at a time, sometimes longer. Then he'd be back for a while, and gone again. I couldn't begin to count the different jobs he'd had over the years. But he'd never seemed to be able to manage bills or payments, or anything else important.

I hadn't had much of a relationship with Ivy until recently. She'd been eight when I was kicked out of the house at sixteen for flunking out of school, thanks to a lot of bad behavior and poor choices. For several years I didn't see much of my family. I was too busy being an asshole and screwing up my life. That has changed since we opened Inked Armor five years ago. I'd gotten my shit mostly together, and I'd been helping my mom out with money.

For a long time I still wasn't allowed to see much of Ivy, but that changed in February when their furnace took a crap and my mom needed some help. Since then, I'd even been invited to Ivy's birthday—but only because John had been on the road.

For Ivy's nineteenth, I'd bought her a cell phone. My only condition was that she keep it hidden from John. Otherwise I knew he'd take it because I gave it to her, and sell it because he was an asshole and wanted the money. Now that she had a way to, she'd been reaching out more, and it helped that John wasn't around to monitor her all the time since work had him traveling. While I wasn't the perfect role model, I wanted to be part of her life. I was still her brother, so I figured it was time to act like one.

I listened to the voicemail first.

"Uh… hi, Chris. It's Ivy. Your sister…" She paused and mumbled something before she was clear again. "I guess you're probably busy… um… uh… Can you call me when you have time?"

The text messages were much the same. It was already after eleven, so I sent a text rather than return the call. I didn't want to risk John catching her if they both happened to be at home.

At this time of night, if he wasn't on the road, he'd likely be either up to his armpits in empty beer bottles on the couch or out at a local bar doing the same. He really was a waste of oxygen.

Lisa came out of the office, rubbing her eyes. "I think I'm going cross-eyed from staring at those spreadsheets."

"I'll take them home and check them over," Hayden said, pushing out of his chair.

"I still have a couple things to add, so it's pointless tonight." Lisa grabbed her purse from behind the counter. "We need to think about hiring some extra help. I can't stay on top of things anymore."

"It'll start to slow down soon," Hayden said.

"We're booked through to the end of August, and then we'll get the college kids. I don't think it's going to slow down at all," Lisa replied.

Hayden poked at his lip with his tongue. I could tell the idea of hiring someone new stressed him out, but Lisa had a point. We were all drowning in work.

"Even if it was just someone part time to run the cash, that'd be okay, right? Or maybe we could train someone new for piercing to take the pressure off Lisa," I suggested. It was too soon to say anything about a new tattoo artist, which we could also use. It was always one step at a time with Hayden, especially when talking about significant change.

"Why don't you make a list of the things you need help with, and we'll see what's possible," he said after a long pause.

Lisa threw her arms around him. "I can definitely do that. I promise it'll be a good thing."

Jamie came out of the back room, wearing the same blanket of fatigue as the rest of us, as Lisa let Hayden go.

"What'd I miss?"

"Hayden's going to let me have an assistant, or an apprentice, or something." Lisa's smile was its own reward, and Jamie returned it.

He patted Hayden on the shoulder. "We'll find a good fit. Don't worry, brother."

Hayden brushed his hand off with a roll of his eyes, but we all knew how hard it would be for him to bring someone new into the fold. We'd been four for a lot of years.

We were quiet as we filed out of the shop and headed to our vehicles.

By the time I got home, I still hadn't heard back from Ivy, so I made myself a sandwich and stretched out on the couch. I couldn't settle though, worried now not just about Sarah, but my sister as well.

If I didn't hear from Ivy by morning, I'd stop by the house to check on her. I might be shut out of protecting Sarah at the moment, but my sister was willing to accept help where I could give it.

THREE

SARAH

I measured the quality of my night by comparing total tips to the number of times some jerkoff put his hands on me. Tonight had been relatively mauling free, and the money was decent—decent enough to blow a regular waitressing job out of the water, though nothing like what I could be making if I'd taken a page from my mother's book.

But I was trying hard not to do that.

I had no interest in being totally dependent on someone else for my financial well-being. Strip club waitressing, while often degrading, was far less reprehensible than being a serial mistress like my mom, as long as I could stay on the floor and off the pole.

So far I had managed to avoid that scenario, even with Xander's constant nagging. But it wasn't easy. Having grown up in a situation where men rotated through my mother's life almost as regularly as the seasons, I had to remind myself that not all males were assholes— just pretty much every one of them who came through the doors of the club. I'd believed no one could ever be faithful to one person. Then for a while, Chris had made me believe it was possible to love someone and be only theirs, until I screwed that up, too.

Anyway, I hated that the job I was now forced to keep was the very thing I'd been trying to escape. More than my loathing for The Sanctuary, I wished I'd never taken the job at The Dollhouse when I first moved to Chicago. My mother had been the one to give me the contact there, and I should've recognized her help for what it was—another attempt to get me to follow her path. If I hadn't, the allure of the tips and the flow of money wouldn't have been something I was now afraid to be without. Part of that came from the constant roller coaster I'd been on as a kid; the temporary excess, followed by a plunge into poverty, wasn't something I wanted to contend with ever again.

I sat on the bench in the changing room, cash and receipts spread out in front of me. I never did my count at the tables with the other girls, and I quickly shoved my tips into my bra—except for two hundred dollars, which I shoved in my pocket—before anyone had a chance to see what I'd pulled in on a relatively not-so-great night. Sometimes I made a lot more than even the girls serving center stage.

I had no idea why my brand of sex appeal sold so well. Regardless, this was the money I needed to pay down school debt. And while the girls who worked left stage made a good two to three times as much as I did, the level of touching expected to be tolerated there made my usual section seem positively chaste. The one time I'd served there had been a colossal clusterfuck and had opened my eyes to more reality than I would've liked. The money I could make on that side of the club wasn't worth the price, but I'd learned that lesson the hard way.

Candy sat at her station, peeling off her fake eyelashes. She'd been giving me dirty looks all night, more than was typical for her, anyway. Her hair was almost the same shade of white-blond as mine, except hers was artificial. Her narrow waist was courtesy of her coke habit—and whatever other illegal substances she managed to score through favors.

Candy and I didn't have much use for each other, seeing as our one common interest was the same man. I'd broken it off with Chris a couple of weeks ago. Not because I wanted to, but because I'd been put in a position where I felt I had to. I hated how this job impacted my life, and that it had cost me someone so important.

I'd wanted out pretty much as soon as I'd taken the job. But

Xander had kiboshed any attempt at quitting when he mentioned how difficult it must be to juggle work with such an exclusive master's program at Northwestern. He'd discovered I had a partial scholarship, and that there was a propriety clause because of the donors—something I hadn't paid much attention to until he'd pointed it out.

I'd stupidly assumed it pertained only to in-school and internship behavior. The message was simple: Don't screw your teachers, don't screw the boss at your internship, that kind of thing. I hadn't taken into account how my job at The Sanctuary might factor in, but Xander assured me he thought they'd be very interested, should they have reason to find out. If I violated the propriety clause, the donors could take back what they'd given me.

At first I thought maybe he was just trying to scare me. Then one of the girls at my internship got caught blowing an account manager in the copy room. I'd expected her to get some kind of reprimand, but that wasn't what happened. I was shocked when she was expelled from the program, losing her degree. Plus she had to pay back the entire cost of her tuition because her scholarship was revoked.

If that happened to me, I'd also owe the whole six-figure cost of my graduate degree, not just half, on top of my undergrad loans.

During our chat, Xander had shown me a still shot from one of the video cameras. He'd captured me screwing around on one of the poles at the end of a night. Taken out of context, it looked bad. Xander, being the asshole he was, mentioned how natural I looked up there on the stage. He'd gone on to suggest that there were plenty of ways to make my school loans go away faster, and he'd ensure no one ever found out about this job. I declined his offer, but the threat had been clear. He'd bound me to him and the club for as long as I was in school and my scholarship was at risk.

I'd thought that leverage was bad. It was nothing in comparison to what happened two weeks ago.

My car had died on my way to work. I'd known it needed some work, but I'd been waiting until I had enough money set aside to pay for repairs before I took it into a garage. It wasn't going to be cheap to fix. My car troubles had made me late, and Xander had been pissed. He'd been ready to send me home. But rent was due, along with my tuition payment, and I couldn't afford to lose a shift.

So instead he'd offered a proposal. He'd loan me the cost of car repairs, and I'd serve left stage that night. There was no other option because I was late, he'd explained. And I'd also owe him a favor. He called it interest on the loan.

I'd considered, for a moment, asking Chris if he could help me out, but he'd just bought his mom a new furnace. I didn't want to put my financial troubles on him, too.

In hindsight, that would've been the better choice. I should've known owing Xander wouldn't end well, especially combined with the leverage he already had. But I'd been backed into a corner, so I'd made the deal.

All the suited-up men with their wandering hands and vulgar requests that night should've sent me straight into a scalding shower to burn away their unwelcome advances. It had reminded me far too much of the things my mother tolerated from the men she "dated."

Chris's bed was the last place I should've gone, but I'd wanted the comfort being with him always brought. I needed his gentleness to wash away what the shower couldn't. And I knew I wasn't going to have it much longer with the way things were going now.

The sex was amazing, as it always was, but the emotions tied to it, for me at least, weren't something I could compartmentalize any more. In the morning, as I lay there beside him, tracing the ink he refused to put on me, I knew I'd ruined what we had by making a deal with Xander.

While Chris didn't talk to me much about his family or past girlfriends, he'd been honest about why his relationship with Candy had ended. When they'd gotten together, she'd been like me: a waitress, not a stripper. He'd managed her transition from serving drinks to taking her clothes off for a while, until he couldn't any more.

If the favor Xander called in was serving left stage again, or something worse, I wasn't sure I could live with myself. Whispers of his predilection for humiliation fluttered like nervous hummingbirds in the dressing room. Some of the girls seemed intrigued by him, but a thick undercurrent of fear permeated my interactions with him. His constant reminders about how easy it would be for me to lose my grad school placement spiked my anxiety every time I came to work. I hated that he had such control over my life.

Additionally, if the favor was anything more than left stage, I wouldn't be able to go to Chris after, leaving me with no real support system. Not that I'd had much of one anyway. If he ever found out about any of this, it would make things so much worse. Chris had made it clear that if I ever made the move from waitress to pole, he was done.

So I'd broken it off, thinking it would make the situation easier on me.

It hadn't. I was miserable without him.

I took a deep breath, pushing away the sadness that came with thinking about Chris, and how I'd ruined what we'd had with one bad choice. Maybe I was destined to be like my mother. Maybe I'd never figure out how to love someone without being hurt.

I focused on the stack of twenties, flipping the bills so they all faced the same direction. Xander liked things organized, and I liked to be in and out of his office in as little time as possible. He made me nervous. Especially now that he had so much to hold over my head. The car repairs had cost more than twenty-five hundred dollars. Compared to my school loans, it was nothing. Juggling bills to back the loan was the easy part. But waiting for him to collect on the favor made me anxious, which was likely purposeful.

For all the time and energy I'd put into not becoming my mother, one decision had shifted me far too close. Money had always been her motivation. She'd done horrible, degrading, desperate things for the illusion of luxury. I'd made it my goal never to have to ask someone else for something I needed. I never wanted to be indebted to someone who could turn that on me for personal gain—and now I was.

"Guess who I had breakfast with this morning." Candy was loud-talking across the room.

"Is it that guy you were talking about last week? The one who drives the Mercedes?" someone asked.

"Nope. That guy's a jerk, and that car is leased. You'll *never* guess."

I went back to counting, uninterested in who Candy was screwing. She reminded me of my mother, but with none of the finesse. Then I heard her say, "Chris."

My stomach dropped, along with the wad of cash. I got down on my hands and knees and gathered the bills back into a pile. Chris was a common name. It didn't have to be my Chris. It could be anyone, really.

"Who?"

"Who do you think? Chris Zelter."

I caught Candy's reflection in her vanity mirror. She was staring right at me, a smug smile plastered on her makeup-caked face.

One of the other girls started to comment, "But I thought—"

Someone shushed her with a whisper, and she checked over her shoulder, looking in my direction. I focused on the money in my hands, not wanting Candy to see my reaction.

I hurriedly restacked the bills, desperate to get away from her before I said or did something I'd regret more than breaking it off with Chris. I was ready to punch her in her stupid, coke-blown nose, except I'd seen her fight one of the other girls. She was a hair-puller and a scratcher. Dark circles were enough of a problem to hide without claw marks on my face and bald patches on my head.

My stomach turned at the thought of Candy in Chris's bed, at the idea of his hands on her, or hers on him. Why would he get involved with her again? It wasn't like she'd become a better person since they'd last dated.

As I gathered the money, I was thankful I'd changed out of my slutwear and into street clothes before I counted my tips. Clutching the money and receipts, I left the dressing room, Candy's high-pitched laugh following me down the hall. I took a deep breath as soon as I was away from her. I could get emotional about this later. Right now I needed to be angry—Chris had to know she'd say something. Or maybe that was the point. Maybe he was getting me back for the way I'd dealt with us.

Which was not dealing at all.

I couched all the feelings and made the trek to Xander's office, anxiety creating a roll in my stomach. I'd cried in front of him once and given him a weakness to exploit. I understood now what Chris had always been so worried about. One step down the wrong path had already created more problems than I could fix.

I was almost relieved to find Trixie sitting on the edge of Xander's desk. She was still dressed in her last on-stage outfit, a short skirt and a bra. Trixie had only been working at The Sanctuary for a few weeks, and she was Xander's pet.

She tossed her hair over her shoulder, barely glancing my way, though I knew she saw me. She spent most of her time in the protective cover of Xander's office when she wasn't on the stage. It was a smart move on her part. Many of the girls weren't happy with the shift in dynamics since she'd started working here. She got the best shifts, the most lucrative dance spots, the nicest leased car—whatever the best perks were, she had them. The rest of the girls had banded together, starting rumors, causing drama, and making Trixie generally miserable when they could.

Coked-out dancers—high on E and whatever uppers Xander and his goons provided—were irrational and volatile. My friend Tenley thought it would make an interesting research paper. I would've agreed if that wouldn't have made me one of the lab rats. This life wasn't anything she understood, apart from second-hand accounts and witnessing the drama from the outside. She couldn't fully appreciate what it was like from the inside.

More than anything else, I wanted to be free of this.

Xander leaned back in his chair, fingers steepled under his chin. "How was your night, Sarah?" he asked in his thick, European accent. I wasn't sure exactly where he was from since Xander didn't like chitchat or questions unless he was doing the talking.

"Fine." I passed over the envelope and waited, like always, for him to count it in front of me. I wasn't stupid enough to walk away without confirmation the numbers matched.

"Trixie, be a good girl and go get me a soda water. Two lemons. No fucking limes this time."

"Two lemons, no limes." A flush crept into her cheeks as she slid off the desk, her skirt flipping up to reveal a lack of underwear.

"And close the door behind you." Xander didn't look away from his computer screen as she flounced to the exit.

My heart rate sped as the door clicked shut. It wasn't locked, though. That was good. I didn't like the idea of being locked in a room with Xander.

He gestured to the chair across from his desk. "Have a seat."

"I'm good standing."

His smile was sinister as he stared me down. "Sit."

His power trips, which had increased in frequency, were infuriating, but I wasn't about to push him. I was certain he enjoyed how tense he made me these days. Before I dropped into the chair I pulled the two hundred dollars out of my pocket, smoothed it out, and passed it to him.

"You sure you want to hand over this much?"

"The faster I pay it down the better, right?"

One side of his mouth lifted in a leer. "Soon you'll be all paid up, except for the interest, of course." He nodded to the chair behind me.

I hated his constant reminders that money wasn't the only thing I owed him. I tried not think about the bodily fluids the fabric might hold as I took a seat. Everything I wore would go directly into the laundry when I got home anyway.

"I trust your internship is going well? You're at Media Mogul aren't you? Specializing in marketing management?"

The small talk wasn't innocuous. It was Xander's way of reminding me of his hold on me.

"It's fine, and yes."

He continued to stare in that unnerving way of his. "Just fine? That's a very renowned company. I'd think someone with a background like yours would be an exceptional asset to them. What was your undergrad again? You double majored in programming and marketing?"

None of this was information I'd ever shared with Xander. He'd done all the digging on his own to prove he could find out whatever he wanted about me.

I tried not to let derision seep into my tone. "It's a good placement. I worked hard to get there."

"Yes, well, I imagine you have a vast array of talents that extend far beyond serving drinks, don't you?" His smile was lecherous. "You look tired tonight, though."

"It was a busy one." I kept my hands clasped in my lap to prevent myself from fidgeting.

"Yes, I see that. You pulled in five grand in sales on a Tuesday? Impressive."

"Men like slutty librarians."

His eyes shifted to me. "Men like the idea of fucking someone they think is untouchable."

I tried not to let my anxiety seep through into my words, because showing weakness, especially fear, wasn't going to help me. "Until it isn't untouchable any more. Then it's just another body everyone gets to see naked, right?"

Xander chuckled. The sound was dark, like an unfilled grave. "Aren't you even the slightest bit curious what I've been offered for an hour with you?"

A shiver forced its way down my spine, real fear settling under my skin. Head still bowed, his eyes lifted, making him look as demonic as he was turning out to be. Xander's blond hair, icy blue eyes, high cheekbones, and white smile might've made him beautiful to look at, but under that stunning exterior I could see a terrible, terrifying man. He wasn't a wolf in sheep's clothing, he was a viper, and he was going to taunt me with this for as long as he could. Draw it out and make me sweat over it. In the meantime, while I waited for the ball to finally drop, Candy would taunt me with Chris. Unless I did something about it.

I didn't have an opportunity to hear Xander's next veiled threat. Trixie burst through the door, glass in hand. He turned his hard glare on her, and the simpering smile melted off her face.

His usually calm veneer slipped as he slammed his palm on his desk, sending sheets of paper fluttering to the floor. "How many fucking times do I need to tell you to knock before you come into my goddamn office?"

Her drawn-on eyebrows came down as she looked from him, to me, to the glass in her hand. "But you asked me—"

He pushed up out of his chair, all six feet four inches of him rising in a tower of menace. He rivaled Chris in height and breadth. "I asked you to get me a soda water, and I asked you to close the door. What does that mean, Trixie?"

Her eyes went wide as she realized her mistake.

"What does that mean?" Xander barked.

"That I should knock when I come back."

"Why?"

Her voice trembled. "Because you want privacy."

Xander snapped his fingers. "Come here. Now."

She scurried over, shooting a hateful glare in my direction. She bumped the corner of the desk, and the drink in her hand sloshed over the edge of the glass, spilling across the smooth wood surface.

Xander grabbed her by the back of the neck and forced her face to the desk, her cheek displacing the spilled contents into a wider puddle, soaking papers in its radius.

His voice was gravelly with barely restrained rage as he leaned down to whisper next to her ear. "Do you see the mess you've made? Clean it up." His eyes lifted to me. "Unless you plan to be part of this, I suggest you get the fuck out."

I jumped up, nearly toppling the chair in my rush to follow his order.

"And close the fucking door." Xander's malicious grin and Trixie's fearful eyes were the last things I saw as I pulled the door closed. I hurried through the small waiting room and burst through the door to the club, jumping as it slammed shut behind me.

Grant, head of security and Xander's shadow, snapped to attention at the loud noise, and his right hand twitched by his side. His brows pulled low as he looked me over in his assessing, clinical way. Despite being in Xander's back pocket, he always seemed to be looking out for the girls.

I took a deep breath, trying to shut down my visions of all the scenarios that could be taking place in Xander's office, and was relieved Grant was there to run interference. I'd never seen Xander lose it like that. From what I'd heard the girls say, Trixie was an E-head, but it hadn't erased her look of terror when I left her in there alone with him.

Grant pushed off the wall. "What happened?"

"Trixie." It came out a croak.

He crossed the empty, low-lit club in three easy strides. He stopped several feet away when I raised my hands in defense, as if to ward him off. His usual flat demeanor dropped for a second, and his expression softened. Well, as much as it could.

"I'm not gonna hurt you, Sarah. Now, breathe and try again."

"Trixie didn't knock. And she spilled Xander's drink on his desk, and then he got… mad."

"Mad how?"

"Aggressive."

"Shit." He palmed his walkie-talkie, muttering under his breath about not signing on for this. "Max, I need you in here stat. We've got an office issue." He clicked off and shoved the walkie in his back pocket, his eyes returning to me. "You should go."

"I should go," I repeated.

"Now."

When I didn't turn right away, he put his hands on my shoulders, thumbs smoothing down the sides of my neck. The severity of his expression didn't at all match the softness of the contact. It was foreign and slightly unpleasant because of the intimacy in it. "You did the right thing by walking away. I've got this. Go."

I whirled, as much to get away from the feel of his fingers on my skin as the trouble in the office, and walked quickly back toward the dressing room. Max rushed past me, lips set in a grim line as he followed Grant into the office.

When I'd worked at The Dollhouse, my manager had been female. Sienna had been volatile and manipulative, just like Xander was turning out to be. But Xander had the physical presence and ability to do real damage to the girls when he lost it. That was terrifying.

There were still a few girls hanging around when I passed through the dressing room, but at least Candy was gone. I headed for the small room off the dressing area where wait staff like myself had separate lockers to keep our things and a place to get changed and do makeup. The dancers all had vanity stations where they prepared for their sets. The tremor in my hands was hard to hide as I struggled with the combination lock.

"Max ran through here like his ass was on fire." One of the girls eyed me suspiciously.

I slung my bag over my shoulder. I wanted to get out of here, but Dee, short for Destiny, and one of the few girls I spoke to on a regular basis, stepped into the doorway. She'd waitressed with me at The Dollhouse, and she'd been the one to tell me this job would be better. Yet recently she'd gone from serving drinks to dancing. I worried about her a lot these days.

"Do ya know what's up with Max?" she asked.

The chatter stopped, all eyes on me.

"Something with Trixie," I mumbled.

"I hope that bitch gets it, stepping in on Candy's territory like that."

Maybe she was the reason Candy was no longer on center.

"I have class in the morning. I should go." As far as the rest of the girls knew, I went to community college and was undecided on my major. They had no idea I was in the last months of a MBA. The truth would only serve as more ammunition to make my life difficult. It was bad enough that I was in college at all. My potential escape would be impossible for most of these girls, and they hated me because of it.

"Hold up. There's no one on the door. I'll go with you." Dee grabbed her bag from her station. "See you later, girls."

Dressed in a pair of white terry shorts and a sheer tank top, complete with four-inch heels, Dee had started to look the part of a stripper both inside the club and out. Her long, dark hair fell in waves almost to her waist. Her eyes were also dark, and at the moment highlighted by fake lashes and pale eye shadow. She was pretty, prettier still without all the makeup. And she wasn't gossipy in the same spiteful way as some of the others.

Once we were outside with some distance between us and the club, Dee asked, "Is Trix okay?"

"I don't know. Xander was pretty pissed."

"I told her not to get involved, ya know? Like, it was a bad idea, but she doesn't listen. It's like something isn't right in her head."

"Sometimes people need to learn on their own." I certainly had. I stopped in front of my Tercel. It now ran better than it had in a long time because of Xander. But his generosity didn't come without a significant price.

"I don't think she's ever gonna learn. She's killed what's left up there with all the blow and the E." Dee surprised me when she grabbed my wrist. "You stay where you are. Don't do what I did. It's not worth it."

"I won't."

"Promise," she said fiercely.

"Of course, Dee. I promise."

The look on her face made me want my words to be true, although when it came to my debt, I had no idea what Xander was going to ask for. I could only hope it wasn't me on a stage. My regret over losing Chris hit me again. It seemed magnified in the wake of Candy's recent revelation.

The back door opened, and a couple girls came out. Dee dropped my wrist and walked away without another word. But her relief at my promise would haunt me for weeks to come.

I didn't have to unlock the doors to get in my car. I never kept anything in it besides the owner's manual and a box of tissues.

Tonight, after I slid inside, I reached across and slapped all the buttons, locking myself in.

The scene in Xander's office had unnerved me. I was sure he'd done it not just to show Trixie who was boss, but also to garner a reaction from me.

I left the lot, wanting to get as far away from The Sanctuary as possible, but at a red light I checked my messages. Ones from Lisa and Tenley took up the top spots. The unchecked ones from Chris weren't too far down. He'd messaged me the night before last, and several other times since we'd broken up. I'd left them all untouched, worried that if I checked them, I'd respond. This time I gave in.

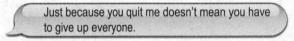

> Just because you quit me doesn't mean you have to give up everyone.

There were messages before that one asking if I was okay, telling me he was around if I wanted to talk, and another saying he'd bring my stuff to the shop if I wanted it back.

A loud honk behind me alerted me to the green light. I took a right, heading for Chris's place instead of mine.

I sent a one-word message:

> Candy?

Ten minutes later I pulled into the lot behind his apartment building. His bike was parked at the top of his spot, maybe out of habit since it used to allow enough space for my car, too. I wasn't sure what I expected. It was after two in the morning. I didn't have a key anymore, so unless the door to the building was propped open, which it often was, and I somehow managed to wake him up—he slept like the dead—all I'd accomplish was looking like a desperate idiot haunting his building in the middle of the night.

I tapped the steering wheel, my attention moving to the dashboard where one of Chris's old Post-its still clung. He left them for me all the time. Or he used to. Some were sweet sentiments or little notes, other were instructions.

Usually I'd peel them off whatever surface he'd stuck them on and tuck them away in a box. I'd left this one on my dash for no other reason than I liked the reminder of his sweetness, particularly after a long shift at The Sanctuary. It said EAT ME. It had been attached to a bag of my favorite candies, which Chris had thoughtfully left in my car. He'd stuck the note on my dash and proceeded to eat half the contents of the bag. The hot pink paper had now been bleached almost white by the sun.

Cutting the engine, I shouldered my bag and rounded the building to the front entrance. The door was propped open with an old newspaper. I slipped in, tossed the newspaper aside, and climbed the stairs to the third floor. A pungent air freshener had been deployed, but it didn't mask the scent of stale cigarettes or body odor.

Chris should've been able to afford to live in a better neighborhood, but he helped out his mom and his sister a lot. This past winter he'd replaced their furnace, and he constantly seemed to be paying bills for them. It was another reason I hadn't wanted to go to him when my car broke down. I didn't want to seem like I was using him the way his mother did, which was something I understood only too well.

I didn't stop to think about what I'd say if he happened to answer the door. I gave a few sharp raps and waited. I could hear the TV. If I'd still had a key, I was sure I'd find him sleeping on the couch.

I rested my head against the cold steel, considering my options. This favor Xander would eventually call in could be a bad one, and I would have that hanging over me until it happened. But right now it seemed like I'd given Chris up for nothing. I didn't want to drag him into a situation he had no interest in handling, or go to him after I'd compromised myself, but I also didn't want Candy to have him again.

But I couldn't tell him about the deal I'd made with Xander. If I did, he probably wouldn't want me back. I wouldn't feel good about giving him half-truths, but there didn't seem to be any other choice.

And if he ended up back with Candy, that would be far worse. She deserved him less than I did.

She was the reason I knocked one more time, softly. Just as I was about to give up, the heavy tread of feet made the floor vibrate.

I backed up so he'd be able to see me through the peephole. The seconds seemed endless before the door finally swung in, revealing a heavy-lidded, half-dressed Chris. Sweats hung low to reveal a large dragon snaking up his ribs on the left. Ink climbed from his wrist along the tight, thick muscles of his forearm to his shoulder. Dark blond stubble accentuated the heavy line of his jaw. His tongue dragged across his plush bottom lip as he blinked. His steel blue gaze moved slowly over me, and he ran a hand through his blond hair. He was as gorgeous on the outside as he was on the inside, and I'd stupidly given him up.

Hopefully I could fix that, unless he'd already decided Candy was the one he wanted.

FOUR

CHRIS

Sarah was standing in the hallway outside my apartment. It kind of felt like Groundhog Day. She'd shown up like this months before, knocking on my door before she had a key to get in. She'd been wearing a similar outfit: worn jeans with tears at the knee and a loose-fitting shirt that hung off her shoulder, the strap of her tank top peeking out, her duffle crossed over her chest. Like those days early in our relationship, she was still wearing her face from the club. Even with the unnecessary and overdone makeup, she was gorgeous.

Her gaze moved over me quickly before it dropped to the floor, and she adjusted the strap of her bag. "Hi."

"What're you doing here?" It wasn't the friendliest greeting, but I was still half-asleep, trying to figure out if this was a dream or real.

"I-I don't know."

"You don't know?" If I had a million dollars, I'd bet Candy said something to her about seeing me. Which had sort of been the point. Sarah showing up at this hour hadn't been expected, though.

She shook her head. "I didn't really think this through. I'm sorry."

"What are you talking about?" She was fidgety and quiet, not her usual fiery self.

"Me coming here like I have some kind of right."

She turned as if she was about to walk away, so I grabbed her wrist. "Hey. Where are you going?"

"Home. It's the middle of the night. It's not the best time for a conversation."

I pulled her into my apartment, closing the door and turning the lock—not so she couldn't get away. Well, mostly not. Mostly it was to keep the neighbors where they belonged, on the other side of the door. There was a woman down the hall who'd wandered in before when I'd fallen asleep on the couch. I'd woken up to her rifling through my fridge.

"You must have a pretty good reason for showing up in the middle of the night, so you might as well come in and tell me what it is. Unless you're just here to get screwed. I'm not down for that."

As much as getting naked with her would be awesome, I was past the point of us being about just that. So there was a conversation we needed to have before that was even a remote possibility.

"You think I'm here for a booty call?"

"I've been used for less." I crossed over to the couch and flopped down, patting the cushion beside me. "Might as well sit."

Sarah dropped at the corner, instead of right beside me. "I'm not here for sex."

"So you thought you'd stop by for a chat at three in the morning? You do realize I work right across the street from your apartment, right? You can pop by any time you want. I'm pretty much always there."

"Did you sleep with Candy?" she blurted.

"What?" There was the fire I was used to.

"Candy. Did you sleep with her last night?"

"Is that what she said?" Candy was pretty good at embellishing, and it would be just like her to pretend that's what had gone down.

"So you did?" She looked halfway pissed and half ready to cry, which was atypical. Normally, Sarah had a backbone of steel. It was one of the many things that had drawn me to her. I'd later learned that under all that attitude was a soft, sometimes self-conscious woman who was afraid to get close to people. Just like me. Which was why we'd worked. Until we didn't.

"You came here in the middle of the night to find out if I fucked Candy?"

"It's one of the reasons." She ducked her head so all I could see was a veil of pale blond. "I'm guessing that means yes."

"Uh, no. I didn't."

She raised her mascara-heavy lashes. "But you had breakfast with her."

"I met her at a restaurant." I couldn't quite figure Sarah out right now. The fire was gone again, making her subdued in a way I wasn't used to.

"Oh." She picked at the frayed threads of her jeans, making the hole at her knee bigger.

"Not quite sure how you made the leap from bacon and eggs to screwing." I was actually one hundred percent sure Candy had made it seem like that's what happened on purpose to needle Sarah.

"I guess I assumed that if you were having breakfast with her it was because you'd spent the night together."

"You know what they say about assumptions." I stretched my arm across the back of the couch. I wasn't sure I liked that my potentially screwing Candy had been the motivation that brought her here. But at least I could get an answer to the question that had been eating at me since yesterday morning.

Before I could ask, Sarah spoke up. "I made a mistake."

"What kind of mistake?"

"I shouldn't have asked you for a break. I don't really want one." She rested her cheek on her knee and regarded me with sad eyes.

Well, that sure wasn't what I'd expected. "So why'd you ask for one?"

She was quiet for a few long seconds before she finally said, "I panicked."

I waited for more of an explanation, but all I got back was silence. "Wanna elaborate on that, or am I gonna have to drag all the answers out of you?"

Sarah huffed out a laugh and gave me a half-smile. "I'm sorry. I should've planned this out a little better. Just... Candy was bragging in the dressing room about seeing you, and it wasn't the best night. The last couple of weeks have been hard without you." She scooted forward until my fingers brushed her shoulder. "I miss you."

I wanted to run my fingers through her hair and skim the pale, smooth skin along the curve of her jaw. But I kept my hand mostly to myself, because Sarah was talking, and I wanted to keep it that way. "That still doesn't explain what the panic was about."

"That night I stayed at your place, all I could think about was how hard my internship was going to be combined with work. Finding time to see each other is already hard. I got scared."

"Scared of what?" I wasn't following, and I didn't think it was because she'd woken me up.

"Of this thing between us." She ran a soft finger across one of the lines of my tattoo, following the movement with her eyes instead of looking at me. "I figured you'd get frustrated eventually and... I guess I thought... I don't know, that if I took a break from you, I could take a break from how I feel about you."

Sarah and I didn't talk about feelings, or make plans for the future, so this honesty and vulnerability was new. For a long while I'd avoided pushing her to talk, but now that she was, I wanted more of it. I just wondered how I could avoid having to do the same. "How'd that work?"

"Not very well. I like being with you. It's one of the things I look forward to the most, and not having it—you... I didn't like it."

This rationale might explain what happened the last time she stayed here, but it sure didn't answer any of the other questions Candy had raised. "So you asking for a break didn't have anything to do with serving left stage?"

Her eyes went wide, and a hint of irritation colored her voice when she said, "I guess Candy told you about that."

"Seems to coincide pretty nicely with what went down that night."

"I knew you wouldn't be happy about it, but that wasn't the reason I panicked. Not really."

My stomach twisted as I considered that maybe Sarah hadn't been opposed to serving there. "How'd you end up on left?"

"I had car trouble, and I was late for my shift. It was either Xander send me home or I take left stage, so I did it because I needed the money."

I'd been after her for a while to get her car looked at. The rattle under the hood had been a sure sign it was in need of repairs, or a trip to the junkyard. I'd even offered to make an appointment with Hayden's mechanic, but she'd kept putting it off, saying she'd get it taken care of. Obviously she'd waited until it was too late.

"Why didn't you call me? I would've come to get you. I would've driven you in."

"You were with a client. Remember how you stopped by to see me before my shift?" Her cheeks flushed pink.

I sifted back through my memories and understood exactly why she was blushing. We'd had a frantic make-out session, cut short by my early client and her having to go to work. I'd still managed to get her off, though.

"Was I the reason you were late?" If she'd been forced to serve left stage because I'd been looking for an early-evening orgasm, it served me right that she'd broken up with me in the first fucking place.

She shook her head. "I would've made it on time if my car hadn't broken down. It wasn't like you dropping everything to pick me up would've changed that, so I called a cab. Xander was pissed that I was late, and all the other sections were taken, so I took the one still available."

"And that's all you did? Serve left?" I didn't want the answer to be anything but yes.

"I just served the tables."

"You didn't get pushed into anything else?" I wondered if I could get past security to punch Xander in the dick.

She held my gaze. "No. I mean, someone asked for a lap dance, but Xander told him I wasn't available."

Of course he did. Sarah was stunning, and she didn't need all the caked-on makeup to look that way. She was girl-next-door meets Barbie—an incredible commodity to a guy like Xander. He wouldn't waste her like that.

If he was anything like the owners of The Dollhouse, he'd be wanting to make her into something only the very privileged could have, like they'd tried to do with Lisa all those years ago. And those men were the worst kind. They would ruin a woman like Sarah. I was almost surprised Xander didn't want Sarah for himself. Or maybe he did.

I gave in and picked up a lock of her hair, letting the pale strands sift through my fingers. "Xander been looking for you to serve there again?"

She kept her eyes down when she said, "He's always pushing some angle."

She wasn't going to give me more, which meant there was likely something happening that she wasn't willing to share. It frustrated me that in protecting myself, I'd helped create the wall between us. During and after the trial Sarah had pushed, albeit gently, for me to talk to her about things, but I always shut her down. I hadn't wanted to taint the thing we had by revealing any more of my shit. In doing so, I'd closed off the possibility of real connection. But that was mostly okay. Even if this thing between us lasted a little longer, it wasn't going to go on forever.

"Was the money good?"

Sarah lifted a shoulder and let it fall. "It's all relative. You get paid for what you put up with."

It was a loaded response. I threaded my fingers through hers. Seeing Candy had ended Sarah's silence, as I'd hoped. But I didn't like what had caused it.

"You know he's going to keep pushing until you break, right?"

She bit her lip, her expression sad. "I'm not going to be there long enough for something like that to happen."

"So you're quitting?"

"As soon as my internship is over, I'm out. Hopefully I'll get a job from my placement."

"That's a couple of months away, though, right?"

A lot could happen in that time. I didn't want to think too far ahead, because Sarah getting a job in her field would change a lot of things. Still, getting her out of The Sanctuary was something I'd wanted since she'd taken the job. "Why wait so long? What about that friend of Tee's, the one who works at that bar? You could try to get a job there."

"I'm supposed to see Tenley and Lisa tomorrow night. I can talk to her then."

I nodded. "That's good."

Sarah focused on our twined fingers. "Can I ask you something?"

"Sure."

"Why'd you see Candy in the first place?"

"You weren't talking to me or the girls, and she started messaging. Things weren't adding up."

"And you thought Candy was a good source of information?"

"Not particularly, no. But she was willing to see me when you weren't."

"And you knew I'd find out."

Lying was pointless. "I was banking on it."

"So you used Candy to get my attention?"

"I'm not going to apologize for it. Candy was using me to get to you, and I used her back. It might've been an underhanded way to go about it, but she presented the opportunity, so I took it. Candy's nothing if not a manipulator, and she always wants the things she can't have the most." Ironically, I was the same in a lot of ways.

I probably belonged with someone like Candy rather than Sarah, but Sarah seemed to be choosing me, and I'd take it, for however long it might last. Whether it was for the right reasons or not, I decided not to analyze.

"Well, your plan worked."

"Good. Then it was worth having to sit through breakfast with Candy."

Sarah breathed out a laugh, then gave me a shy look. "You're not seeing her again?"

"Fuck no. Once was painful enough."

"So no more break?"

"Not if you don't want one."

"I don't."

"Then me neither." I leaned in to kiss her.

She put a palm on my chest. "I still smell like the club; I should shower first."

I tilted her head up, barely touching my lips to hers. "Let's wash away everyone else's sins so we can commit our own."

A wave of goose bumps pebbled her arms. "That's the best idea I've heard in the past two weeks."

I stood up, our hands still laced, and led her to the bathroom. I closed the door, not because we needed the privacy, but because I wanted the heat and warmth for Sarah.

She waited while I turned on the faucet and adjusted the temperature. Sarah liked hot showers. Her pale skin was always an angry pink when she was done. I toned it down a bit, since I assumed the heat was a sort of punishment for other people's transgressions.

Once I was satisfied, I turned to Sarah. She stood on the bathmat, hands clasped in front of her. A lot remained unsaid between us, but what she'd given me in words I'd thank her for with touch, because I couldn't match her honesty. Not yet.

I brushed her cheek with the back of my hand and traced the contour of her lip. Sarah's tongue peeked out. I knew why she was so popular at the club; she exuded a kind of purity that made her both desirable and unattainable. Except I had her. She'd let me put my hands all over every part of her perfect body.

"Jesus Christ, you're so fucking gorgeous." I made another pass with my thumb, this time wiping away residual lipstick—a garish red too severe for her fine features and pale skin. I followed with my mouth, sucking that pouty bottom lip.

Sarah gripped my shoulders, but I didn't take the kiss any further. First we'd shower, then I'd take her to bed and show her how much I'd missed having her there. I backed up, and she whimpered.

Trailing gentle fingers down her side, I found the hem of

her shirt and slipped my palm underneath, lifting the fabric over her head. Her bra was white cotton, with a front clasp. I carefully unfastened it, hooked my fingers under the straps, and pulled it down her arms.

Sarah's nipples tightened in the warm, damp air. I caressed the swell of her breasts, but moved on to her jeans, unbuttoning and unzipping, then dropped to my knees in front of her so I could drag them down her legs.

Her panties matched her bra, a pair of white Hanes bikini briefs. I pulled those down, too. I took a few moments to appreciate that she was here with me again, and that in the past two weeks no one had touched her like I was about to, that my worries had been unfounded. For now.

I ran my hands down her sides and over her hips on a deep exhale, then kissed below her navel before I stood. I was already shirtless, having fallen asleep on the couch.

As my sweats hit the floor, Sarah's eyes dropped to my hard-on, which had been hiding, tucked into my waistband. She ran her hands down my chest, but I caught them before they could get past my navel.

"Let's get wet."

She laughed, helping to temper the heavy mood, and let me pull her into the shower. I checked the spray before I put her under it. Her pale hair turned dark blond as water cascaded over her. I passed her the shampoo first, letting her take care of the important stuff while I lathered up her sponge-poof thing and dropped to my knees again.

I started at her feet and worked my way up her shins in slow circles, then moved around to her calves and up along the back of her thighs, coming around to the front again. I didn't pause to get between her legs, even though she'd parted them. I had plans.

By the time I was done washing her legs Sarah had finished with her hair. Showers were usually functional for her. I stood and washed the rest of her while she trailed her fingertips over the ink on my shoulder and the dragon running down my side.

I didn't spend a lot of time on her breasts, or the other sensitive areas where I knew she liked my hands. Instead I skimmed and teased, appreciating her soft, slightly impatient sighs.

When I'd been over every inch of her body, save one part, I stepped back to watch the suds pool at her feet and swirl down the drain. "Okay, all clean."

"You missed a spot," she said softly.

"I did? You look perfect to me. What'd I miss?"

Sarah's already flushed cheeks darkened further. She took my hand and dragged my fingertips from her navel to the neatly trimmed triangle of blond, guiding me to that sweet spot between her thighs. Her eyes fluttered as I went lower.

Sarah's lips parted as she swayed forward, grabbing the back of my neck.

"Is this what I missed?" I asked, gliding my fingers back and forth over slick skin.

Sarah nodded. I caressed her cheek with my not-busy hand. "Let me see those baby blues."

Sarah's eyes opened slowly, and I smiled when they finally met mine. "Feel good?" I asked.

"Uh-huh," she whispered.

"We almost finished washing away all the bad things?"

She nodded, her grip on the back of my neck tightening as I increased the pressure but not the speed.

I kept rubbing, slow and steady, and Sarah's eyes stayed on mine. My name formed on her lips, but it never came out as a sound. When she started to tremble, I backed her against the wall to help her keep her balance. Her mouth dropped open, eyes rolling up as the tremble became a quake. I eased a finger inside and used my palm to keep the pressure on her clit, feeling the heavy pulse within.

When she finished coming, Sarah wrapped her arms around me, her face pressed against my chest, lips moving in a slow path up my neck. "I missed the way you make me feel."

"You should let me make you feel even better then, don't you think?"

She nodded against my shoulder. I cut the water and wrapped her in a towel, then grabbed one for myself. We dried off and left them in a heap on the floor, too interested in getting back to the good stuff to care about the mess of wet clothes.

We ran naked through my apartment, Sarah shivering as she climbed up onto the mattress. The fan was on, the fluctuation in May temperatures making it difficult to sleep sometimes. I threw back the covers, flicked on the bedside lamp, opened the top drawer, and slapped the box of condoms on the nightstand so I wouldn't have to fumble around for it later.

Once prepared, I faced Sarah and propped myself up on my elbow. She lay on her side of the bed, wet hair soaking the pillow. She palmed the back of my neck and drew me down for a kiss. Her skin was pebbled, and she shivered again, so I wrapped an arm around her waist and pulled her against me.

Sarah's small moan vibrated against my lips. She threw her leg over my hip and pressed her warm, strong body along the length of mine, trapping my cock between us. We stayed like that for a while, kissing, hands roaming, until hers went to my ass and she pulled me on top of her.

"I want you." She smoothed her hands up my arms.

"You'll get me." I dropped a kiss on her chin. "First I need to reacquaint myself with this gorgeous body of yours. You down?"

She smiled and bit her lip. "Totally down."

Grinning, I lowered myself so we were chest to chest. I took my time kissing along Sarah's jaw while she ran her hands down my back. She pushed on my ass, maybe hoping to encourage me to grind up on her, but I was saving that for later. It had been too long since I'd been inside her, two weeks of uncertainty.

I pushed up again, hovering above her. "Show me where you want me to kiss you."

Sarah wasn't a talker in bed. She wasn't silent, but she was more prone to soft sounds and encouraging actions than exuberant affirmation that she was getting off on what I gave her.

She pointed to the spot below her ear, so I ran my tongue over the sensitive skin, following with gentle teeth and lips. The tightening of Sarah's legs around my waist indicated I was on the right track.

"Where to next?"

Sarah walked a trail down her body with her fingers. I skirted her nipples on purpose, because I wanted her words, not just gasps and moans.

"Chris," she whimpered, arching her back.

"Yeah, baby?" I kissed the center of her stomach.

She touched close to her nipple. "You missed right here."

I licked a line over the swell of her breast. "Here?"

"No." She shook her head. "Here." This time she brushed her nipple with a fingertip.

I covered the peak with my mouth, applying suction. Her hands went to my hair, holding me there. I waited until she loosened her grip before I moved to the other nipple, then continued my guided descent.

Sarah's lip was between her teeth when I finally reached her pussy. "Now where?"

She parted her legs and touched the juncture of her thigh, so I kissed her there, following with a slow lick that barely missed her clit. She moved her finger to the other side, so I did the same thing again. Sarah's eyes were on me as she grazed her clit, so I kept mine locked on hers as I pressed a tiny, soft kiss there. Then I waited.

A hint of a smile tugged at her mouth. She touched the same spot. I kissed there again and drew back.

Sarah propped herself up on an elbow and swept her finger across my bottom lip before she tapped the spot again. "French me," she whispered.

I grinned and closed my lips over her clit, stroking her with my tongue, doing exactly as she'd asked. She stayed propped up on one arm so she could run her fingers through my hair until she was close to coming. Then she dropped back down and writhed against my mouth, her faint moans growing louder. Her toes curled under my forearms, and I slipped two fingers inside her while I licked, once again feeling the pulse as she came on me, for me.

Then I eased back up her body and reached for a condom. I lost myself in her, in the way she whispered my name and kissed my neck and bit my shoulder, asking for my mouth. I gave her what she wanted, because it was the same thing I wanted. Just her. For as long as she wanted to keep making this mistake. At some point she'd figure it out, find someone who could give her all the things I'd never be able to, but until then, I'd love her, even if I couldn't tell her that's what I was doing.

FIVE

CHRIS

Sarah took off early the next morning for class. I didn't go back to sleep after she left. Instead I stared at the ceiling, trying to figure out why things still didn't feel quite right. Everything was tied up too neatly. Sarah was back in my bed, where I wanted her. Maybe the problem was me wanting something I wasn't going to get to keep, and being mostly okay with it.

New texts from Ivy made my phone buzz on the nightstand, distracting me from my continued worries. The first message apologized for not getting back to me sooner—she'd been at work— and the second said she'd be home until eleven this morning. It was barely past eight. I didn't have to be at work until 10:45 since I'd set up for my first appointment last night. I got dressed and grabbed my keys and my spare helmet.

Warm May sunshine greeted me as I stepped outside, but it didn't lift my mood. Hopefully whatever was going on with Ivy was less complicated than what was happening with Sarah.

I left my neighborhood and headed south toward Midway Airport. Rather than taking the rush hour-snarled highway, I took surface streets past Pilsen's bodegas and indie art galleries, then through Chinatown before I angled west on Archer and eventually found myself in an area that hadn't changed much since the 1960s. Dated apartment buildings and tiny houses in various states of upkeep crowded next to storefronts as I rode down potholed streets.

The house I'd grown up in hadn't changed in the years since I'd been kicked out, except to succumb to the weathering of age and disrepair. The constant stream of airplanes overhead didn't help much with the ambiance.

John had never been much for maintaining things, too busy drinking or out with his friends to care about what was or wasn't falling apart. And my mom had never been particularly healthy, even when I was young. As time and a hard life continued to wear her down emotionally, the rest of her had declined as well, making it nearly impossible for her to manage maintaining the house on her own.

Bad habits and lack of ability, or motivation, to seek proper medical care had prevented her from achieving any real goals. Not that she'd had big goals anyway. Getting pregnant before she finished high school had fucked things up pretty good for her. It was hard to beat down someone who was already half buried.

She couldn't take care of things, so the dilapidated state of the house had grown progressively worse. I'd only been allowed back into their lives recently, apart from paying the occasional bill, so I hadn't had much in the way of time or resources to help with upkeep. The first time I'd been back here was a few months ago, right after the trial started. The sorry state of the house had been shocking.

The pale blue exterior had faded to a muted gray, peeling in spots to reveal the washed-out sunny yellow it had once been when I was a kid. Today plastic still covered the windows, even though spring had arrived. The screen in the door was torn, and the frame hung askew. The front steps were wonky, having shifted from the repeated freeze-thaw cycle of winter over the years, settling on an angle and cracking at the edges. Ivy's bike—one with pedals, not an engine—was double locked to the rotting wooden slats of the front porch. No one who wanted to steal it would have to try very hard—not that the bike was worth anything anyway.

An old, broken love seat rounded out the disheveled front with its stained, brown flowered fabric. The lawn, or what was left of it, hadn't been mowed in a long while. Weeds had taken over, climbing halfway up the chain-link fence. This shitheap was a festering sore amid other blemishes on the landscape. In the absence of care, the decay had become too pervasive to cure.

I parked my bike in the gravel drive, noting John's rig (currently without a trailer) on the street. Just because it was there didn't mean he was home. Pocketing the keys, I headed up the front walkway, picking up pieces of broken beer bottle as I went. I hadn't been here since my mom had called about the furnace being broken. Guilt over having left her and my sister here in this dump of a house sledgehammered me every time. Not that I'd had much of a choice.

John had been the one who sent me packing, and my mom hadn't been in a position to take my side. I'd been a handful as a teenager—always getting into fights, messing around in school instead of listening to my teachers, talking back to John, and arguing with him until words and yelling became slaps and fists. I'd always lost those fights up until right before I got kicked out. Ivy had been young. My mom didn't want her exposed to my bullshit, and I couldn't blame her. But things were different now. Ivy wasn't a kid anymore, and living like this wasn't good for her. It made my apartment look like the Taj Mahal.

Ivy slipped out the door and jumped over the front steps to meet me. She threw her arms around me, but kept her voice low, her excitement tempered with nervousness. "Hey! What are you doing here?"

"I figured I should stop by and see you after you sent those texts." I returned the hug, disturbed by the too-prominent ribcage beneath her threadbare shirt. After I set her down, I nodded in the direction of the rig. "Is he home?"

"Mom said one of his friends picked him up around midnight. He hasn't come back yet."

"When'd he get in?"

"Two nights ago, I think. I've been working a lot, so I haven't been around much, and Mom had double shifts."

"How is Mom?"

"Worried. She's at work already." Ivy chewed on her chapped

bottom lip. "Her cell phone got cut off last week 'cause we're behind on payments, so she hasn't been able to make calls. I went to a payphone earlier to try to check in, but Dad didn't pick up. I couldn't call him on my cell or he'd ask questions about the number—you know, like we talked about?"

I hated that she made excuses for him. But I'd made the same kinds of excuses for our mom, so I could hardly fault her.

"Why don't I take you out for breakfast and drop you off wherever you need to be after?"

Her eyes lit up. "Really?"

"Yeah. For sure. You pick the place."

"Okay! Let me get my uniform and my purse."

I both loved and hated that something as simple as taking her for breakfast created that much excitement.

Ivy ran back into the house and reappeared a minute later, shoving clothes into a ratty backpack while fighting with the door. The back of her shirt rode up, exposing the edge of a tattoo placed right above her tailbone. From what I could see, the artist had been either an amateur or high when they'd done it. I bit my tongue so I didn't say anything. If I'd been in her life sooner, I could've made sure she had a decent artist to work with, even if it wasn't me.

The stairs creaked as I climbed them, protesting my weight.

"Watch the third board to your right."

I looked down to find a gaping hole in the front porch. Splintered wood littered the space around it, the rotten board having given way under someone's foot. This place was an infestation of cockroaches away from condemnable.

I took the bag so she had a free hand. "We need to do something about this before someone gets hurt."

"I keep meaning to put a board over it."

It shouldn't have been her responsibility, but John, waste of space that he was, rarely took care of anything but himself.

Ivy yanked on the door, and it finally slammed shut. Locking up, she followed me down the steps to my bike. I adjusted the spare helmet and passed her the leather jacket I'd gotten for Sarah. I hadn't wanted to risk any of that beautiful skin of hers when she rode with me. The jacket was way too big for Ivy, Sarah being much taller, but it did the job.

Ivy decided on an all-you-can-eat buffet. I followed behind her as she loaded up a plate. "Oh my God, Chris, there are so many options. I want everything."

"You can have everything." I stole a strip of bacon from her plate.

"Hey!" She elbowed me in the side.

I motioned to the giant tray full of bacon. "They're not going to run out, Ivy. You can come back as many times as you want."

"I'm hitting the waffle station next."

"Good call."

Once her plate was heaped with food, we sat down, and she dug in. I could tell she was trying not to scarf everything down, but had trouble holding back.

"I can't remember the last time I had a buffet breakfast," she said between mouthfuls.

"I'll bring you here anytime you want," I replied.

My mom had never been much of a money manager. Neither had I when I first started out on my own. But I'd learned quickly what it meant to have money in the bank, and that living paycheck to paycheck wasn't something I wanted to do for the rest of my life.

Cutting out drugs and limiting booze sure helped a lot. Getting into business with Hayden had forced me to manage myself better. I may not have had much in the way of education, but I had good people to keep me in line and make sure I didn't fuck things up.

My mom didn't have that kind of support, and she'd never figured out how to make what she had last. I had no idea how much of that was John and how much was her. But lack of education, low-paying jobs, and a loser husband weren't a good combination.

Watching Ivy stuff her face made me wonder how difficult their financial situation had become. She ate with one arm wrapped protectively around her plate, as if someone was going to steal it from her.

She looked just like our mom had at nineteen. Except she didn't already have a two year old hanging off her hip. Her hair was the same shade of coppery brown, with a slight wave. She had chocolate brown eyes, framed by thick lashes, and a heart-shaped face. She was pretty in a sweet way. But way too thin.

I'd seen more than one guy check her out since we came into the restaurant. I didn't like the idea that she was probably dating by this point. Ivy had grown up in a home with a dick for a dad who treated our mom like shit. I didn't want her to end up continuing the cycle—being taken advantage of by some asshole who could sense how broken she was.

It took me a long while to recognize I'd made a habit of seeking out broken women, though not to take advantage. And I didn't honestly believe I could fix them. People can only fix themselves. But the closer they matched me in their level of damage, the safer I felt—the easier it was to keep up my walls. Until Sarah. She might be broken, but she'd put up a good front at the very beginning. Since then she'd slipped through my cracks and fractured them, making me covet the possibility of something more, although I doubted she knew that even now.

"What?" Ivy asked, swallowing a mouthful of scrambled eggs and swiping at her chin with a napkin.

Shit. I must have been staring. "You doing okay? You're looking thinner these days."

Her eyes dropped to her plate. "I'm all right. I get busy with work and forget to eat."

"You sure you forget, or are you coming up short for grocery money?"

She tensed and shoved a forkful of pancake into her mouth.

"Come on, Ivy. You leave me these cryptic messages and then wanna pretend there's nothing going on? What's happening?"

She set her fork down and finished chewing. When she lifted her gaze, she seemed put out by my questioning.

"I just wanna help however I can, okay? Is it John?"

The waitress stopped by to freshen our coffee. Ivy was on her fourth cup.

"Can you bring her one of these smoothies?" I pointed to the card at the end of the table, advertising fresh fruit blended with yogurt. "You want this?" I asked.

"Regular juice is fine."

"She'll have one of these as long as they're made with real fruit and not some sugary syrup junk. Please." I tacked on the niceness, hoping I didn't come across as harsh.

The waitress assured me they were indeed made with real fruit. Once she was gone, I turned back to Ivy.

"You didn't have to do that. I would've been fine with orange juice or something."

"Screw that. I'm treating my baby sister to breakfast. You get the good stuff, not the crap they reconstitute with water."

Her smile was exactly what I'd wanted to see, but it faded at my next question.

"Now tell me what's going on. Is Mom okay?"

She smoothed her napkin out on the table. "She's got another cough."

She'd also had one this winter when I was there about the furnace. "She been to the doctor?"

"Uh-huh. She told me he said it wasn't anything to worry about, but I found this in the garbage." Ivy pulled out her tattered wallet. I recognized it as one I'd gotten for her for Christmas a couple years back. I'd left it in the mailbox since I wasn't allowed in the house at that point. I'd never even known if she'd gotten it or not until now. It was girly, a faded teal with a white and yellow daisy pattern. She withdrew a small slip of paper, unfolding it and pushing it across the table. It was a prescription for antibiotics issued three days prior. If she still had the paper, it hadn't been filled.

"Shit."

"She needs that medication. I can pay for it, but then I won't have enough to cover the water bill."

"What about John? Didn't he just come back from some big job?"

Ivy poked at her food but wouldn't look at me.

"Ivy? Why doesn't John pay for it?"

"Things aren't real good between him and Mom right now. He hasn't been staying at the house much when he comes back between jobs. They got into a big fight a while ago about money, and then he left on one of his runs, saying maybe this time he wouldn't come back at all."

I bit back all the nasty things I wanted to say. John was still her dad, even if he was an asshole. "Obviously that was an idle threat if his rig is parked at the house." Our mom wasn't very good at standing up for herself. Or her kids.

"You know how it is sometimes. Dad's got a temper and Mom gets… Well, he told her she wasn't grateful for what she had. He was gone for a few weeks, and she figured he'd calm down. She kept calling him until her phone got cut off. I guess he must've forgiven her since he's back and all. But she's been really upset about it. I think all the stress must've made her sick. She took on all these extra shifts at both jobs to cover all the bills, and so did I, but I guess we got behind a bit."

That explained why I hadn't heard from my mom recently. While we weren't especially close, we usually talked every couple weeks, sometimes more, even if it was only for a few minutes, or because she needed money for something.

"Why'd you wait to call me? I could've helped you out."

She mashed up a strawberry with her fork, the liquid soaking into her half-eaten pancake, turning the edges pink. "You put out all that money in February for the furnace and stuff. I didn't want to ask you—"

The waitress stopped by with the smoothie. Ivy seemed relieved by the interruption. Her eyes fluttered shut as she took a sip, like it was the best thing she'd ever tasted.

I held up the piece of paper. "I want you to call me for stuff like this. What about the cell phone bill? How much is owed on that?"

She looked both grateful and embarrassed. "A few hundred maybe? I'm not sure."

"Can you get me the bill?"

"I should be able to."

"You get it for me, and I'll pay it directly."

I'd learned the hard way that if I handed over cash, it never went where it was supposed to. My mom would invariably either give it to John for whatever bullshit expenses he deemed important, or he'd find it squirreled away in one of her hiding places and take it. At least that's what she'd told me in the past.

"Thanks, Chris. I didn't know what else to do. I can cover the basics for food and stuff, but the bills keep piling up, and I don't know where the money goes."

I had a pretty damn good idea where it was going. I imagined any threat from John about my mom managing on her own would be accompanied by some kind of purposeful sabotage on his part. If I didn't think it would do more harm than good, I'd have a talk with him. But since I didn't live in that house, I could never be sure what the repercussions of something like that would be.

"Calling me was exactly the right thing. We'll get this sorted."

"I'm sorry to put you out like this."

"You're not putting me out." The alarm on my phone buzzed in my pocket, alerting me that I should get to the shop if I didn't want to be late for my first appointment. "You need another round at the buffet? I gotta get to work soon, but I don't want you leaving hungry."

She glanced longingly at the waffle station and rubbed the flat expanse of her stomach. "I wish I had more room. If I eat anything else, I'll go into a food coma."

I signaled the waitress over. "Can I get a takeout box?"

She gave me a nervous smile. "There's no takeaway with the buffet, sir."

"I know, but my baby sister here would love another waffle; she just doesn't have the room for it right now. How about you charge me whatever it costs for an extra breakfast, and she can get one to go?"

"You don't have to do that." Ivy's cheeks went pink with embarrassment.

"You can have breakfast for dinner, or lunch," I replied.

The strain in our waitress's polite smile faded. "That's so sweet. I'm sure that'd be fine."

She came back with a takeout box. Inside was a huge Belgian waffle, with covered plastic ramekins of fresh strawberries, sauce, butter, and whipped cream lined up on the side. "I would've brought you the ice cream, but it'd melt, unless you want it in a separate container with a lid that seals?" She looked to Ivy.

"That'd be great. You're a doll," I answered before Ivy could say no.

"I only charged you for the extra waffle, not a whole breakfast." She slid the check across the table with a wink, and I passed her my credit card.

When she returned I added a generous tip, bagged up the takeout, and hit the road.

I dropped Ivy off at work. It was the first time I'd ever seen her place of employment. She should've been in school, in some kind of art program. I'd seen her transcript on the table when I'd been over about the furnace. She'd had great grades in high school— so good that she should probably be on a scholarship somewhere, getting a diploma she could use to get a better paying, less physically taxing job. But if there wasn't enough money to cover a prescription for antibiotics, there sure wouldn't be enough to cover any of the expenses associated with college.

I wasn't pleased about the seedy location and the even seedier exterior of the sports bar. Apparently Ivy had gotten the job a few months ago through an acquaintance of John's. Before that she'd been a cashier at a convenience store close to the house.

"My buddy's girlfriend can probably get you hooked up with a better job than this. She's got a friend who works in one of the popular bars on the north side." I used the term *friend* loosely.

Hayden hated that douche, Ian, who worked at Elbo. I wasn't so sure I wanted Ivy working with someone like him, but it had to be better than this skeezy joint. Plus I could keep an eye on her, and that guy was already scared of Hayden, so it wasn't like he'd try something on my sister.

She passed over the jacket and helmet. "That's nice of you to offer, but I'd have to take the bus, and they don't run very often after the bars close. I can bike here in twenty minutes. They give me lots of shifts, and my manager is pretty nice about letting me take home food on the house."

I couldn't imagine them serving anything healthy, but I kept my mouth shut. "If you change your mind, let me know. You could get away with fewer shifts and still make more money."

"I can think about it." Her tone told me she'd already dismissed the idea.

"I'll get that prescription filled at the pharmacy a couple of blocks back so you can pick it up after work, okay? In the meantime, see if you can't rustle up that cell phone bill for me."

"I will. Thanks for everything, Chris." She put on her ancient backpack and went inside.

I stayed there for a minute, watching as a few early patrons filed in through the grungy, black door. It was a dive, and the clientele reflected as much. The current crowd seemed to consist of a bunch of men in their fifties who worked at the dilapidated factory across the street. Next time I'd check out the inside.

Before I headed to work, I stopped at the pharmacy, as promised. No wonder my mom had tossed the prescription in the trash; it cost nearly a hundred bucks to fill. I sent Ivy a message to let her know she could pick it up later in the day.

I took the highway for my return trip, admiring the view of the buildings rising along the lake as I skirted downtown Chicago on the way to Lincoln Park and Inked Armor.

Lisa was sitting at the jewelry counter when I arrived. A takeout coffee from Serendipity sat next to her, along with a brown bag. She looked up as I approached. "How're you doing this morning?"

"Pretty good." I glanced at the schedule. I'd already prepped for my first client last night, so it was just a matter of setting up the ink.

She pointed to the bag. "I picked up some bagels if you want something quick before your first appointment arrives."

I patted my stomach. "I just took Ivy out for breakfast, but thanks."

The door tinkled with the arrival of my client, so I didn't have a chance to get into it with Lisa.

After minimal chatting, I got started on my client, but she had questions from time to time, and it was hard to stay focused on the conversation. I kept thinking about my family and Sarah. My mom had made a lot of bad choices, her first one being getting pregnant in high school by my asshole of a father. It sucked all the potential out of her life.

Being a teenager with a kid made a hard life harder. All the challenges, all the money worries were magnified by so much responsibility. That was the main reason I still insisted on bagging it with Sarah. She'd told me plenty of times she was on the pill, but that wasn't a foolproof guarantee against baby making.

'Doming up meant added protection against fucking up Sarah's life. When she graduated from that MBA program, she was going to have more opportunities than I'd ever dreamed of. I wasn't going to be the one to take that away from her with an accident, like I'd done to my mom.

I stopped shading the yellow flower on my client's ribs, aware it was a sensitive place to get inked.. "We're almost there, you need a short break so you can power through the rest?"

She smiled and exhaled a breath. "That might be good."

Want me to grab you a water while I'm at it?"

"That'd be awesome, Chris."

I rolled off my gloves and dropped them in the trash. "I'll be right back, you just lay back and breathe."

The short break was enough to get us through to the end.

After six, I finally had a gap between clients. I hadn't had a chance to talk to anyone all day, having had back-to-back sessions in the private room. If I'd had more time, I would've run across the street for a quick visit with Sarah. Although I wasn't likely to be quick the next time I clocked some serious alone time with her.

I came out of the room in time to see Tenley walk into the shop. "What's going on, Tee?"

"I brought treats!" She set a white box on the glass-topped jewelry counter as I swallowed her up in a bear hug. Where Sarah was tall, willowy, and fair, Tee was petite and dark.

Hayden came out of the storage room as I set her down. A wide grin broke out across his typically serious face. "Hey, kitten. I thought I heard your voice."

A coy smile turned up the corner of her mouth as she stroked the box on the counter. "I brought something to share."

"As long as it's not you, I'm good." He cupped her face, dipping down to kiss her.

"Take it to the private room," Lisa said, but she was smiling.

I reached around them and flipped the lid open, inside were Hayden's favorite treat: vanilla cupcakes with vanilla buttercream frosting. Made from scratch. Tenley liked to bake in her spare time. Like Sarah, she was a master's student at Northwestern. Unlike Sarah, she didn't have a job to manage as well. She used to work for Cassie in the bookstore, but she and Hayden had decided a while back that she should focus on her studies—and she also had the financial backing to make it work after her settlement from the plane crash.

I nabbed one of the cupcakes and stuffed the entire thing in my mouth.

Hayden took a break from sucking off Tee's face to give me a dirty look. "Don't even think about taking another one."

Dude had a cupcake fetish. It was pretty unreasonable the way he got worked up over them. Cupcakes—mainly the ones made by Tenley—had the same effect on him as, say, complete female nudity might've on another guy.

"There are plenty at home. I even made mini ones," Tee assured him.

Hayden's eyes lit up. "Yeah?"

"Mm-hmm."

His grin was lecherous. "Eat as many as you want. I'm going on a treasure hunt later."

"You two are disgusting." Lisa grabbed her bag and ducked out from behind the counter.

The tinkle of the door drew everyone's attention again as Sarah walked into the shop. No one said anything at first, eyes darting from her to me. Seemed neither one of us had had an opportunity to fill anyone in on what had happened last night, or early this morning.

"Hey." Sarah lifted her hand in a tentative wave and looked to me, like she was waiting for me to say or do something.

I hid a half-smirk behind my hand as I pretended to scratch an itch on my chin.

"I guess we should go?" Lisa asked, her gaze shifting uncomfortably between us.

Sarah gave her a bright smile. "Sure." She turned to me. "Are you coming by Hayden's later?"

"I can." Yesterday the plan had been to go there so I could finally talk to her. Now I had a different reason.

She dangled a key from her finger. "Want to drive my car over instead of your bike? It might rain later."

I held out my hand, and she dropped it into my palm. "Does this mean I'm staying at your place tonight?"

Her shy smile widened. "If you want."

"Oh, I want."

"Um, does someone want to tell me what's going on here?" Lisa asked, hands on her hips.

"Sarah and I had a chat last night. We figured a few things out," I said.

Lisa pointed at me. "And you didn't think to say anything about it?"

"I've been holed up in the private room all day."

"It's a one-sentence conversation that goes something like, 'Sarah and I got back together.'"

"There's no such thing as a one-sentence conversation with you."

Lisa swung around to Sarah. "Let's go. You need to fill us in on the details."

"I'm going to suggest censoring out the ones that ended in moans," I called as Lisa and Tenley pulled Sarah out the door.

SIX

CHRIS

I followed Jamie and Hayden to his place in Sarah's car. When we arrived, empty martini glasses littered the counter, along with a mostly empty bottle of vanilla-flavored vodka. There was a good chance the girls were drunk.

Hayden called out our arrival. He didn't get a response right away, so panic tilted his voice on the second shout out.

A door slammed somewhere upstairs, followed by girly giggles.

"If you're having a naked pillow fight, you best be taking pictures," I called up.

Hayden punched me in the shoulder.

I rubbed the spot. "I was kidding, H. Don't get your balls tied in a knot."

Tenley came into view, her long hair sweeping the banister as she started down the stairs. "Hey! Sorry. We didn't hear you."

Sarah and Lisa followed her. They all held the railing and watched their feet. They were definitely feeling the drinks.

Hayden took one look at Tenley and sighed. "Did you eat anything while you polished off that bottle of vodka in there?"

Her eyes widened, and her palm came over her mouth. "Oh! I forgot to clean up. We were just—um, I... we—"

Sarah cut in, her grin devious. "Tenley was showing us your birthday present. It's a surprise."

"Is that right, kitten?" He slid an arm around her waist, pulling her close. "You know how I feel about surprises."

"I think you're going to like this one," Tee said.

"A lot," Sarah added, giving Lisa a sly look.

Now I really wanted to know what those girls had been up to this evening. I might get it out of Sarah later—when no one else was around and I could bribe her with favors.

I headed for the kitchen. "I'm grabbing beers. Anyone else need anything?"

"I'll make another round of drinks for us," Sarah said to the girls. Her cheeks were flushed pink, her lips the same shade, a sure sign she'd had more than a couple of drinks. Most of the time Sarah limited her alcohol consumption. Hard liquor made her loopy, and it seemed the three of them had been at it for a while, without a food buffer.

Once in the kitchen, she grabbed the belt loop on my jeans to keep me from getting away. Her arm came around my waist, and I felt her forehead on the back of my neck.

"Hey."

"Hey." She ducked under my arm, coming around in front of me.

I absorbed the hug as she snuggled into my chest. When Sarah got sauced, she became super affectionate. Most of the time she was pretty reserved with the PDA, but not right now. I liked it when she got all touchy.

I rested my chin on top of her head. "You girls get up to no good?"

"We dressed Tenley in lingerie and took pictures."

"You what?"

She pinched my earlobe. "Shh. Don't ruin the surprise."

I dropped my voice. "Like sexy pictures?" I'd seen the photographs hanging in Hayden and Tenley's bedroom—the ones of her half-naked with her back piece on display. I fought the accompanying visual.

"Exactly. We're making an album for his birthday."

"He's gonna blow his load over that. You have her holding cupcakes, too?"

Sarah's eyes widened with excitement. "I should've thought of that! We'll have to get her back in one of her outfits and snap a few extra shots."

"You know, I've got a birthday coming up in a few months. You could put together something like that for me."

She stiffened. "I don't really have sexy stuff. Mostly it's just slutty."

"I'm talking about your non-work stuff."

She snorted. "Yeah, right, because white cotton is so super sexy."

"I think you underestimate the impact of white cotton on me." Just thinking about all that pale, simple softness made me super hard for some reason. I liked that Sarah didn't feel the need to cover her body in things that distracted from her natural beauty.

She didn't do provocative outside of the club, but she had lots of pretty outfits hanging in her closet and filling up her dresser. Today was no exception. She wore a pale green tank, gauzy and sheer, over a thin-strapped white one, paired with gray leggings that ended below her knee.

"Well, I have an underwear drawer full of boring cotton, so you're totally in luck."

I cupped her face, lips hovering close to hers. Her breath was sweet with vanilla and alcohol. "You should model some of that for me when we get back to your place."

"The bikini briefs or the boy shorts?"

"Mmm. Tough decision. I have so many favorites."

"I'll just model them all, then." She tilted her chin up, waiting for me to kiss her.

Which was exactly why I didn't.

"If you can stay awake that long. I put money on you passing out in the car on the way home. Your eyes are drooping. Or are you practicing your sexy face on me?"

She pinched my neck. "They are not. I'm just a little buzzed."

"You need me to take you home? Put you to bed?" I was definitely getting to her.

"You can put me to bed later, like you did last night. Right now I want a kiss." She pushed up on her toes.

I dropped one on the tip of her nose.

"Chris."

"Sarah."

She dug her nails into my scalp. "Keep it up and no sleepover for you."

Her eyes lit up with satisfaction when my smile dropped.

"How're you gonna get home if I don't drive you?" I asked.

Her satisfaction fizzled when she realized I had a point.

I angled her head and pressed my lips to hers. She wasn't having the slow and easy tonight, though. Her tongue stroked along the seam of my mouth, looking to get inside.

When I parted my lips, she took full advantage, as if she wanted to make up for our time apart. Which would have been perfectly fine with me if we hadn't been in someone else's kitchen with our friends in the next room.

"Whoa. Maybe I should come back in a few minutes." Jamie backed out of the kitchen with his hands in the air.

"What's going on in there?" Lisa asked, somewhere close behind him.

Sarah sucked on my bottom lip, nails digging in harder, little punishments for making her wait before she broke free.

"We were saying hi." She ran her hands down my chest as she stepped back. "You know I was joking about not sleeping over, right?"

"You're sure you want me hogging your bed?"

"I want."

"Then I'm all yours."

As much as I would've liked to take Sarah back to her place right then and enjoy some naked snuggles, she was tipsy, and we hadn't spent much time with the Inked Armor crew outside of work lately, especially not all together. So we stayed.

It was hard not to compare what Lisa and Jamie had, or Tenley and Hayden, to the uncertainty of me and Sarah. We were together for now, and I'd have to be content with what it was, for as long as I got to have it.

The girls, who didn't seem all that interested in slowing their drinking roll—despite it being the middle of the week—decided the deck wasn't the place they wanted to hang out. Instead, they all ran up to Tenley's room to get bathing suits so we could make use of Hayden's hot tub.

He'd had it installed for Tenley, because the hot water was good for her hip, especially in the winter when the cold made it ache. She had all kinds of pins holding her together, although I never heard her complain about it.

I'd been smart about keeping a pair of swim shorts here for such impromptu occasions. I'd only had to borrow a pair from Hayden once. He was a wiry guy, tall and lanky compared to me, so his shorts hadn't fit all that well.

Sarah came down the stairs in one of Tenley's little bikinis. She was perfectly curvy and long limbed, so the scraps of fabric didn't leave much of her smooth, pale skin to the imagination. Good thing I was already in the tub, otherwise I might've embarrassed myself.

Hayden set his beer down and stood up. Wrapping his arms around Tenley, he lifted her over the edge and into the tub.

"I can get in on my own, you know," she said, but she was grinning.

"Any reason to get his hands on you," I replied.

"I was being helpful." Hayden adjusted the strap on her top, getting close to her boob.

"I'm going to sit between you two if you can't knock it off." Lisa slipped in beside Jamie, her lavender hair pulled up in a loose ponytail, covered by a bandana.

"Like hell you are. You've had her for the last three hours. You don't get to monopolize her now that I'm here."

"She was kidding, Hayden." Tenley patted his cheek as he pulled her down into the water on his lap. She made no move to find her own space, more than happy to be wrapped up in him.

Sarah settled in the tub, sidling up to me. I moved her legs so they were in my lap and put an arm around her.

"So what exactly were you girls up to tonight, apart from getting all sauced and not eating dinner?" Hayden asked.

"Yeah, no one's telling you anything," Lisa said.

"I'm pretty sure I can get this one to talk if we keep feeding her drinks." Hayden nuzzled Tenley's neck.

"Not likely," Sarah snorted.

"I'm pretty sure you'll be happy about it," I chimed in.

Sarah elbowed me in the side. "You're not supposed to say anything!" she whispered in my ear. At least she attempted to whisper, but her level of drunkness made her louder than she meant to be.

"Sarah! You were supposed to keep it a secret!" Lisa scolded.

"You're going to tell me later, right?" Jamie asked her.

"Seriously?" Hayden's expression went dark. "You all fucking suck with this shit."

Tenley whispered something in his ear, and his eyebrows furrowed more, then lifted high.

"Okay, you two, break it up. No one wants to watch you get it on in the hot tub," Lisa said.

Hayden flipped her the bird, but Tenley moved off his lap, her cheeks pink and her wide smile matching his.

A couple hours later, by the time we were ready to call it a night, Sarah was sleepy drunk and using me as a crutch on the way to her car. I'd passed on more than one beer, aware that we'd be spending the night in a spare room instead of her bed, otherwise. Sarah got self-conscious about sex when there was a chance someone could hear her, even though that was unlikely under any circumstances, since she was so quiet. But I hadn't wanted to chance it, not that it mattered much by the time I got her into the car.

Sarah fell asleep on the short drive home with her hand on my junk. The car was running a lot smoother now that she'd had it fixed. Waking her up proved to be more difficult than I'd expected, and I half-carried her up the stairs to her apartment.

She used me as a brace while she kicked off her shoes, face mashed into my chest. She bypassed the bathroom and stumbled her way to the bedroom. Too bad she wasn't in any state to be doing something more than sleeping off her oncoming hangover.

Sarah struggled out of her clothes, leaving them strewn across the floor, until she was left in a pair of nude cotton panties and a matching bra. I followed behind, picking up articles as I went, pausing to watch as she did a little spin and flopped back on the comforter.

Sarah was difficult to resist at the best of times. Mostly undressed made it that much more of a challenge—unless she was so tired she couldn't stay awake long enough to finish an entire sentence. Then she was amusing, but untouchable.

"C'mere." Head lolling to the side, she extended a hand in invitation.

I went to her dresser first. Opening the second drawer, I rummaged around until I found a white camisole. When I turned around, she was spread out on the bed, arms wide open, legs hanging off the edge, eyes closed again.

I sat down beside her. "Sarah, baby, let's get this on you."

She batted my hands away and felt around on the comforter, close to my leg, like she was searching for something.

"You gonna help me out, sugar lips?"

She blew out an exasperated breath and pried her eyes open. "I'm trying, but you're making it hard."

Some parts of me sure were hard. "I should probably get you a glass of water."

She arched her back and shoved her hands behind her, fighting with the clasp on her bra.

"I could help with that," I offered.

"I got it." Her tight, perky breasts appeared, with their sweet little nipples. "You should get me your dick." It came out with a heavy slur.

I laughed, pushing her hair away from her face. Sarah wasn't one to use crude language, so it was a bit of a shock to hear, and it made me harder than I already was, which was pretty damn hard. "What do you think you're going to do with it?"

She looked up at me, her blond lashes fluttering as she tried to focus. "Sit on it."

"You think so, huh?"

"I know so." She rolled onto her stomach and put her head in my lap. With uncoordinated fingers, she fought with the button on my jeans. I let her have at it for a few seconds, entertained by her attempt at the impossible.

"Baby, you can't even sit up, let alone sit on my dick. You'll be lucky if you get in a cuddle tonight."

She made a discontented noise and dropped her head on my thigh. Sliding forward, her cheek rested on the bulge straining against my fly.

"You're prolly right."

I let her stay there, smoothing her hair while she gave me cheek-dick snuggles through my pants. I'd have to whack it something fierce before I fell asleep, but there'd be other times to make good on her desire to get all up on that and ride.

Her hair was in her face again. I swept it back, stroking along the long column of her throat. She was flawlessly beautiful, even as messed up as she was right now. It terrified me that she worked in a place where someone could get her into this kind of state and take full advantage of it.

When her eyes stayed closed, I moved her off my lap. I hadn't managed to get the cami on her, so I took the throw blanket folded at the end of the bed and laid it over her instead. Kissing her forehead, I left her sprawled out on top of the covers while I got her a glass of water and Tylenol. It took all of maybe two minutes, but her breathing was even by the time I got back. Getting her to sit up and drink the water took a lot of coaxing.

"You're real tired, huh, sugar?" I rearranged her until she was under the comforter.

"Uh-huh." She hugged her pillow, curling into a ball.

I kissed her temple and pushed up off the mattress, needing to take care of my problem before I joined her.

"Chris?" She grabbed my wrist, bleary eyes struggling to focus on me with something between sadness and panic.

"What's up, baby? You need something else?"

"I'm sorry."

"For what?" I dropped down on the edge of the bed.

"For drinking too much. I didn't mean to."

"You don't have to apologize for having fun with your friends. It's good for you to let loose. I don't think you do it enough." Although I wasn't sure she'd be feeling all that awesome at work tomorrow, despite the water and Tylenol. I went to stand, but she tightened her hold on my wrist.

"Can you stay a while longer?" She pushed through the sheets until she could curl her body around me.

"I'm just gonna hit the bathroom. I'll be back in a few minutes."

"You're not leaving?" She seemed confused.

"I wasn't planning on it."

"Okay. That's good. I don't want you to go, even if there's not really anything for you to stay for." She pressed her lips against the back of my hand. "I'll make it up to you next time, okay? Just stay with me tonight." Her eyes fluttered shut, and she settled back into the warmth of the bed.

It took me a few seconds to get what she was trying to say. "Sarah?"

She had to work hard to pry her eyes open. I touched her cheek and her lips parted on a sigh.

"I didn't just come here for the sex. I came here for you."

She smiled softly and mumbled, "I'll still make it up to you."

I waited until her breathing evened out again before I went to the bathroom. It bugged me that she'd think the only reason I wanted to sleep over was for sex, but then maybe I'd never given her a reason to believe otherwise. That was something I'd need to find a way to change.

My toothbrush was in the top drawer of the vanity. She hadn't gotten rid of it while we were on our break, which made me feel better. I gave my mouth a quick brush, then took a few minutes to alleviate the hard-on that wouldn't go away.

On the way back to her bedroom, I paused at the coffee table. Papers were strewn around in a disorganized mess. While Sarah wasn't super tidy, her place wasn't usually this bad. It looked as though she'd been searching for something, and maybe she'd been in a rush. The clutter would make Hayden go exorcist crazy.

Sarah's résumé—the one for her internship—sat on top of the pile. Not surprisingly, neither The Dollhouse nor The Sanctuary was listed among her places of employment. According to her history, she'd done some temp work for a small marketing company—just secretarial and filing—about a year and a half ago, before she moved to Chicago.

There was a gap in her employment history after she moved here, but grad school could account for that. Her program was tough, and a lot of her peers didn't take on jobs as well. If only Sarah could afford to do that.

Under the résumé was a copy of a project she'd been stressing about since before she called for the break. It was marked now. She'd gotten a ninety. I flipped through it, skimming the contents. She'd laid out an entire marketing plan for opening a small business. It was neatly organized in a clear portfolio with pic charts and graphs outlining projected start-up costs, and potential profit and losses. It was impressive. Beside that were her bank statements. Looking at them would be an invasion of privacy, but I did it anyway.

The statement was dated a week ago. Bi-weekly automatic deposits denoted the lame-ass paychecks from The Sanctuary, the hourly wage pitiful in comparison to the tips Sarah pulled every shift. There were additional weekly deposits of a couple hundred or so, but it didn't come close to the cash I assumed she pulled in. I'd watched her count out the stack of bills at the end of a shift once she got home, double checking figures. Most nights she pulled in at least two bills for slinging drinks. Weekends she made a lot more.

Under the bank statements was another official looking

document detailing her student loans which totaled more than fifty grand. I'd never owed that amount of money in my life, or *owned* it, for that matter. I could and did make more than that in a year, but I would never be able to help Sarah pay off her debt. Not when I was passing over money to help out my mom on a regular basis.

As I looked over the statement, I understood exactly why she stayed at The Sanctuary, even though she hated it. I knew her home life growing up had been unstable, a lot like mine. It had just been her and her mom. That she'd managed to get through undergrad and move on to grad school facing that kind of uphill battle was impressive.

My guilt trips over her job probably made her feel worse. It was selfish insecurity on my part, borne out of fear that Sarah would take the same path Candy had, and not only ruin her potential, but erase my temporary blip of happiness before I was ready.

It would disappear, though. No one took on a school loan that size if the job they'd eventually be walking into was going to pay less than it had cost to get the degree. Soon Sarah would be fully immersed in one world, not two. There'd be no reason for her to stay at the bottom with me when she could climb to the top with someone better suited to the journey.

Beside the coffee table was a basket of clean laundry. I couldn't help Sarah financially, but I could make life easier in other ways, make myself useful beyond the bedroom. I sat down next to the basket and smoothed out her panties the way I'd seen them in her drawer, arranged by style. Most were Hanes, with a few nicer ones thrown in, all in various pale shades. They came in two styles: bikini briefs and boy shorts. Halfway through the basket, I found one of her work outfits. The naughty nurse uniform was a one-piece zip up number.

I'd seen her in it a couple times when I used to go to The Dollhouse. It was low cut, her cleavage squeezed together with a white lace and satin push-up bra that made her boobs look way bigger than they were. The skirt barely covered her ass. She'd worn a pair of lacy shorts under it and white garters. A stethoscope drew more attention to her breasts. I'd tried real hard not to look at them when I ordered a drink. Or I'd tried not to let her catch me, anyway.

The outfits had never done it for me with Sarah. They'd never done it for me period. Strip clubs were like costume parties on Halloween—everyone dressed as the sluttiest version of themselves. Women in fetish outfits wasn't what had drawn me to the club in the first place. It was that everyone there seemed the same as me. We were all damaged, and the girls who went to the private rooms and offered services were the most fragile of them all, even if they put on a good front.

I wasn't a knight in shining armor coming to save them; I was a kinder, safer option than someone who would abuse them, because I knew what it was like. I wasn't sure what kind of person that made me.

Sarah was different than those girls, and that had been clear from the beginning. I'd asked her out, fully expecting the *no* I got back. But I'd kept asking, and she'd kept saying no. And the more she said no, the more I wanted to make it happen.

I'd see her working the tables, smiling the way she was supposed to, shredding egos in that subtle way of hers where I couldn't quite tell if she was joking or serious when she cut someone down. And when she thought no one was looking, I'd see that smile slip. Her sadness leached the warmth out of her gaze whenever she turned toward the stage to watch the girls strip down to thongs, offering the tiny straps for bills to be shoved in.

Her expression when she thought no one was watching made me re-evaluate my strategy. I wanted to understand why someone so well-spoken and gorgeous would choose to put herself in a position where she was regarded as a thing to be had and discarded.

After nearly two months of persistence, Sarah finally agreed to meet me at a juice bar. She'd driven herself and had been determined to hate me. I'd been determined to change her mind. I wanted to be someone better than I was. I hadn't even tried to kiss her at the end. She'd been the one to lay one on me, and she'd looked pretty pissed about it. I'd called her an hour later and left a message asking to see her again. It took her two days to get back to me, but she'd agreed. That time she let me take her to dinner.

She'd been guarded at first, which was understandable. Her walls were like mine, which was another part of the allure. I understood walls. They'd kept me safe from people most of my life. Only my Inked Armor crew got past them, and even then, I only let them into the rooms I wanted to. There were locked closets no one but me could enter. But by keeping my walls in place with Sarah, I'd created a distance I didn't know how to cross any more.

Part of me wanted to let her in, tell her all about my shitty childhood and the way I struggled with how to help my sister and mother with the poverty they couldn't escape. I thought she'd understand, and maybe she'd empathize, and maybe she'd even give me some piece of her in return, but it was a dangerous slope. And it might tangle me deeper in something I wanted but couldn't have. Not with any real permanence.

I finished folding the laundry, stuffing the nurse outfit under everything else. Then I went around turning off the lights. I stripped out of my shirt and pants, but left my boxers on.

Sarah was starfished on the bed. Most nights she'd roll over and give me space, not that her double bed had much to give. Tonight she burrowed through the covers, grumbling in her sleep. She did that sometimes when she was stressed. Xander's name came up often. Tonight it was mine as she shimmied in closer.

"I'm glad you decided to stay," she breathed. Her arm came around my waist, and she smoothed a hand up my chest, stopping on my left pec. I covered it with my own.

"I told you I would."

"I thought maybe you'd change your mind."

"Not a chance. I thought you were asleep."

"I am."

I smiled against her hair.

"I had to change the sheets today," she muttered.

Now I knew she was only half awake. "Oh, yeah?"

"Uh-huh. I didn't want to, but they'd lost your smell. Now I'll get it back."

"My smell?"

"Mmmm."

"What do I smell like?"

"Safe."

I let the word sit, like oil floating on top of water; it didn't mix with the answer I'd expected.

"I like that I can feel your heart," Sarah whispered, her sleep-fuzzed mind drifting again.

She wasn't really present in the moment. I knew that. So I said the thing I wanted to, but couldn't when she was truly listening.

"It's all yours, baby. All you have to do is want it enough to take it."

SEVEN

CHRIS

I woke up to an empty bed. Sunshine streamed in a muted haze through the gauzy curtains, the sound of traffic on the street below buffered by the fan running in the corner of the room. I had a vague recollection of Sarah kissing me goodbye this morning, but it must have been at some god-awful hour.

I stretched out, my back aching from her hard mattress. That was part of the reason we preferred staying at my place; my mattress was a pillow-top. There were few things I spent good money on. Nice sheets and a good mattress were right up there with a comfy couch and my ride.

I checked her closet, hoping I'd left one of my T-shirts behind the last time I slept over. I could go to work in the one I wore yesterday, but I doubted I'd feel very fresh by closing. The other option was to ride home and get changed. It wouldn't take that long, but the convenience factor of staying over would be lost if I had to make the trip.

Sarah's closet had two distinct sections. One side held a selection of dress pants, blazers, and skirts in dark colors, as well as mostly white blouses. The other side was comprised of summer dresses, old jeans, and shirts. On the far right was one of my Inked Armor T-shirts, huge beside her clothes.

I took it with me into the bathroom. Sarah's shower was weak compared to mine, the spray more light rainfall than thunderstorm. I took my time anyway, using her soap to take care of the morning wood and wishing there'd been time to get in some action before she left for work. I knew it was unlikely, but I'd still kind of hoped she would've woken me in her special way after we had to take a pass last night. Regardless, it had been good to see her let loose.

I couldn't recall any other time where I'd spent the night with Sarah without the expectation of getting busy under the sheets. Maybe there had been a night or two during the trial when we'd ended up in bed without the intention of nakedness, but it had usually happened anyway—more as a distraction and a comfort than a means to get off.

Sitting through the trial had been a real mind fuck. All the memories I'd left behind when H and I broke free from Art Addicts became new again. We all had shadows in our pasts. But I had a lot more demons than I wanted to acknowledge. Hayden was much the same for very different reasons.

Pushing aside the black thoughts, I finished my shower and got dressed. I went commando rather than recycle my boxers. It took me a while to find Sarah's hair products. She didn't usually put anything in her hair unless she was working. Sometimes she'd do this updo thing when she dressed like a fifties pinup girl. It was the only outfit I actually liked.

I searched the vanity for gel or mousse—anything that would keep me from having to wear a hat all day. When I was done, I cleaned up and put everything away. I even took the time to make her bed. The living room had been tidied; the papers on the coffee table had disappeared, including the bank information.

My stomach growled, so I hit the fridge, hoping to find something to take the edge off. I'd stop at the café downstairs before heading over to Inked Armor, but even a glass of juice was better than nothing. I found a note stuck to the fridge with a magnet.

CHRIS,

I'M SORRY ABOUT LAST NIGHT. I WISH I'D BEEN ABLE TO
TAKE ADVANTAGE OF HAVING YOU IN MY BED. THANKS
FOR FOLDING ALL MY PANTIES.

NEXT TIME I PROMISE I'LL MODEL THEM FOR YOU. I
NEED TO DO GROCERIES, BUT THERE'S CEREAL IN THE
BOTTOM CUPBOARD.

XO
SARAH

I opened the fridge. Aside from condiments and some bruised apples, the contents were pretty dismal. I checked her cupboards. They weren't much better. It was only ten; I had plenty of time to remedy her grocery situation. Pocketing the key she'd left on the counter, I took the stairs to street level and hit the closest market. It was only a five-minute walk, but Sarah's hours made it a challenge for her to make use of its convenience.

I stocked her up with fresh fruit and vegetables and picked up some of her favorite snack foods. I could only cover the essentials since I'd walked, but she wouldn't come home to bare cupboards tonight. It was nice to do something for her, even if it was insignificant, much like the laundry folding.

That afternoon she stopped by between school and work to

thank me, but I was busy with a client, so I couldn't fully appreciate her gratitude.

The next week held more busy-ness for both of us. Xander seemed to be piling on the extra shifts, despite Sarah's internship. I had begun to worry about how little sleep she had to function on. I avoided offering sleepovers or taking her up on her requests during the week, knowing full well it would mean she'd get only two or three hours of sleep before she had to be up for work again.

Her ability to handle the internship wasn't a question—she'd been offered the placement, working at one of the major marketing firms downtown, on the spot. She'd been handed some pretty detailed marketing plans to implement already, and she spent a lot of time outside of the office reviewing paperwork and spreadsheets.

If she didn't have shifts at The Sanctuary to manage, it probably would've been a lot easier to get it all done, but she had to squeeze it in between coming home from one job and going to another. Exhausted as she was, it would be much easier for Xander to persuade her to do things she normally wouldn't.

We tried to make time to see each other, but it was tough with our conflicting schedules. She came in looking for a key on Thursday afternoon while I was working on a partial sleeve.

With the weekend on the way, I caved, especially since her request had been preceded by texts citing exactly how she still wanted to make up for last week—not that she needed to, we'd seen each other on the weekend. But my dick would happily take contact from something other than my hand, especially if it was Sarah.

Despite the plan, I woke up at four in the morning to an empty bed. Disappointed by the lack of a warm, soft body, I got up to take a leak and latch the chain lock.

I found Sarah passed out on the couch with a half-eaten sandwich in her lap and the TV on mute. I hated seeing her like that. I carried her to bed and made sure her alarm was set. All she left behind in the morning was the key she'd borrowed, a note, and a lip gloss mark on my cheek.

Though I saw less of Sarah than I liked, I'd heard a little more from Ivy since our breakfast. The antibiotics seemed to have had a positive effect on my mom's cough. Ivy reported that she was only using her puffer, and the horrible rattle was better. I'd also managed to pay down the cell phone bill and added a month buffer so they didn't have to worry about it for a while.

I would've bought her an entirely new phone if she'd let me. But Mom didn't want to make John angry, and of course she figured it was her fault they'd gotten so behind on the payments, like every other bill. I didn't give a shit if I pissed him off, but I didn't have to live with the asshole, so I didn't push.

I mostly kept my thoughts about John to myself and continued to check in with Ivy, making sure I was a consistent, reliable presence in her life. If I wanted to get her out of that house, I needed to earn her trust and give her a way to make it happen.

Now that we were talking about hiring someone to help take the pressure off Lisa I'd started considering whether Ivy might be a good fit. She'd only been in the shop once before, but despite the brief visit, everyone had been taken with her, particularly Lisa. I'd also taken her by the café to meet Cassie, who instantly fell in love.

If Ivy was willing, there might be an opportunity for her. She was definitely organized and far more capable of managing money than anyone else in her house, and the pay would be steady. If it worked out, my sister would be safe, and I could do what I hadn't been able to before now: take care of her.

The next day I got confirmation that I was earning a place of trust in Ivy's life when she called me at ass o'clock in the morning. It wasn't that early, but eight-thirty wasn't a time I usually rolled out of bed feeling chipper. She started with small talk, but I cut her off.

"Ivy, what's going on? You're not calling me this early to chat."

She was silent for a few seconds before she heaved a sigh. "I'm sorry, Chris. I know you had to pay a lot for the prescription and the phone bill—"

I sat up, suddenly way more alert. "Is Mom sick again?"

That cough could easily have turned into pneumonia, even with the antibiotics. We might not have been close, but that didn't mean I wanted anything bad to happen to her—or anything worse than what already had.

"No. No. She's fine. That cough has cleared up really well. It's just... I think there's something wrong with the hot water. All I got was cold when I tried to shower this morning. It'll cost a couple hundred to have someone come out to look at it. I thought maybe you could check before I go forking over money for no reason."

"I can stop by in twenty, if that works for you."

"Thanks, Chris. You're an awesome brother."

"Thanks. See you in a bit."

I didn't know shit about hot water tanks. But if I couldn't figure it out, I could easily call Hayden. He'd reno-ed the house he and Tenley lived in, so he had a much better idea about home maintenance than I did. The only downside would be him seeing the shithole my family lived in.

As close as we were, Hayden hadn't been inside my family home. I'd been exiled for a long time when he and I started hanging out. On the one or two occasions that we'd driven by my mom's back in the day, Hayden had been just as fucked up as me on a steady stream of booze and drugs, so I doubted he would remember much about it.

I hadn't been invited to a holiday function since I was eighteen. The last time I'd spent Christmas with my mom, John and I got into a fistfight, and I broke the dining room table with his body. It ruined dinner. I also broke his nose. Ivy was ten at the time. That had been the last time I saw her prior to the past few months.

The rig wasn't around when I got there, and Ivy met me at the door. "Thanks for coming."

"No worries. I'm glad you called." I nodded at the empty street. "John out?"

"He left real early this morning, before Mom or I woke up." She stood in front of the mostly closed door looking embarrassed.

"Dad had some friends over last night, and I haven't had a chance to clean up."

"It's cool. You don't have to apologize."

She opened the door and ushered me in. I stopped just beyond the threshold, gaping at the mess. The house was a sty, worse than it had been the last time I was here by far.

"I should've tidied up."

"You're not the fucking house maid."

I could see she'd tried to clean the worst of it before I arrived, but didn't have time to make it happen. Magazines and newspapers littered the coffee table beside the lounger. Two ashtrays, overflowing with butts, sat on top of the mess. Half-empty beer bottles lined the perimeter of the chair and most of the space on the table. There were even a few bottles on top of the TV, still half-full with butts floating in the murky liquid.

I wanted to pour them all together and force that asshole to drink it.

"Where's Mom?"

"Still in bed," she whispered as we passed her room. "She worked both jobs yesterday, and Dad was up real late with the guys. You know how she doesn't sleep well. I have to get her up soon, but I thought I'd let her sleep as long as I could."

"Is he gone for a while again?"

Ivy shrugged. "He didn't say."

It was a damn good thing John wasn't here, because I probably would've wiped the floor with his ass. But I didn't want to make Ivy feel worse, so I didn't comment. Her memory of my departure would always include busted drywall and stitches in her dad's face. And she'd had ten years of hearing what a loser I was from him. We were making progress now. I didn't want to mess that up.

The house didn't have a full basement, just a four-foot crawl space accessible through a hatch in the floor of Ivy's closet. There was another hatch in the ceiling for the attic, and the furnace had been partitioned off with some cheap divider. It was amazing she could fit any clothes in there at all. Her room in no way reflected the shabby disorder of the living room and kitchen. The twin bed against the far wall was made neatly, its threadbare comforter folded back to reveal faded pale blue sheets with a flower print. A few library books were neatly stacked on her desk in the corner, along with an ancient-looking computer I wasn't sure could still work. Beside that sat a small dresser with mismatched knobs on the second and third drawers. The white paint on the walls was now nicotine yellow, the result of John's years of smoking in the house.

Ivy had already taken care of clearing out her closet so I could get to the hatch. A small plastic laundry hamper, both handles broken, was pushed against the wall beside it. Her closet was pitifully bare. Three pairs of black pants and four pairs of jeans hung from cheap metal hangers. One pair stood out from the rest, maybe a splurge on her part. They boasted jeweled back pockets. A few shirts hung on the opposite side, as well as several hoodies. Nothing seemed very new.

I could always ask Lisa about getting her some clothes, since they were close to the same size, or even Tee maybe. If Sarah had the time I was sure she'd help me shop for Ivy, but she already had enough going on, and I didn't want to put this on her, too. I wasn't too keen on sharing this part of my life with her. It was a little too much reality.

I dropped down into the space below Ivy's closet, then reached up for the flashlight as she handed it over. Flicking it on, I looked around. A couple of old cardboard boxes were tucked away in the corner. The water heater was on the other side, covered in dust and cobwebs. It didn't look broken, but then I had no idea what I should be checking for. The tank was cool to the touch, which for sure wasn't right.

"You got water pressure?"

"Yup. It's just not hot. I can handle the cold water, but it could make Mom sick again."

That going without hot water was an option she'd considered made me ragey. Sinking into a crouch, I crab-walked around the perimeter, looking for obvious issues. When I found none, I checked out the pipes above. They were covered in cobwebs, fat spiders clinging to them.

I should've brought Hayden with me in the first place, though I wasn't sure he could manage his OCD self in this level of disorder or filth without saying something that might hurt Ivy's feelings. The sorry state of the house was an embarrassment, as well as a testament to the poverty I'd grown up in and couldn't seem to help my mom find a way out of.

Instead of admitting I didn't know the first thing about water heaters, I hoisted myself out of the hole. "Where's the water meter at?"

"Out back." She gestured for me to follow.

I felt bad about trekking my dirt-covered shoes through her bedroom, so I took them off and carried them to the hall.

"It's usually not like this. I try to clean the floors once a week, just last night…"

I braced myself against the door frame, slipping my boots back on in the hall. "You don't need to explain. You're not the only one who lives here." A hole marred the drywall next to her door. I stopped, sweeping my finger around the perimeter, it came away powdery. "What happened here?"

She looked away as she spoke. "I knocked into the wall."

"With what? Your fist?"

"I had a friend over. We were fooling around. My elbow hit the drywall."

"Were you doing the Chicken Dance? 'Cause it sure looks like those knobby elbows of yours were up by your ears."

She shoved my shoulder, but when she spoke, she didn't look at me. "My elbows aren't knobby! It was an accident."

Ivy walked down the hall to the back door. There was a small, shittily built porch tacked onto the main house that was relatively new. It was filled with all sorts of random crap, probably belonging to John. The rickety steps groaned as I descended. The backyard was in a worse state than the front. It had developed a serious case of alopecia. Patches of green dotted the mucky sludge from a recent rainstorm, weeds having choked out the grass. The lawnmower sat on its side, parts strewn over the cracked patio stones. Dog shit bombs littered the yard, even though there were no pets in the house, some of them white from having been there so long.

"I'm working on fixing the lawnmower." She was already defensive without me saying a word.

I didn't comment. What the fuck could I reasonably say that didn't include some sort of asshole remark about how the nineteen year old in the house had to take care of everything? I waded through the grass to get to the gas meter. The bright red lock attached to it explained the problem.

"This is why you don't have hot water." I tapped the lock. I'd gone to all the trouble to have a new furnace put in, and the gas had been cut off.

"But I gave Mom the money to pay the bill last week."

"You gave it to her in cash?"

"From my tips."

I sighed, not wanting to make her feel bad. "You can't do that, Ivy. You gotta know that by now. Why'd you have to use your tips?" I'd direct-deposited funds into Ivy's account the same day I took her for breakfast.

"She said she was going to take it right to the bank."

"I'm sure she was. Except I can bet that isn't what happened. How much did you give her?"

"Two hundred."

"Shit."

Ivy's eyes went glassy, but she blinked back the tears, clearing her throat. "I was going to use it for this course I wanted to take this summer, but then she needed it—"

"What happened to the money I gave you?"

"It's a joint account."

I closed my eyes, tamping down on the sudden spike of rage. "Aw, Ivy."

"I'm so sorry. That was so stupid of me." Her chin lifted skyward. The tears she'd been holding back ran down her temples.

I held my arms open. "C'mere, little sis."

"I'm fine."

"You're not, and that's okay. You don't have to be all strong around me. I get that it sucks."

I felt sick that she'd had to learn these kinds of lessons from her family. This wasn't how it was supposed to be. She shouldn't have to worry about paying bills or not having hot water. She should earn money for new jeans and frivolous things, like nail polish and nights out with friends, not have it stolen out of her account by her dick of a dad. I wished I could've saved her this kind of pain, taken her out of this place long ago and given her something better.

Her thin arms wound around my waist, holding on tight as her body shook with silent sobs. She pushed away just as quickly, swiping under her eyes to hide the evidence of her emotions.

"Let's see if we can find the bill somewhere. Then we're going to the bank to set you up with your own account."

"I don't think Dad will like that."

"I don't give a fuck what John does or doesn't like. He's not taking care of you, so he doesn't get a fucking say."

"He's just bad with money."

This was about more than poor money management. He was a greedy, selfish bastard.

The door to mom's bedroom opened as we came back inside. She blinked blearily, eyes widening when she saw me. "Chris? What're you doing here? John isn't home, is he?"

No welcoming hug, no, "It's good to see you." Just panic. The lines around her mouth deepened as she glanced toward the living room. Her fingers tightened on the lapels of her rob, holding it closed.

"Dad's not here," Ivy said, stepping out from behind me.

"Oh. Well, of course not. He's probably got a job to take care of."

My mom sure knew how to pick 'em. That she pretended he had a legitimate job was another reason I didn't stop by the house very often. I couldn't stand listening to her lie her way around another missing chunk of cash.

Her limp hair, peppered with gray, barely brushed her shoulders. The soft waves were matted, like someone's hands had been in them. Maybe her own. I didn't want to look too closely, afraid I'd see things that would make the guilt I carried heavier.

"When'd they turn the hot water off?" No point in beating around the bush.

"I got the notice last week. Ivy gave me money, but then John—"

I cut her off, uninterested in the excuses. "Can you get me the bill?"

Shame dragged her eyes to the floor and hunched her shoulders. She shuffled down the hall, pale pink slippers turned mucky gray from having trekked through the filth John constantly left behind.

In the corner of the living room was a roll-top desk. She fought with the latch and the rolling mechanism, struggling to pull it up. I stepped in, putting a gentle hand on her arm. She jumped.

"Sorry, Moms, didn't mean to scare you. Let me get it."

Once I had the roll top open, she sifted around through a file folder. Most of the notices in there had red stamps, indicating they were long overdue. When she finally found the one she was looking for, she passed it over with trembling fingers.

I scanned the sheet, seeking out the total. "A grand?"

"I didn't mean to get so far behind."

"Almost half of this is interest. Why didn't you call me months ago? I would've taken care of it before it got to this."

I had more than enough in my savings account. I'd been putting money aside to get a better place eventually, or maybe even buy Hayden's old condo above the shop when his tenants rolled over. But every time I thought I was getting ahead, my mom would call, and I'd lose a little ground.

"You'd had the new furnace put in, and I didn't want to ask for money again. I thought I'd be able to make it up with some extra shifts at the factory, but they're not giving overtime these days, and then there was that cough."

"Which you weren't even going to get the prescription for."

"I figured it would go away on its own."

The things I'd hidden from for years came into sharp relief. I'd spent all this time trying to protect her from John, thinking I was keeping her from going without the necessities. In reality, I'd been giving her the tools to make a martyr of herself and a fool out of me. It was a painful realization, especially knowing the kind of damage it had done to Ivy—how it would impact the rest of her life, like it had mine.

My mom wasn't a victim; she was a perpetrator of her own demise.

It was pointless to continue the discussion. Mom would protect John every time; it didn't matter what was at risk—her kids, her health, her goddamn home. Getting angry wasn't going to solve anything either. This life was the only thing she knew. There was comfort for her in the predictability of her circumstances. You couldn't rise above what you didn't truly want out of.

I shoved the bill in my back pocket. "I'll pay this, but the money's going right into the account. Do you have to work this morning?"

"I work at the factory at three, but I've got a few hours at the deli this morning."

"You're back on afternoons?" Last time I'd been by she was on days.

"This way I can pick up mornings at the deli a few days a week."

"Let me guess, John thought it was a good idea. Does he pick you up at the end of the shift?"

"He's not home much these days, and he had to sell the car to get the rig." She shifted from one foot to the other, nervous in the face of owning her choices. She hated the conflict I brought with my questions, but reveled in the abuse her husband dished out.

"If I get off early enough, I ride my bike over and we go home together," Ivy offered.

As if that made it better. My nineteen-year-old sister was riding her bike into an industrial park in the middle of the night to make sure my mother got home safe because her husband couldn't be bothered to make sure she had a car.

"Why don't I make coffee and some breakfast?" My mother scurried across the room. The kitchen was a mess, food-crusted plates and empty pizza boxes strewn across the counter. She opened the fridge door, but the inside was almost as empty as Sarah's had been. "I have to do a shop." Her tone was full of apology.

"I'm gonna take Ivy out with me to pick up some groceries."

"If you get cream, I'll have coffee ready for you by the time you get back."

This was the way she worked: avoid and pretend the bad things weren't happening.

She opened a cupboard and pulled out four pots. Checking to make sure they were clean, she filled them with water and turned on every burner. A memory from when I was a kid floated around in the back of my consciousness and broke the surface. That was what she used to do when I was real young. Before Ivy. Before John, even. So they weren't the root of these money problems.

She'd made it normal. When the water wouldn't heat up in the taps, we'd boiled it in pots until we had enough in the tub to wash with. It had never been more than lukewarm.

Ivy followed me out the door and took the helmet I passed over. Wordlessly, we got on my bike and stopped at the bank first. I paid the gas bill, and Ivy set up a new account, one that didn't have anybody else's name on it. We transferred almost all of what was left in the other account—which wasn't much—leaving twenty-five bucks behind.

Then we made the trip to the grocery store. We couldn't pick up much, only what would fit in her backpack, but I tried to make it count.

Outside, before I passed the helmet back over, I turned to her. "Is he beating her?"

"What?"

"Does he smack her around?"

"No." The response was immediate, automatic. She pursed her lips. "I don't think so."

"Have you seen him hit her before?"

"It's not like that."

"Has he ever hit you?"

Her eyes stayed level with mine. "He only hits the walls."

I wasn't sure if I believed her or not.

EIGHT

CHRIS

A couple days later I found myself holed up in the private tattoo room with Sarah. There was no aboveboard business going on. I wasn't putting a tattoo on her perfect, unmarked skin like she'd talked about fifteen minutes ago. Instead, I was taking full advantage of her pretty, convenient sundress and its accessibility factor. We were making out like teenagers expecting to get caught by our parents. Except our situation was much more comfortable, and no one cared what we were up to.

I sat in the tattoo chair with Sarah straddling my lap. I untied the thin halter strap behind her neck and pushed down the top on one side to reveal a perfect, perky breast.

"What're you doing?" she asked in a hushed, slightly anxious, albeit excited, whisper.

"Kissing one of my favorite parts of you." I pressed my lips to her collarbone, then forged a path over her breast until I reached the tight peak of her nipple. She gasped quietly and arched, shoving her fingers into my hair. My hat was on the floor since this wasn't the first time she'd done that in the past five minutes.

"We should stop." Her words in no way matched her actions. She pushed her chest farther out and ground up on me.

"Fuck that," I mumbled around her nipple.

"When's your next client?" She punctuated the question with a hip roll.

"We got lots of time."

"You should've come up to my apartment." Sarah snuck a hand between us and palmed my erection through my jeans. "We could go now if you want."

"This isn't comfortable enough for you?" I pulled the left side of her dress down until the other breast popped out.

Sarah covered her nipple with her palm. She was still holding on to my hair with the other hand, though. "There are people on the other side of the door—clients, our friends."

"Baby, you have the quietest orgasms in the entire world. Everyone'll think we're talking in sign language in here. Besides, the speakers are on. All they can hear is music."

"You want to give me an orgasm? Here?"

"You don't want me to?" I flipped her skirt up, revealing a pair of pale pink cotton panties. I fucking loved them. I loved that they were simple, and what I loved most was how damp they were when I slipped my finger under the elastic. "I think you want me to give you an orgasm."

Sarah dropped her hand to cover mine, but it wasn't to stop me. Her eyes closed as I brushed her clit with a knuckle. I eased the fabric to the side. I'd already planned to make a trip around the bases when I took her back to my place later, but no one said I couldn't have a sampler now.

"Do you have a condom?"

Or maybe I was getting a full meal. "Weren't you worried about someone hearing us a few seconds ago?"

"I think I can get over it."

"Can't wait until later for a piece of this?" I wagged my brows.

Sarah gave me a look that told me I was treading the fine line between funny and infuriating. I sat up and threaded my fingers into her hair, brushing my lips over hers.

"I'm playing, baby. There's one in my wallet, if you're interested in using it."

Sarah slid her hand into my back pocket. "You locked the door right?" she asked on a whisper.

"Fucking right I did."

She got up on her knees and pushed her panties over her hips, removing them one leg at a time while I unbuckled my belt and popped the button on my jeans. Then she pulled her dress over her head and let it drop to the floor. Sarah's body was incredible. She was the kind of beautiful that should never have been on display for the masses. She was too perfect for public consumption. Hers was a body to worship privately.

I rolled on the condom while she straddled me. If we'd gone to her apartment, I could've taken more time with her, but this was hot—and not something Sarah was usually up for. She was more of a get-it-on-in-a-bed kind of woman, which was why I appreciated even more that she was willing to do this right here, right now.

I ran the head of my cock back and forth along her slit a few times before I let her sink down. She dropped her face to my shoulder and exhaled a shuddery breath, along with my name.

I stroked down her back, palming her ass to pull her tighter against me. "No one's gonna know. It's just you and me, baby."

She lifted her head, and I cupped her cheek, kissing her when she started to move—slow, easy circles that were going to send me to the edge a lot faster than I wanted to get there. Not that this was a bad thing, considering where we were and what we were doing.

"Later tonight I'm gonna kiss every inch of this perfect body."

She bit my lip, muffling a sexy moan. The whole-body tremor that followed, along with the tight clench around my cock, told me she was coming.

"I got you, baby." I held her hips, shifting her over me when she lost her rhythm.

I followed right after, having been holding off pretty much since the second I got inside her.

She rested her forehead against the crook of my neck and traced the lines of ink on my forearm. "One day we should use this room for its intended purpose."

It didn't take long for her to come back to that topic. "I'm not letting you near my tattoo machine."

She bit my neck. "Don't be a jerk."

"I don't wanna mar your perfect skin with something you might regret later."

"You're an amazing artist. You wouldn't mar me, and I won't regret it."

"What if I fuck it up?" I didn't want her to have a permanent reminder of me that she couldn't erase. I wasn't talking about the art.

"Every design I've ever seen of yours has been gorgeous. I can't imagine you putting something on me that would be anything less than that." Sarah lifted off me and grabbed her dress from the floor. "You could put it in a place no one else would see it but you."

When she talked like that, it made me think there was something to this thing we had going on. It was one of the reasons I'd avoided putting any ink on her. Tattooing was an intimate process, regardless of the tattooist-client relationship. I'd seen Hayden and Tenley's relationship consume him while he put the wings on her back.

It had worked out for them in the end, and that process had brought them together, but then Tenley's tattoo had been symbolic of a massive loss. Sarah's motivation for getting a tattoo was nothing like Tenley's, but it would still be intimate regardless.

But I did want my art on her body, and the idea that it would just be ours made it seem a lot like I was someone she wanted to keep around. There was clearly an upside, but also a downside to that. With permanence came openness and honesty, and I wasn't sure I knew how to share all my truths with her.

I removed the spent condom, tied it in a knot, and tossed it in the garbage across the room. Then I grabbed her by the waist and pulled her between my legs. "What kind of tattoo do you want? A little heart right here?" I tapped her hip. "Or maybe something sexy right here." I brushed over her ribs.

"Not a heart, and not on my hip."

"No hearts? Too cliché?"

"Totally cliché."

"You think about it, and when you come up with a design and a location, we can talk."

"I already have some thoughts."

"Oh, yeah? Like what?"

"I'll tell you later, when I have designs I can show you." She ran her fingers along my jaw. "You'll come get me as soon as you're done with your last client?"

"If you still want me to, yeah."

"Didn't you say something about kissing every inch of me?"

"I did. You wanna be my late-night snack?"

"And breakfast." She leaned in for a kiss at the same moment my phone buzzed on the tray beside me.

I reached over and grabbed it, checking the number. "Hold that thought. I need to get this." I answered the call with, "Is everything okay?" It had been a few days since I'd taken Ivy to the bank, and she'd texted a couple of times since then, but we hadn't had a phone conversation.

When I got calls from her, it was usually because something was going down.

"It's my sister," I explained to Sarah as Ivy's high, panicked pitch made me pull the phone away from my ear. "Whoa, hold up. What happened?"

"Dad came to my work looking for me, but I was on a split shift, so I'd gone to see a friend. One of the girls I worked with said he was super mad about something, asking about my paychecks and whether I was getting them. I think he knows about the bank account. It's the only reason I can see him doing something like that."

"You didn't tell him, though, so how can he know?"

"I don't know. Maybe we shouldn't have emptied the account. I should've left more in there."

"How often does he take money out of your account?"

"It used to be once in a while, but it's been a lot more lately."

I glanced at Sarah, who looked concerned. All the most important women in my life were controlled by men whose only intention was to take from them. It made me feel like I was constantly failing. I gave Sarah an apologetic smile.

"You want to come to my place tonight, until the dust settles?"

"I can't leave Mom here to deal with Dad alone."

"You're not responsible for her. It's supposed to be the other way around."

"I know that. It's just hard, Chris."

We went on like that for a couple of minutes, me trying to get her to come to my place, her feeling like she needed to stay to make sure Mom was okay. I hated that she felt like that was her job. In the end, she wanted to be home to make sure Mom was okay when she finished work.

"What happened?" Sarah asked after I hung up.

"Family shit. My sister's caught in the middle, and she doesn't know how to get out of it."

Sarah swept her fingers up the length of my arm, tentative and uncertain. "If you need to be with her tonight, I'll understand. And if you want to talk to me about it, I'm here."

Her tenderness made the whole thing more difficult to manage. Sarah didn't know how bad my family stuff was. Part of me wanted to tell her about all the crap I'd learned over the last few months with Ivy, but then she'd know exactly what a mess my life was. Inked Armor and my crew here was only part of the package. The rest was seriously fucked up.

I'd been trying to keep the women in my life safe from the things that could harm them, and now I'd become one of those things for Ivy. Again.

"She's gonna keep in touch, let me know if things get any worse."

Maybe I was the common denominator. Maybe despite my best efforts, I only made things harder for everyone.

Ivy was fine. Or that's what she said when I called back a while later to check on her. I offered her a spare key to my apartment, in case she ever needed somewhere else to go. She said it wasn't necessary, and if things didn't look good at home, she had a friend she could stay with. But she remained committed to running interference for

Mom. Which I continued to hate. However, forcing things only made them harder for Ivy, so I went back to my standard operating procedure: keeping my mouth shut.

I still felt unsettled, though, so after the shop closed, Hayden, Jamie, and I drove over to my mom's to check things out. I'd figured it would be a quick stop, and then I could go back to get Sarah and spend a few hours with her. It had been a lot of years since we'd driven by the house I grew up in, and they'd only had the pleasure of meeting John once. It'd been pretty easy to keep that part of my life separate since I mostly wasn't allowed to come home.

I could've gone on my own, but it wouldn't be good if John was there and I didn't have anyone to back me up, or hold me down and keep me from making bad choices. Like kicking John's ass. Now that Ivy was involved and I had Sarah in my life, the stakes were a lot higher. I couldn't afford to be arrested. I had too much responsibility.

"This looks different than I remember." Hayden rolled to a stop at the curb.

I could see very clearly the changes that had taken place over the years through his eyes. It had never been a nice house, not like the one he'd grown up in, or the one he'd recently renovated for him and Tenley. And not like Jamie and Lisa's funky little apartment in Pilsen either.

"I'm gonna see if my mom's home yet." I checked the time. It was past eleven. If she took the bus, she'd be here already.

"You want us to come with?" Hayden asked.

The rig wasn't around, which meant John probably wasn't here. "I should be good."

I made sure to avoid the hole in the porch on the way up the steps. I knocked and waited, listening for movement inside. The lock turned, and the door opened. My mother's tired eyes appeared in the crack.

"Chris." Her voice held a nervous waver.

"Hey, Moms, can I come in for a minute?"

"I'm not sure that's a good idea. John might be home soon."

"I wouldn't mind talking to him. Apparently he stopped by Ivy's work looking for her paychecks. You know anything about that?"

Her fingers came up to her mouth, tapping at her chapped lips, but she still made no move to let me in. "He needed to pay some bills, and there's no money in the account she usually uses."

"So you told John to hunt her down at work and ask her about it? Since when are her paychecks his to spend?"

"I didn't tell him to do anything. She gets paid every Friday, and her paycheck wasn't in there. He wanted to know where the money went. He thought I'd taken it out and hidden it somewhere. He went through the whole house looking for it, even though I told him it wasn't here. It's gonna take me a month to get this place back in order thanks to whatever meddling you've done!"

"Meddling? I'm trying to *help*. Ivy's paychecks belong to her. John has his own job, right?"

"Why can't you leave things alone? Why do you always have to cause problems? We were doing fine. Ivy was perfectly happy working at that restaurant, and now she's talking about school and wanting things I can't give her. Why you gotta give her dreams she'll never make happen?" She started to cough, the watery, rattling sound shaking her slight frame. She'd always had asthma, and John's smoking certainly did nothing to help it.

I took her by the elbow and led her inside. I could see now why she'd kept me out on the porch. While the place had been a cluttered, disorganized mess before, it now looked like a tornado had ripped through here. Paper and magazines littered the floor, topped with tumbled couch cushions and turned-over bottles. Drawers had been yanked out, their contents dumped on the floor. Things were so much worse than I could ever have imagined. And I'd made it this way.

Ivy had lied about things being okay—unless she hadn't been here to witness the catastrophe. I wanted a timeline to verify what I hoped wasn't true.

With a firm grip on my mom's waist, I navigated a path through the mess to the ancient couch in the living room. It was barely a step up from the one on the front porch. She continued to hack, the rattle growing more pronounced the longer the fit went on.

Wading through the debris, I went to the kitchen and opened a creaky cupboard, locating the glasses. They were the same ones we'd had when I was a kid, the patterns nearly worn off now with washing and age. I filled it from the tap and sank down in front of her, holding it out.

"Here, Moms."

She took it with shaking hands, spilling some of the contents on her robe. She was already in her pajamas, her shoulder-length hair pulled back in a clip. She looked well beyond her forty five years, lines and creases crowding out any remnants of youthfulness.

I stayed crouched beside her, rubbing circles on her back until she set the glass on the side table. Unlike the one beside John's recliner, this one was clear of cigarette butts and half-empty beer bottles.

I gestured around the room. "When did this happen?"

"Just 'afore I went to work."

"Ivy hasn't seen this?"

She shook her head. "Ivy left early 'cause her manager called her in for a double. John was real upset about the money, Chris. Real upset."

"Is this the only room he trashed?"

She looked down the hall, toward Ivy's bedroom. "I haven't had time to clean it up yet."

I push out of my crouch, and she grabbed my wrist, her grip startlingly firm. "I'll clean it up before she gets home. I was already starting."

I gently pried her fingers away and went down the hall. Ivy's room had been ripped apart. Her clothes littered the floor, and her bed had been turned over, the mattress hanging over the edge of the metal frame. The few knickknacks she owned lay in pieces on the scuffed parquet.

I stood there for a long while, fists clenching and releasing. I wanted to beat the living fuck out of John. And I could. I'd done it before—the day he'd kicked me out of the house. I'd had nothing left to lose since he'd taken it all anyway.

The problem was, I wasn't sixteen anymore. As satisfying as it would be to lay him out, he'd press charges for sure, and then what? I'd walk right into the stereotype: deviant loser who beats on an old guy. My mom would never back me up on him having deserved it. On top of that, John was shady, and I was sure he knew shady people. If I laid a beating on him, he'd retaliate. It wasn't worth the risk for Ivy or me.

I turned to my mom, still sitting on the couch, hands clasped in her lap. "You gotta get out of here," I told her.

"And go where? Everything I have is here."

"I'll help you start over."

"He was just angry." She bent down to pick up scattered papers.

"Why are you making excuses for this?"

"You don't understand. John has had a hard time of things lately being on the road all the time. The jobs haven't been paying so good, and then me being off for a bit back in February set us back—"

I raised a hand to stop her, and she shrank back. It seemed like a conditioned response.

"I'm not going to hit you, Mom."

She smoothed a hand over her hair. "Of course not. I'm just jumpy after what happened with John."

"Is this kind of thing a common occurrence?" I motioned to the mess, in case she wasn't sure what I was referring to.

"Like I said, it's been stressful, and John's trying to be good about the gambl—" She stopped mid-sentence, maybe realizing she'd given me information she shouldn't have.

"Wait a fucking second. He's gambling?"

"He's been better about it, but lately, with all the missed bills—"

I couldn't listen to her spew more bullshit. She was like a broken record, as if repeating the excuses would somehow change the outcome. I wanted to leave, to walk away from the latest nightmare

I'd left my sister to grow up in. But I couldn't. Because I didn't want Ivy to see the damage my attempt at helping her had done.

"Hayden and Jamie are in the car. You remember the guys I work with at Inked Armor?"

My mother nodded.

"I'm gonna go get them."

"But the house is a mess."

"Exactly. I can't let Ivy see this. She'll feel guilty about it like she does everything. And you can't clean this on your own before she gets home."

She seemed to realize I was right and slumped back against the couch. I went to get the guys from the car.

Hayden rolled down the window at my approach, a deep frown hardening his features. "You all right, brother?"

"Not so much. I need some help."

He didn't ask any more questions. The window went up with a whir, and he cut the engine and opened the door. "What happened? Is your mom okay?"

"That's a question I really don't know how to answer without turning it into a therapy session. John trashed the place, including Ivy's room. I just need to put it back together before she comes home."

Hayden spun his car keys on his index finger. "You think it's a good idea for Ivy to stay here?"

"Definitely not, but she won't leave my mom here on her own, so this is the best I can do for now."

"We could wait until she comes home and get her to come with us." Jamie pretzeled himself out of the backseat.

"Tenley and I have plenty of room at our place if she needs somewhere to crash," Hayden added. "She has options, if she wants them."

I nodded, but Ivy was as stubborn as me. If she didn't want to do something, she sure as hell wouldn't be coerced by us. "I honestly don't know that she'd go for it."

"Well, the offer stands. Whatever you need, you got it."

Hayden clapped a palm on my shoulder. "Let's get things under control, yeah?"

"It's pretty bad," I warned. Hayden had issues with clutter. This was going to blow his mind.

"We'll deal." Jamie followed us up the steps to the front porch and into the house.

My mom stood in the middle of the living room, holding a black garbage bag.

"Holy shit," Hayden breathed on an exhale.

"Sorry about the mess." My mom patted her hair and ran her hands down the front of her robe, maybe realizing she wasn't exactly dressed for company. "I should change."

Jamie graced her with one of his warm smiles. "No worries, Mary. You don't need to get changed on our account. We're here to help get everything back in order. Right?" He elbowed Hayden in the side.

"Yeah. Definitely." Hayden's eyes bounced around the room.

"You boys have grown up since I last seen you." She gave them a weak smile.

"Happens like that, doesn't it? Ivy's all grown up, too, isn't she?" Jamie crossed the room and picked up the cushions from the floor, then lined them back up on the couch.

"She is. She's a real smart girl. You got a girlfriend? Maybe Chris'll introduce you."

Jamie laughed, while I tried not to cringe. "I've got a fiancée."

She patted his cheek. "Of course you do. Now I remember Chris telling me about her."

I tried not to let it affect me, but it was hard to watch her share warmth with other people and keep it from me.

"And you—" She looked to Hayden, eyes soft. "Chris told me you found yourself someone special. Can't say you don't deserve someone after everything you've been through. Chris says she's been through her own hard times."

Hayden shoved his hands in his pockets and rocked back on

his heels. "She has. Tenley's the best fu—uh, I love her. I'd probably marry her if she'd let me."

Both Jamie and I turned to stare at him. Not once in all the years I'd known Hayden had I ever heard him say something like that. Of the three of us, Hayden lived the furthest outside the rules.

"Handsome man like you? She'd be crazy to say no."

Hayden snorted. "Handsome isn't a word I hear very often."

I clapped him on the back. "Pretty is a better way to describe him, wouldn't you say, Moms?"

She gave me an admonishing look. "Handsome suits you just fine."

"We should get to it, yeah? What time's Ivy supposed to be home?"

"She said she'd probably be working late tonight 'cause there's some big game on, so she won't be home 'til close to two. She might stay at a friend's house near her work, though. I don't like her riding around in the dark on that bike of hers."

There it was, the façade of parental care. I gritted my teeth.

"She said she'd call to let me know if it wasn't too late."

I deliberately turned away and began to work. Hayden was like a machine once he got started, driven to make order out of chaos. I tried to tell him it didn't matter if everything was perfect, but he couldn't help himself. It was a compulsion. By the time he was finished, the kitchen was cleaner than it had been in probably twenty years.

It took almost two hours to clean the mess in the living room and Ivy's bedroom. There was nothing we could do about the broken things, so I tossed them in the garbage with the rest of the trash, hoping she wouldn't notice. I'd reviewed with my mom that Ivy didn't need to know about the blowout, otherwise she'd feel responsible, and I didn't want that. Mom said she was in agreement, but that didn't ensure her silence. I hoped for Ivy's sake she would keep this under wraps until it couldn't do any more harm.

I messaged Ivy around one to make sure she was still at work.

I got a response a few minutes later saying she still had a couple of tables, and that she'd be fine to get home.

We left at one-thirty in the morning, passing the bar where Ivy worked on our way out. The closed sign flashed in the window, which meant she'd be home soon. I didn't bother shooting Sarah a message. She had to be asleep by now. At least I hoped she was. She was in desperate need of rest.

Hayden dropped me off at my place. Beat and filthy, I ignored my mail and the stack of newspapers piled on the floor and climbed the stairs to my apartment. I came to a dead stop at the end of the hall. Propped up against the door was Sarah.

She'd pulled her knees up to her chest, her cheek resting on top of them, long blond hair covering her face. Her purse was tucked into the space between her ass and her feet. A suit hung on the doorknob, the skirt a few inches from touching the floor. I dropped into a crouch and swept the hair away from her face.

"Baby?" I whispered, not wanting to startle her.

It didn't work. She came awake with a jolt. Her hand went immediately to her purse.

"Hey, hey. It's cool. It's just me."

She blinked a few times, her confusion shifting to relief, then she threw her arms around my neck, setting me off balance. I braced myself against the doorjamb so I didn't land on top of her and wrapped my free arm around her waist. She held on a long while, her face buried against my neck, lips on my skin.

When she finally let go, I leaned back to look at her. Her eyes were red and a little puffy, whether from just waking up or crying, I didn't know.

"What are you doing out here?" I asked.

"Lisa said you went to your mom's, and Jamie messaged her saying you guys were cleaning things up and you'd be a while. I knew you wouldn't come back to my place. I wanted to make sure you were okay, but then I realized I didn't have a key any more."

"You didn't need to do that. I'm fine." It wasn't really true, but worse than all the shit that had gone down tonight, I didn't like that she'd felt compelled to sit outside my door on grimy carpet to wait for me. Some of the people in this building were real lowlifes.

"Why didn't you just call me?"

"I didn't want to be a disruption."

"You're not a disruption." I got to my feet and extended a hand. "I should have let you know what was happening myself. Come on, let's go inside."

As we entered she hung her suit on one of the hooks by the front door. Unsteady in her groggy state, she used my chest for support as she kicked off her shoes.

Her arms came around my waist, her forehead resting against the side of my neck. "I was so worried about you. What happened tonight? Lisa said it was bad."

I absorbed the affection like desert sand soaking up rain. She was so soft and warm, and she smelled like rosemary and mint—better than the stale cigarette smell that had seeped into my clothes from my mom's house.

"Lisa's exaggerating. It's not that big a deal. You've got your own stuff going on."

She lifted her head, fingers gliding along the edge of my jaw. "You can talk to me, Chris, about anything."

I dropped a kiss on her lips, pulling back before I gave in to the urge to deepen it. "I need a shower. Why don't you chill out on the couch?"

She stared up at me for a few long seconds. "Do you want company?"

I smoothed my palms down the sides of her neck and tapped my temple. "Usually I'd say yes, but I need a few minutes to get this in order."

"Okay." She kissed my cheek and stepped back. "I can go home if you want to be alone."

"No, baby, I don't want you to leave."

"You're sure?"

"Positive. Give me five." I kissed her forehead and stepped around her, heading for the bathroom.

I half expected her to be asleep when I came out. But she was lying there on the black leather three-seater, waiting for me. She'd even gotten a beer out of the fridge and made me a sandwich. I wasn't particularly hungry, but I ate it because she made it. I didn't like how good it made me feel to have her here after a shitstorm like tonight.

"Do you want to talk about what happened?" She tucked her toes under my leg.

I set the plate on the table, thinking about how this worn-out apartment was a huge step up from the house I'd been raised in, and how someone like Sarah should be living in a fancy condo, or a house like Hayden and Tenley's.

"You don't want to hear about my fucked-up family drama."

She put her hand on my forearm and squeezed. "You don't have to keep this all inside. I know the last few months have been hard with the trial, and now this stuff with your sister. I want to listen, if you want to talk."

I went with the one basic truth that explained everything and nothing at the same time. "My stepdad's an asshole. That's all there really is to say."

She sat up on her knees, getting in real close. "What happened tonight?"

"I'm tired, baby. We should go to bed. You gotta be up early for your internship, right? I don't want to be responsible for fucking that up with my garbage."

I went to push up off the couch, but she grabbed my arm.

"You're not going to screw up my internship. Just talk to me, please."

It was such a temptation to unload my shit, to tell her the things I kept locked up inside. All that fear and hate and uncertainty, the sense that I was destined to screw things up, and to screw up the people around me. All the responsibility I felt because I couldn't get my mom to leave the man who would eventually destroy her. My worry that Ivy would waste all her potential, like my mom had. How I wished I'd been present in Ivy's life sooner so I could've saved her from the things she'd been through. That I worried my early circumstances would follow me forever and pull everyone I cared about down with me.

I wanted to give in and tell her what had gone down tonight. But then I'd be opening a door, one I couldn't close again. She'd see the weakness and the parts of me I'd worked to keep hidden.

I could get lost in her for a while, though. Fuck out the bad thoughts, replace them with the sound and feel of Sarah, the one good thing I had in my life aside from Inked Armor and my sister.

I swept a thumb along her bottom lip. "You being here is enough. Let me put you to bed."

There was resignation in her eyes as I leaned in and kissed her. Talking complicated things. But being with Sarah? That was simple. Easy. And right now, I couldn't handle any more than that.

NINE

SARAH

I didn't fight Chris as he picked me up off the couch and carried me to his room. As much as I wanted him to tell me what was going on, I hardly had the right to expect him to open up. Not when I was hiding things from him—things that could, and likely would, end us permanently.

The more time that passed without Xander collecting on his favor, the more nervous I became about what exactly it would entail. That whole incident with Trixie still terrified me, as did Dee's conversation with me in the parking lot. It had been nearly two weeks since I'd witnessed Xander's aggression with Trixie, and the shift in her fortunes since then had been extreme. She'd been moved from center stage to left, and her vanity station had been relocated to the end. Dee was getting shifts on center now, and Candy seemed to be back in Xander's good graces again.

I'd been seeking out Chris as much as I could lately, even though he was worried about my lack of sleep. My feelings for him had become like weeds, growing faster than I could contain them. I should've been protecting my heart instead of trying to hand it over so it could be crushed later.

So tonight, instead of pushing him to talk about whatever was making him hurt, I let him have what he wanted: an escape. I could be that.

I was exactly that every night I worked in the club. I was my customers' escape from life, from the wives who ignored them, or from the girlfriends who didn't exist. I smiled and batted my eyelashes and pretended their lewd comments were funny.

Tonight I could easily be whatever Chris needed, and if that was naked and a distraction from the things outside of his control, so be it. Or that's what I told myself as I pushed his boxers over his hips.

My clothing took a little longer to remove since I was fully dressed. Chris wasn't as slow as usual, or gentle. There was an urgency in him I'd never experienced before. What he wouldn't give me in words, he gave me in actions. Desperation leaked through, making him frantic as he pulled my shirt over my head and fought with the clasp on my bra.

"Fuck," he groaned. "I just wanna get my hands on all of you."

I brushed him away, taking care of the bra for him. Sitting on the edge of the bed, I opened my legs and welcomed him between them. He locked shaking fingers around the waistband of my jeans and paused, his expression clouding.

"You sure you're okay with this?"

"With you wanting me?" I popped the button.

He lifted his gaze. "I fucking *need you*."

I shivered at his tone, wishing it indicated a different kind of need—a sustained one that was more than physical. But I pushed the feelings down, locked them inside my aching heart, and released my zipper. "Then you should have me."

He tugged, and I lifted my hips so he could take my jeans off, along with my panties. Yanking them free, he tossed them on the floor. His palms slid hard and heavy up the inside of my thighs, pushing them apart.

"I'm tryin' so hard..." He caressed slick skin with his fingertips, then pushed in. Surprised, I arched into the touch. He usually took his time with foreplay, waiting until I was a total mess before he went ahead and gave me what I craved—or in this case what he needed.

Tonight there was nothing playful in him. He curled his fingers up, pumping into me as he reached for the nightstand with his free hand.

"We could go without," I said softly.

He stilled, dark eyes meeting mine. A whirlwind of emotions passed through as I watched—lust, want, fear, and sadness among them. The briefest hesitation preceded a vigorous shake of his head. "No chance I'm screwing up your life like I do everyone else's."

There was so much weight in that statement, and it made me wish all over again that I could be more than just his escape. He grabbed the box of condoms, nearly crushing it in his fist. Turning it over, he dumped the contents on the bed; two packets fell out. I went for them, but he was faster.

"You come first," he said, voice rough.

Dropping to his knees, he slid his free arm under me, pulling me to the edge. His mouth was hard, tongue laving, teeth nipping, fingers pumping furiously. The sensation was too much, too fast. The orgasm crashed over me, blanketing out sound and sight. I turned my head into my shoulder, biting down to stop my moan.

His fingers and mouth disappeared. The absence was a secondary shock to my system, and I pulsed around nothing on a whimper. I attempted to close my legs, but I met Chris's hips as he rose up. I turned to look at him, confused as to why he'd stopped. His dark expression was almost sinister as he towered over me and tore open a condom. Rolling it down his thick shaft, he bent his knees, abs flexing, shoulders tight as he stroked over my still-sensitive clit. I shuddered, so he did it again.

"Does it feel good, Sarah?"

"Yes." It was more sound than word.

A low noise followed as he entered me on a heavy thrust.

Still standing, Chris hooked his arms under my knees, resting my heels on his shoulders. And then he started to move. It wasn't slow. It wasn't gentle. But it was incredible. I wanted him to need me like this all the time, because in so many ways, this was how I felt about him. The ache in my chest when we'd been apart before would likely take over and ruin me if we were separated again.

His hands were tight on my hips, the angle creating sensations that overwhelmed, but couldn't quite push me over the edge. When he sped up, I grabbed the sheets to hold myself in place.

He was too far away, the physical distance an echo of the emotional walls between us. For all the times I'd sought this intimacy with him, on this night he finally seemed to need me in the same way, even if it was only physically. I found his thigh with shaking fingertips. "Please."

"What do you need, baby?"

"You. I need you."

"What part?"

"All of you. Every part."

He faltered for a second, his grip on my hips tightening further. I ran my palm up his forearm, over the cityscape, and tugged, urging him closer. With one knee on the bed, he leaned forward, going deeper.

The sound that came out of him was part fury, part lust. With my feet still on his shoulders, he bore down, his massive body positioned above me. My knees hit my chest and his mouth pressed hard against mine, tongue pushing past my lips, aggressive and dominating. Releasing my thigh from his grip, his fingers twined in the hair at the nape of my neck, holding my mouth to his as he went harder and moved faster.

"You gonna come again for me?" He nipped my bottom lip.

I breathed out a soft *yes*.

Any thread of civility evaporated. He was like blazing fire, untamed and all consuming. Eyes holding mine, his lip curled into a sneer. "I wanna hear it. None of this holding back shit you pull every fucking time. You think you can give me that? Let me know you like it when I make you come?"

Chris was a lot of things—rough around the edges, closed off, secretive, sensitive, stunningly gorgeous, attentive, affectionate. But one thing he had not been was demanding in bed. Until now.

Before this he'd always been careful with me to the point of reverence. He sweet-talked and teased; he went slow and made me feel like I was something precious. Whatever had happened tonight had caused a shift. I couldn't tell if it was good or bad, but I liked it, even though it created conflict I wasn't sure how to manage.

Instead of fighting the moan when the orgasm rushed me, Chris's name tumbled out on a scream.

A low groan rumbled up from his chest, and words I couldn't make out hissed through his gritted teeth on his final, deep thrust.

He collapsed on top of me, his legs still hanging off the bed. He shifted mine so they were no longer on his shoulders but beside his ribs. He breathed like he'd run a marathon, which wasn't far off. It was the most unhinged sex we'd had since we started seeing each other. I'd be sore tomorrow, and I wouldn't mind at all. I was a limp, boneless mass of complete satiety.

"Shit." Chris pushed up on his arms, panic setting in. "That was way out of line."

"What was way out of line?"

"I shouldn't have fucked you like that."

I ignored the twinge in my chest at his choice of words. To me it had been more than that. I placed a palm on his cheek, drawing his mouth back down to mine. "I want you to need me like I need you." The honesty was unintended.

Chris shuddered, and a dark sound passed over his lips. His kisses were soft, tentative and gentle. Almost apologetic.

I wanted this to bring us closer; I needed a way to bind us so he wouldn't walk away when he realized I was weak and damaged, and that I'd fallen into a trap I couldn't find a way out of. But sex was the only time he'd let me in, and now that it was over, I could sense the distance expanding between us.

Chris sat back slowly, his hands roamed over my thighs and stomach, eyes following the movement as if he were looking for signs of damage. He wouldn't find any. Even at his least restrained, he was still a considerate—albeit intense—lover.

When he was done with his examination, he went to the bathroom to dispose of the condom. I slid under the covers and snuggled into the pillow. I must have dozed off in the few minutes he was gone, because the next thing I knew he was tucking me into his warm embrace. Chris's apology was the last thing I heard before sleep claimed me.

I left Chris sprawled across his bed the next morning. He'd moved from his pillow to mine as soon as I'd rolled out of bed. Though I remained thoroughly satisfied by last night, our lack of conversation still didn't sit well with me. Chris's inability to let me in was an echo of my issue, a reminder of the emptiness that consumed so much of my life.

And I didn't like it. Being closed out by him hurt. Not because I didn't understand his motivation—I did. Maybe that was part of the problem. What I liked the least was that I'd resigned myself to being an escape for him rather willingly. I hadn't fought to be the person he felt he could confide in.

We'd been doing this for months now, and keeping all these walls up was getting harder. At least for me. I wasn't sure it was the same for Chris, and that scared me. I was certain he'd tell Lisa the whole story today at the shop, and I'd be left wondering exactly how much I had to push before he'd give me more of him, so I could give him more of me.

I didn't want to keep secrets from him anymore, but I had no idea where I stood. I didn't want to be his next Candy.

The tattoos and the danger, as well as that killer smile, might've been what drew me to him, but they weren't what kept me around. In the beginning, his distance made mine easier to maintain, and that's what gave me a sense of control, of invulnerability. Because as messed up as his life might've been, mine wasn't a shining beacon of stability either.

My mother had always gone through men like underwear. She didn't marry them, because she couldn't. She was the woman on the side. Except now that she was in her forties and the plastic surgery needed touch ups, she wasn't quite as appealing. The men who had willingly cheated on their wives with her were now looking for younger, less-used options—or women willing to engage in fringe activities that fed their baser, more reprehensible predilections, because their wives were too precious for that.

In a lot of ways, Mom was exactly like the dancers at the club who found ways to earn more money off the stage than on it. There was more of that going on at The Sanctuary than I'd first realized, and that scared me.

Anyway if I was honest with myself, I wasn't much better than that. I used my body to make tuition money. Maybe I didn't take off my clothes, but it wasn't far away, especially now that Xander had me in his debt.

Hell, who was I to complain about Chris's distance? I'd broken up with him once to protect my own. But now that I was weeks away from finishing my internship, and getting out of The Sanctuary for good looked more plausible, I wanted what I'd never had—what my mother had never had: constancy. More than that, I wanted love.

Which was stupid. Because from the beginning I'd known Chris wasn't a *more* kind of guy. We'd met at a strip club, for God's sake. And his refusal to let me in, even after all this time, should've made that clear. But I still searched for a way to close the distance, though I feared it wasn't possible.

I dressed in the bathroom, putting on my gray pinstripe skirt and conservative white blouse. I felt like a fraud a lot of the time at Media Mogul, even though I loved what I did there, and I was good at it.

The people side of things was the most difficult for me. I was better at analysis, programming, and planning than social interaction. It had been the same in my classes. I'd forgo lunch with colleagues most days to work on projects, but I forced myself to get involved on occasion. I figured that was part of what I needed from the internship experience. I could look at statistics, numbers, and various marketing campaigns and figure out what worked and what didn't, but making small talk with the other interns was painful.

I had nothing in common with most of them. I could tell they'd never dealt with poverty. They'd grown up in nice houses with nice cars, and even if their hundred thousand dollars' worth of education amounted to nothing more than a framed degree on the wall, they wouldn't have to worry about whether they could afford their next meal, or next month's rent.

I understood the girls at The Sanctuary so much better, even though I didn't engage with most of them either. I didn't feel like I fit anywhere—except with Chris and his friends. We'd all fought to get out of the bad places we'd started in, and some of us still were.

So I kept my head down and worked my ass off at my internship. I put my energy into making an impression on the right people. And I didn't care if that made me unpopular among my peers. Guys who felt slighted because I wasn't interested in their version of a date weren't my concern, even if it meant they considered me stuck up. In the end, they weren't the ones who could give me a job.

That night I headed to The Sanctuary without stopping to see Chris. From the window of my apartment I could see he was working on a client, and he hadn't responded to the message I'd sent earlier in the day. So I wasn't going to push it. What had happened with his family was likely still plaguing him. I didn't want to add to that stress, so I gave him space, even though it hurt to do it.

Despite drinking a pot of coffee before my shift, I was exhausted when I got to work. The caffeine only made me jittery and irritable.

Dee leaned against the jamb. Over the weekend private dances in the booths had become part of her routine after her shifts on center stage. It scared me how much had changed for her in such a short time.

"You look like hell," she observed.

"Hi, Dee. It's nice to see you. How was your day?"

She snorted. Her lip curled up in a lazy smile. "My day was shit. Night's shaping up to be more of the same."

"Aren't you on center?"

"To start." She checked over her shoulder. Lowering her voice she said, "Xander booked me a private party after. Some big business dicks comin' in. He wants me to show 'em a good time." A tremor made her hand unsteady as she picked at her fake nails. They had jeweled tips.

"What do you mean a private party? Like, in the booths?"

Dee shook her head. "In the private rooms. Xander says it's real discreet and to keep it all quiet, so you can't say anything to anyone."

I thought back to our conversation in the parking lot, and the look on her face when she'd told me to stay where I was. I couldn't imagine how Xander had worn her down, getting her to agree. Or maybe I could. He'd surely made it seem like a privilege. Like she was special.

"You said yes to this?"

Dee shrugged and looked behind her again. "I get two grand for an hour."

That was a lot of money. That alone would cover rent and expenses for an entire month. But there was a different kind of price to pay for crossing that line.

"Are you sure you want to do this?"

She laughed, but it was high and anxious. "It's only an hour, right? How bad can it be? Plus Xander'll give me lots of perks if I do a good job." Her smiled faded. Her eyes were slightly unfocused as she pulled a pill bottle out of her purse and dropped it in my hand. "You look wrecked. This'll help you get through the night."

I read the label. "What is this?"

"It's a prescription. It'll help keep you alert."

The name was familiar. I racked my brain as to why that would be. Then I remembered: one of the girls in my program had them. Prescribed to kids with attention deficit, the drug was used to calm them down and help them focus. It had the opposite effect on people without the disorder. It was like taking speed, making you hyper focused and able to stay up all night. It was great for cramming for an exam and popular among wealthy grad students. And it had the added benefit of being an appetite suppressant for girls looking to stay slim.

"You're sure that's what's in the bottle?"

"Yeah. I take 'em sometimes when I don't sleep so well."

I held them out to her. I didn't want this kind of thing in my possession, not when I'd managed to stay away from all the illegal substances floating around in this club. Just because it came from a doctor didn't mean it was better. A drug problem was still a drug problem.

She shook her head. "Keep them. Xander'll give me more if I ask. 'Specially after tonight."

Grant called her name as he rounded the corner. His eyes passed over me as I dropped the bottle into my bag. I didn't want to get Dee in trouble for giving them to me.

He pointed at the clock on the wall. "You better hustle if you plan to be out there on time."

My shirt was unbuttoned, and I was shoeless. I rushed to put on the rest of my outfit, adjusting my skirt so it covered more instead of less. Grant turned his attention to Dee, pulling her aside, away from the vanity stations.

He skimmed her arms with gentle hands. "You okay, Dee Dee girl?"

She nodded, but the tremor in her hands showed the truth.

He stroked her cheek in a gesture that spoke of real intimacy, not placating. "You can change your mind."

"Xander would never let me do that." She exhaled in a rush, eyes closing as she nodded again. "It's just an hour, and it doesn't mean anything but a better paycheck."

He dropped his voice and leaned in, whispering something so low I couldn't hear. Dee shook her head. "I don't want you to do that. Get Max to guard."

There was more heated whispering. Grant's walkie went off, and Xander's voice came through.

"He wants you to stop by his office before you go on," Grant told Dee.

"Is something wrong?"

"He wants to make sure you have everything you need." He put his hand on her arm and led her out of the room. "You don't have to take anything he's offering."

She shot one last glance at me before she rounded the corner, her fear overshadowed only by her regret.

Trixie sat at the station closest to the exit, following Dee's departure in the mirror, her eyes the kind of blank I associated with too much chemical coping. Since that night in Xander's office, she'd been relegated to the left stage, first set. After that she disappeared, and I doubted she was holed up in Xander's office any more. I'd thought maybe she was working the private booths, but now I had to wonder if Dee's special party was Trixie's every night.

Whatever Xander's new plans for her, they'd stolen the life right out of her. And now I was trapped here, waiting for Xander to collect his favor from me. I prayed it wasn't going to be something that would ruin me, too.

Xander was still in his office when I came out of the dressing room. He'd given me a section in center, but it was the one closest to left stage, and that meant there'd be some bleed over. Following last night with Chris, and the way he'd shut me out, this wasn't what I needed.

About an hour into my shift, I spotted Xander sitting at the bar with a group of six men, all in suits. They were likely the ones planning on the after party. Just because they were well dressed didn't mean they'd behave themselves. Men in suits glossed their deviance. Formal dress didn't mean dignity in this place. It was such a farce. Here it denoted entitlement and forthcoming degradation.

The blue-collar men, dressed in jeans and T-shirts, were often the most polite—like Chris had been, even though he was outside of blue collar and pushing fringe. His full sleeves and severe face should've scared me, but they never did, mostly because they made him so obviously different from the suits in the club.

Xander seated them over by left stage, close to me, but they were outside my section, so I wouldn't have to deal with them directly.

For the most part.

One of them grabbed my wrist as I walked by. "When do you get up there, honey?"

I forced a smile, aware Xander was out and watching. "I serve the tables."

"Why aren't you serving my table?"

"You're not in my section, sweetie. Maybe next time." I winked and tried to walk away, but his grip on my wrist tightened. I met his sharp gaze. His pupils were huge, a sign that booze wasn't the only thing these boys had been ingesting. They'd been rotating to the bathroom, which meant they were either shooting or snorting, probably the latter since needles were messy. Either way, drugs made men ballsy and stupid.

The girl serving their table rushed over. "Can I get you another Manhattan?"

"I want this one to get me a drink." He tugged my arm, pulling me closer.

Xander stood up, crossing the room. His smile was both smooth and threatening as he spoke to Mindi. "Is there something our guest needs?"

"I want this one, but she says she's not getting up on stage tonight. I want a private dance instead." He let go of my wrist at Xander's pointed look.

Xander's smile stayed in place, but the tic below his eye gave away his irritation. He caressed my cheek with the back of his hand. "She's rather lovely, isn't she?" He shifted his heavy gaze from the suit to me. "I'm afraid Sarah isn't available this evening."

"Well, make her available." The man's hand went to his belt, adjusting it. Or himself.

Xander swept my hair off my shoulder, his fingers sliding across the nape of my neck. I tried to keep my expression neutral, but my panic was hard to control.

"I'm unable to accommodate that request. Sarah has tables to serve. Maybe another time, right, sweetheart?" His squeezed my neck, his thumb close to an artery.

I had to fight with my body not to jerk out of his hold. I smiled, hoping it didn't come across as forced and afraid I was failing. I was petrified.

"Of course. Whatever you'd like."

Xander turned his attention back to the suit. "As I said before, everything has been arranged already. I'm positive you'll be well entertained, and if you're not, I'm sure we'll be able to find a way to rectify that. Now if you would be so kind as to let Sarah get back to her tables, they're waiting for her service." Xander slipped his hand in his pocket, eyes sharp.

The suit followed the movement. I'd wondered for some time if Xander was carrying, as his gesture was clearly intended to indicate. I couldn't be sure if the threat was idle or real, but I didn't want to find out.

I made my way through my section, trying to keep the tremble out of my voice and hands as I took orders and removed empty glasses.

A little while later, the smell of Xander's cologne filled my nose as I stood at the bar, waiting for my drinks. It did nothing to calm my racing heart.

"What do you say, Sarah?"

"Thank you." It came out a broken whisper.

"What, specifically, are you thanking me for?" His lips were right beside my ear.

"For telling him I wasn't available." *For not cashing in the favor I owe you.*

His dark chuckle left a prickle under my skin. "I think you should be thanking me for more than that." He dropped a hand, fingertips following the lace band around my thigh-highs. "I think we've put off discussing the interest on your debt long enough."

TEN

SARAH

Every time I passed the suit's table, I could feel that man watching me. I didn't make eye contact, overtly aware of the message it would send. Xander had taken up residence at the bar. His eyes were on me, too. My grace period was about to end, and I was terrified of what that would mean. What if he didn't say I was unavailable next time, or worse, he put me in a situation like Dee's?

Dee finished her early set at ten, and Candy took her place on the stage. As she began, the table of suits was escorted to the back of the club. Xander went with them, a slick smile plastered on his face as they passed the private booths and kept going. A sick feeling settled in the pit of my stomach.

I'd dedicated myself to getting a MBA to get away from all this, yet I'd been disappointed that so many of the men I'd encountered during my internship were just as much pigs as the ones who came to places like this. Money didn't end up down women's panties in the business world—at least not literally. Climbing the corporate ladder meant better pay and more power, and there were always shortcuts to getting there. One of the other female interns had already been dismissed for inappropriate conduct. She'd been caught blowing an account manager in a copy room. That was a path I would never take. I would earn every damn stripe and fight every last stereotype they threw at me. And so far I was succeeding. I'd earned respect because I worked hard and took my internship seriously.

But here things were different. Here I was the stereotype. My denying that guy meant someone else would have to deal with him. And I had a terrible feeling it was going to be Dee.

The suits passed through the area surrounding left stage, moving toward the doors leading to the private rooms. I searched the club for Grant. While I didn't necessarily trust him, I knew he tried to protect the girls who weren't all that keen on protecting themselves. I'd also seen how he was with Dee. He wasn't like that with anyone else.

I found him straddling the line between center and left stage, his attention focused on the private booths.

"What do you need, Sarah?" he asked at my approach.

"Who's dealing with those suits tonight?"

His eyes narrowed, his bored expression morphing into something hard. "Tonight isn't the night to be looking to switch roles."

"Is it Dee?"

"Does it fucking matter?" His tone was blade sharp. For all his calm veneer, he was lethal when he needed to be. I'd seen him lay a guy out with one well-placed punch.

"One of the guys in that group was a handsy asshole."

"Like that's anything new. Let security do their job and get back to your tables."

He wouldn't look at me, which meant our conversation was over.

I returned to my section, but I kept an eye out for Dee. Five minutes later, she came out of the dressing room, escorted by Max. He delivered her to Grant, who softened as soon he saw her. He pulled her into the shadows, where he thought no one could see.

He tilted her head up, his thumbs sweeping across the hollow under her eyes. I could see his mouth moving. His tenderness made me believe he offered words of solace. And then he brushed his lips across her cheek. Whatever was going on between them, it wasn't just about the job. There was a relationship there, and wasn't that messed up? Because I had a feeling there was nothing innocent or sweet about what Xander had planned for Dee tonight.

When she and Grant drifted out of the shadows, he had his hand on her elbow, holding her steady as he walked her past the private booths. They disappeared through a curtain, and then he reappeared alone. He stood there for a long while after she was gone, talking on the walkie, his expression grim.

Less than half an hour later, there was a ripple in the air, a surge of electric emotion pulsing through the club. Security moved together toward the private booths, and the sick feeling in my stomach expanded.

Xander, who had been at the bar, made it back there before anyone else and pushed through the curtain. Hardly any of the patrons paid attention to what was happening off the stage. But the girls had noticed, and the energy in the room shifted, a current of fear turning the air sour.

Xander was the first to reappear several minutes later. Flanked by two security guards, he'd set his mouth in a flat line and slipped his right hand inside his suit jacket, Napoleon style.

I scanned the club for Grant, because he was usually right up Xander's ass. I caught movement in the back corner, near a door I'd always assumed led to the storage closets. Three large bodies stepped out, keeping close together to create a tight, protective circle. The door across the hall opened and whoever or whatever was being concealed disappeared through it. Whatever was going down, it had to be bad.

The other security guards dispersed, mouths close to their walkies as they scanned the crowd.

Xander returned soon after, his long strides taking him back to the private booths, followed by more security.

Fear slithered down my spine as I stopped at my tables, taking orders for more rounds, checking to make sure customers were taken care of. Once everyone was set for a while, I waited a few minutes, then headed for Xander's office, plagued by the feeling something bad was happening, or already had. Security wasn't guarding the door, so I went inside the small waiting room. The black leather couch was empty, business magazines stacked neatly in the corner: a veneer of professionalism.

The doors to Xander's actual office and the security surveillance room were both closed, as was typical. I glanced at the camera in the corner, waiting to see if someone would come out and send me back to my tables. I didn't exactly have a plan. But I couldn't shake the heavy feeling in my stomach, and I wanted to make sure Dee was okay. I pressed my ear against the door to Xander's office, listening for something—an angry voice, the sound of someone being beaten, I had no idea.

I put my hand on the knob and turned, expecting it to be locked. It wasn't. It rolled smoothly, and I opened it a crack, peeking through the tiny gap.

Dee sat huddled in the chair across from Xander's desk, Grant's massive suit jacket draped over her shoulders. Her knees were pulled up to her chest, her hair was a mess, and her mascara ran in black streaks down her cheeks.

Grant kneeled in front of her, one hand twined with hers, wiping away tears with the other.

He shushed her, whispering words I could barely make out. "It's okay, Dee Dee girl. You're okay. I've got you."

She shook her head and shifted, yelping with the movement. When he smoothed a soothing hand over her hair, she turned her face into his palm, shaking and groaning. That was when I noticed her nails. Most of the diamond-studded tips had been broken off, leaving behind jagged, bleeding edges.

"I didn't finish the hour. I don't want to owe Xander. I can't do that ag—" her broken sob cut off the words.

"You don't have to worry about that. You don't owe him anything, Dee Dee."

"Trix made it sound like it wasn't that bad. I didn't think it was gonna be like that. I didn't think—"

"It *shouldn't* have been like that. I should've been there to keep you safe. I'm so fucking sorry. Fucking Xander. I'm gonna figure out how the feed got cut, and someone's going to answer for this."

She broke down, clinging to him. "I just wanna go home. Can't I go home? I wanna get this off me. I don't wanna look at what they did—" Grant's arms encircled her, his huge frame dwarfing her slight one. I backed away, the sickness in my stomach turning to rot. I didn't want to imagine what could have made Dee break like that, or leave Grant at risk of falling apart along with her. I pulled the door closed silently.

The door behind me opened as I turned to leave, Xander blocking my exit.

The outer door slammed, shutting us in together. His lip curled as he stepped toward me, chest almost touching mine. In my heels I was only a few inches shorter, but he was huge.

"What the fuck are you doing in here?" he demanded.

Anger overrode the typical fear he incited in me, anger at what I'd seen and heard and couldn't unknow.

"You're supposed to protect her," I seethed.

His jaw tightened, eyes flashing with something so dark I feared I'd just gotten a glimpse at what the bottom of my grave would look like. But he had failed Dee, and in doing so, he'd put us all at risk.

"You need to get back to your tables."

I made a disgusted sound and stepped around him.

He grabbed me by the wrist. "You're good at keeping that pretty mouth of yours shut. I suggest you do exactly that unless you want to find out what it really looks like behind the curtain."

I returned to the floor, and the next two hours were torturously slow. Grant never came back out. At the end of the night, when I went back to the dressing room to cash out, Dee's bag was missing from her station.

The rest of the girls were as antsy as me, questioning each other. I stayed out of it, unwilling to share what I knew. If I did, I could very well end up in a place even darker than my current one.

Max was standing outside the door to Xander's office as I approached. "Easy in there tonight."

I nodded, smart enough to understand that was the only warning I'd get.

Xander didn't even look at me as I passed over my receipts and waited for him to check. He barely scanned them before he waved me off. When I didn't leave right away his eyes lifted, fingertips pressing into the top of the desk until they turned white.

"Destiny will be fine," he told me.

"You mean physically?"

"Yes."

"Isn't that convenient for you."

People recovered from physical trauma. Tenley was a prime example of that. Bones healed, bruises disappeared, burns turned into scars. But the loss of everyone she'd loved had left permanent stains on her soul.

I knew all about those. They were the reason I'd ended up here in the first place.

ELEVEN

CHRIS

In the aftermath of the crap with my mom and managing the state of that house, I hadn't dealt well with finding Sarah outside my door. I couldn't decide if it was the unfortunate location I'd found her in, her need to make sure I was okay, or the way I'd fucked her that was the largest source of my concern and guilt.

I'd been aggressive with her, and that wasn't my style—especially knowing most of the men she dealt with on a regular basis were exactly that way. But before that, she'd offered me more of herself, even beyond what I'd been willing to give her, which was ironic. I'd wanted to know more of her for a while now, but when she'd tried to give it to me, I'd shut it down. I couldn't even understand myself.

When she'd messaged me later yesterday morning, I'd been in the middle of a session. By the time I was free, she was already at work. I'd started a message, but never sent it. I wanted to talk to her in person, not text her about my being a jackass.

In hindsight, anything would've been better than nothing.

And as if that poorly managed situation wasn't bad enough, Ivy had messaged me yesterday mentioning the unusually clean state of the kitchen at our mom's, and asking if I'd had anything to do with it. I played it off like I had no idea, but I worried my mom wasn't going to be able to keep her mouth shut.

At this point, it had been more than twenty-four hours since I'd woken up alone in my apartment, wishing I'd been different with

Sarah. The message I'd sent her this morning had gone unanswered. If I didn't hear something before the end of the day, I was seeking her out, one way or another. I didn't feel good at all about the way things had gone down the other night. And Sarah had tonight off, which I only knew because Lisa was bailing early to go for dinner with her or something.

It should've been me taking her out somewhere nice to eat. I'd probably only done that a handful of times thanks to our mutually crappy work schedules. The best I could typically pull off was takeout from Sarah's favorite Italian place a couple of blocks away. Going out on dates indicated a different kind of relationship, and we'd never progressed that far. Except maybe we had. Sarah sleeping in my hallway told me this was about more than just sex and orgasms for her, like it was for me. So I couldn't figure out why things still felt off with us. Or more off than I'd made them.

At four in the afternoon, I finally got the message I'd been waiting for from Sarah.

> Sry. Busy day today, just got your message now. What're you up to tonight?

I sent her one back.

> Hoping I can see you so I can make up for being a jerk last time.

Her response came quickly.

> If that's your version of being a jerk, you're an incredibly sweet, attentive one. Want me to drop a key off?

I flipped one back to her.

> Please.

A little later Sarah dropped off a key while I was working on a back piece and headed out for dinner with Lisa. It was good to see them spending time together again. I spent the next few hours shading the Celtic design I'd outlined earlier this month, content in the knowledge that I would get to spend the night with my girl, hopefully with no interruptions.

"You coming to Hayden's tonight?" Jamie asked as we were closing up. He'd been working in a private room when she'd been by earlier. Sarah was still with Lisa, and apparently Tenley, based on her recent text, so I'd have time to get in a shower before she got home.

"I'm heading to Sarah's."

"I thought the girls were getting up to no good."

"They're doing dinner. Then she's all mine."

"Things okay with you two?" he asked, trying to be all casual and shit, but he wasn't very successful.

I shrugged. "They are what they are."

I could feel him watching me, maybe waiting for more, but I kept clicking away on the computer, checking the schedule for the coming week. We were booked solid as usual, with no cancellations and a waiting list a mile long.

"Lisa got a call from Candy this afternoon."

"Candy called Lisa? Why?"

"I asked the same thing. I have to assume it's because she thinks it'll get back to you."

"Probably. Fucking Candy. It'd be nice if she didn't keep dragging Lisa into unnecessary drama, or using her to create more."

"Agreed. It'll be good when Sarah's out of that place and Lisa doesn't have any more ties."

I could fully appreciate that. I knew it had to be hard for Jamie when crap like this came up, because it meant old memories surfacing, and none of them were good. "So what's the gossip Candy's dishing now?"

"Apparently she's quitting The Sanctuary."

"Yeah, right. What problem did she make for herself now?"

I'd believe that when I saw it. Candy had walked away from The Dollhouse once, after I broke it off with her. I figured it was her attempt at getting out of that business for good. She'd talked about going to beauty school, since she was good with makeup and hair, but the money couldn't compare to what she made stripping, so she'd kept finding reasons to put it off.

Once that shithole closed down, she moved on to The Sanctuary. She was a pretty enough girl, but the drugs had always been an issue for her, and they were aging her quickly. I didn't want to think about what her life would be like five years from now, when the stage wasn't an option anymore.

"Lisa said there was an incident with one of the girls."

Jamie pulled me out of my trip down memory lane.

"What kind of incident?"

"I don't have all the details. Something happened with Destiny, and it doesn't sound good, but that's all I got."

"*The* Destiny?" I nodded toward the storage room where Hayden was running an inventory check. He did it every night.

"That's the one."

"Shit. I wonder what went down."

Destiny had worked at The Dollhouse too. She'd started as a shooter girl and worked her way to waitress. She'd been sweet, if not a little naïve. Hayden had taken a liking to her one night a few years back, thanks to a shitload of beer. He'd managed to get an invite back to her place, where he'd fucked her six ways to Sunday before going home in a cab. She'd thought there was more to it until she realized pretty much every chick in the club had been on that ride.

Hayden had been a legend, kind of like the horsemen of the apocalypse, but his weapon of choice had been his dick and his punishment a stellar array of orgasms, never to be forgotten.

That had changed when Tenley came along. Now she was the sole recipient of his orgasms. She didn't seem to mind, though—about his past or the excessive orgasms—which was good for Hayden.

"Lisa was hoping to get more information from Sarah, but I thought maybe you'd already know."

"I haven't talked to Sarah since she stayed at my place night before last. Maybe it's recent?" Like last night recent.

Jamie drummed the counter, leaving fingerprints on the glass surface. "Could be."

"It could also be Candy blowing things out of proportion like she loves to do."

"Lisa said she sounded pretty upset, but it's possible." He frowned. "I figured this would be something Sarah might tell you. I mean, you two are well beyond the fuck-buddy stage, right?"

I motioned between us. "If we're getting ready to braid each other's hair and sing "Kumbayah," I'm out."

Jamie and Hayden had been on me for a while about what was going on with Sarah, but it was difficult to answer when even I didn't know.

"What're we talking about?" Hayden asked.

I hadn't heard him come out of the back room.

"Chris being a pussy."

"Oh yeah?" Hayden was only half paying attention; his focus was on his phone. His brows came down low, and then his eyes popped wide. "What the—" He hit a couple of buttons and put his phone to his ear. "You want to tell me what's going on over there, kitten?"

There was silence on his end for a few seconds, during which his eyebrows climbed his forehead.

"What time are you planning on coming home?... That's not soon enough... No fucking way. I'll drive over there and get you if I have to. I don't care. It's warm out; the hood of my car needs waxing."

He looked over at us, maybe realizing he wasn't alone. His grin was ridiculous.

"You bet your sweet ass, kitten. Just wait until you get home to see how serious I am."

He hung up.

Jamie and I stared at him, waiting.

"Early birthday presents. Man, I always used to hate my birthday. But now I'm thinking it's not so bad." Hayden shoved his phone in his back pocket. "I'm not a hundred percent on what's going on, but I think I'm going to like it based on the picture Tenley sent me."

"Really? We couldn't tell by the tent in your pants," I said.

Hayden looked down.

He'd been bitchy the last couple of days, moaning about how Tenley had been out late a lot. Tee was Hayden's security blanket. If she wasn't around enough, he got cranky.

He flipped me the bird. "You coming out tonight?"

"I'm gonna have to pass. I'm spending the night at Sarah's."

"That's good. About time you two figured your shit out."

"Yup." I didn't disagree, even though it seemed like we were a long way from that. I considered what Jamie had said about Destiny, and wondered if Sarah and I were going to talk about it. Dee was one of the few girls Sarah actually had nice things to say about. She'd been the one to get her in at The Sanctuary.

Now I was worried there were things Sarah wasn't telling me, and not just because of our crazy schedules. I needed to find a way around the walls we'd put up. And after all my resisting, I'd probably have to take some of mine down first. If there was something going on at The Sanctuary, I'd find out about it tonight.

I was drying off after my shower when I heard Sarah call my name from her living room. I hadn't thought to bring extra clothes, but I was sure I had something clean in her closet.

I came out with a towel wrapped around my hips.

"How perfect is my timing?" Sarah hung her purse on the hook inside the door, almost missing, since her eyes were on my towel and not what she was doing.

I tucked it in tighter to keep it in place. "You have a good time with the girls?"

"It was fun. Tenley's album is almost done."

"Whatever pics she sent Hayden tonight pretty much pushed him over the edge."

Sarah grinned. "Can't say I'm surprised about that."

I turned in the direction of her bedroom and my clothes, hoping I could get something on before she tried to take the towel off. With the way she was looking at me, it seemed like this was her turn not to be interested in talking, unless it included a lot of moaning on her part, interspersed with questions from me about how various things were feeling. I had to change her mind if we weren't going to chase each other in circles forever.

I saw the irony in that, too. Just the other night I'd shut her out and used sex as a distraction from the things I didn't want to deal with. And maybe that was the real problem—here we were, after all this time, still keeping the important shit tucked away in our respective dark places. Worse yet, she'd given me the opportunity, and I'd refused to take it. I was my own biggest problem.

Sarah grabbed the back of the towel. "Hey, where are you going?"

I held onto the ends to keep from losing it. "I thought I'd put on some clothes."

She wrapped her arms around my waist and rested her cheek against my back. "Why would you want to do that?"

I closed my eyes, trying not to get caught up in the sudden affection. My frustration over the situation I'd created grated on me. I'd made it this way between us, especially recently, but now I was tired of keeping up all the walls. Yet I had no idea what to do to bring them down.

"I haven't talked to you since the other night. I figured maybe we could do some of that, unless you're looking to get down to fucking." I didn't mean to add that last part, especially with the bite it carried.

The hand moving down my stomach stilled. "Chris?" She ducked under my arm and came around in front of me. "Is everything okay? Did something happen with Ivy?"

I hadn't heard from Ivy today, but for ten years I hadn't heard from her at all, so it wasn't like daily contact was expected.

"She's fine, as far as I know."

"What's wrong, then?" She ran a hand up my chest, her warm palm coming to rest against the side of my neck.

"How was work last night?"

Her gaze shifted down. "It was okay."

"Yeah? Business as usual?"

She traced the edge of the tattoo on my biceps. "It was the same for me as it is every night."

I raised a brow. She was walking right into it.

"What about Destiny? How was her night?"

She froze, eyes widening in something that resembled fear. "What? I don't—how—"

"Lisa talks to Jamie."

Sarah's defenses went up. "Well, you all work together, so that makes it a lot easier, doesn't it? What did you want me to do, interrupt your tattoo session so I could tell you about stupid work drama? Like you don't already have enough to deal with. You don't need mine, too."

"But you talked to Lisa about it today? And Tee?"

"Well, yeah, because I saw them."

"So you can talk to them, but coming to me isn't on the top of your list? Why didn't you message me last night? Or this morning?" I didn't need to be such an asshole, but my frustration had nowhere to go.

"What would've been the point? I'm seeing you now, and last night you still hadn't answered my message from the morning. I don't get why you're being like... like—" She flailed, gesturing at my face, which I was sure showed my frustration. "This!"

"Because you're keeping shit from me."

"I'm keeping shit from *you*? Jesus, Chris, you win the gold medal for hypocrite right now. Weren't you the one who decided fucking me was a better option than talking about what happened with Ivy on Sunday?"

"I didn't think my family crap was stuff you should have to know about." She was right about me being a hypocrite, but it was damn near impossible to open up, especially when doing that meant giving Sarah insight into all my flaws.

"Right. That would be you letting me in, wouldn't it? And that's not going to happen." Sarah crossed her arms over her chest, her irritation clear. "I knew you'd be upset about Dee, because I sure am, and I figured this was a better conversation face to face. I didn't want it to turn into some kind of argument. But it looks like we're fighting anyway."

"Seems that happens a lot when we talk. Maybe it would be better if we did less of that."

She threw her hands in the air. "Well, we hardly do any of it now. Maybe it's better if we stop all together."

This was the Sarah I'd met at The Dollhouse all those months ago. She'd had her back up, spitting fire at me. I shouldn't be egging her on, looking for a fight we didn't need to have.

I dropped the towel. Sarah's eyes dipped down and came right back up. I was hard. Really hard. Which was messed up because I was also pissed off. The two were not a good combination for thinking. I held my hands out, offering her the one thing I knew how to do well.

I smiled, but it was full of anger and a desperation I didn't know how to control. "I agree. Fuck talking."

She took a step toward me, looking like she wanted to slap me. I didn't think she would. Sarah had never been the kind of woman to retaliate with violence.

She picked up the towel and thrust it at me. I didn't move, didn't speak, waiting for something—her rage, the end again—anything but this emotional limbo I couldn't seem to get myself out of. Or maybe that wasn't true. Maybe I knew exactly how to get myself out of this situation—but I wasn't quite brave (or stupid) enough to put myself through that again. With Candy I'd been a lot younger, and maybe less jaded, but I'd still been wrong for thinking things could've been more than they were. Growing up I'd been shut out by my family over and over again as I looked for some kind of connection with them. I suppose lately I'd finally gotten that, but with a side of extra drama I didn't want or need.

"Dee got pushed into hosting some kind of private party last night, and it didn't go well," Sarah said, her voice flat.

"What do you mean *private party*? And since when is Dee dancing?" I took the towel Sarah still held out for me and fixed it around my waist, my hard-on deflating fast.

"She only started a few weeks ago, maybe a month? It happened really fast. She was serving, and then Candy got herself into some trouble with Xander, and the next thing I know, Dee's up on stage."

"Fuck." That was bad news I should've had already. "What's the deal with the private party? Why didn't you tell me about this?"

"Because I didn't know it was happening until last night, and I'm not supposed to know at all. I don't think anyone was. She said she was going to make a lot of money in a short period of time, which worries me a lot, and now she's not answering my texts."

There was only one kind of party in places like The Sanctuary. I'd once been to one in the private rooms at The Dollhouse, where lap dances turned into fucking for an extra few hundred bucks, or the right amount of blow. Damen had always had a surplus of that. It was the only way he could get anyone to fuck his ugly ass. I doubted Xander had that problem. He was a handsome, albeit slimy, motherfucker.

"What happened that made it not go well?"

She crossed over to the couch and took a seat, eyeing me warily. "Promise you're not going to go off on me again?"

I dropped down on the other end of the couch. "I'm sorry. I shouldn't have done that. I just—"

"—thought I was lying to you?"

"I want you to talk to me, that's all."

"As long as you don't get upset with me for telling you the truth."

"Why would I get mad at you for being honest?"

She chewed her lip for a second before speaking. "So, there were these suits—they were sitting by left stage, at the edge of center. You know where I'm talking about?"

I tried to visualize the layout of the club. I'd only been in there twice, and my focus had always been on Sarah. I nodded, even though I wasn't a hundred percent, so she'd continue.

"I was serving close to them, and one was a real asshole."

"Did he touch you?"

The word no formed on her lips, but then she stopped, exhaled a sigh, and nodded. "He grabbed my wrist, nothing else. He was coked up or something and being a jerk. Xander handled it."

That didn't make me feel better at all. Xander was the worst of all of them.

"I promise, Chris, he kept his hands to himself after that."

That these douchebags could get away with putting their hands on the girls at all was a real problem. The only time that had been permitted at The Dollhouse was after money had changed hands for services about to be rendered. Xander ran a much looser club, and the lax rules put the women at risk.

"Does that happen often?" I asked, trying to keep my voice calm.

"The private parties?"

"People putting their hands on you."

"Security is usually good about making sure that kind of thing doesn't happen."

That wasn't a real answer, which was a problem, but I wasn't going to push her on it now. Not when she was finally talking.

"What happened after Xander dealt with the guy?"

"I went back to serving tables, and Dee finished her set. Everything was fine until Dee went to host her party, or whatever the hell you want to call it. She was gone for, like, maybe half an hour, and then something went down. Almost all of security went to manage the situation. Grant looked really upset, and he usually doesn't have facial expressions, so I figured it had to be something with Dee."

"Who's Grant?"

"Head of security."

"I thought that was Max."

"He's second in command. Anyway, I'm pretty sure Grant and Dee have something going on."

"Like a deal? Like they're cutting out Xander?" Now I

remembered who Grant was. He was a tank. He made me look like a damn dwarf. He and I had had words once, and only once. It was the last time I'd been allowed in the club.

"No. Nothing like that. I think they're involved. Grant—he's different with her. Soft. And that man isn't soft with anyone." Sarah took a deep breath, her gaze dropping. "Dee had been pretty worked up about the party. She was nervous enough to tell me about it. I don't think she wanted to do it, but she'd been pushed, and maybe she needed the money? Anyway, I was worried, so I went to check on her. Something happened back there that wasn't supposed to. Grant said something about the feed being cut."

"You mean security tapes?"

Sarah nodded. "I think maybe someone messed with the cameras so they couldn't see what was happening." She stumbled over the words, her fingers going to her lips.

She didn't need to say anything else. It was pretty fucking clear. "Shit, Sarah. How'd you find out about all of this?"

"Dee was in Xander's office with Grant. She was… really upset, and Grant was beside himself. She has these fake nails, and she freaking loves them even though they're crazy long." Sarah closed her eyes and sucked in a high-pitched breath.

I couldn't understand what the hell fake nails had to do with anything.

When she opened her eyes again, they were glassy with the promise of tears. "Except they'd been ripped right off. Like, her fingers were bleeding and everything. But all she was worried about was not finishing the hour. She told me she was getting two grand for the party."

I breathed out an expletive. Two grand was a lot of money. But I could guarantee it was less than half of what those men had forked over to Xander for the services to be provided. I imagined they would've expected fairly extensive services for that kind of money. I'd been privy to conversations about that with some of the girls at The Dollhouse, back when I'd been living in the house with them.

"You see why I didn't say anything until now? This wasn't a

phone conversation or a text message," her voice wavered, breaking at the end.

I cupped her cheek. She'd dealt with this all day without talking to anyone until she saw Lisa and Tenley a few hours ago. And my silence yesterday had made her feel like she couldn't come to me.

She closed her eyes and leaned into my touch. "I'm sorry."

"For what?"

When her eyes opened, a single tear leaked out and pooled in the crease in my hand. "For all the drama. You don't need it."

"You gotta get out of there, Sarah. This isn't good for you."

"I know. I want to. I'll talk to Tenley again about Elbo and see what I can do." Her soft palm came to rest on the side of my neck, her thumb sweeping back and forth over the vein connected to my heart.

"Just let me help you if I can, okay?" I ran my hand along her arm. "I want you to talk to me. This stuff about The Sanctuary, I want to know. I just want you to be safe."

"Me too," she whispered.

I dipped my head to meet her lips. I knew I needed to give her something back, but it wasn't going to be in words tonight. She was carrying enough of her own burdens.

I worried that no amount of loving Sarah could change the way things had shaken down recently. I could see the escalation at the club that she refused to. It was like watching a train speeding toward a broken bridge. There seemed to be nothing I could do to stop the fall. Hers or mine.

It was late by the time I woke the next day. I was sprawled over Sarah's side of the bed, her pillow tucked against my side as if it were her body. I rolled off her rock of a mattress and headed for the bathroom. Next time we were sleeping at my place.

I passed the kitchen table groggily, knocking into her duffle bag hanging from the chair. It dropped to the ground, the contents barfing out all over the floor.

A black lace bra and matching boy short panties with a serious ruffle were among the items scattered across the hardwood. They weren't anything I would ever see Sarah wear in the bedroom. It wasn't her style; it was her uniform. I knelt down, intending to shove it all back in, when I noticed the wad of rolled cash fastened with an elastic band. Beside that was a bottle of pills—not the store brand variety Sarah always carried with her to offset aching calves after killer heels, but a prescription.

I picked it up, rolling it between my fingers until I could see the label. The prescription wasn't for Sarah, but some other name I didn't recognize. However, it was the contents of the bottle that concerned me most. I knew exactly what the pills were for.

As a kid I'd had trouble listening in school. They'd decided my inability to focus meant I needed medication to manage my distractibility. No one took into consideration that maybe, just maybe, part of the issue had been that most days I came to school without breakfast. And when I did eat, it was usually white bread with cheap margarine and brown sugar. On a good day there might be some cinnamon to sprinkle on it. Or that sometimes my mom let me have sips of her coffee because it was so hard to get me up in the mornings.

But then, that's what happened when my afternoons were spent hanging out in the back office of a store, waiting for my mom's shift to end at eleven because she couldn't afford to pay someone to watch me. The rare times she could, it was the lowlife neighbor who let me eat candy for dinner because she was too overworked to make real food. Bedtimes were late, mornings were early. At seven, it meant I was unregulated and often underfed. No shit I had trouble paying attention.

So they'd put me on meds—back then it'd been Ritalin. The doctor had given my mom samples since we couldn't afford to pay. It had killed my appetite and made me even more wired. After a while I'd figured out the pills had the opposite effect of what they should've, so I stopped taking them and started selling them to the high school kids in the neighborhood. It wasn't the potheads or the acid trippers who bought them. It was the smart kids.

I'd used the money to buy lunches at the deli down the street from school—huge sandwiches spread with real butter, piled high with meat and cheese and slices of fresh tomato, crisp leaves of lettuce, sharp rings of raw onion, and real mayo. I'd bought milk to go with it—white, not chocolate. It was heavenly, and nothing like the powdered shit my mom had to buy because we couldn't afford the stuff that came in the gallon jug.

I righted the chair I'd knocked over and dropped down in it, still rolling the pill bottle between my thumb and finger.

I dumped out the contents on the kitchen table, separating them into piles of five. The bottle told me there should be thirty in there. I counted twenty-two, twice. The numbers confirmed what I didn't want to believe. But why would she have the pills if she wasn't using them? I finally had to own that Sarah was heading in a direction I didn't want her to, and maybe she was okay with that. Maybe I had to be too, or I had to bail.

I scooped the pills back into the bottle and capped it, leaving it on the kitchen table. I left her duffle bag open, the contents still all over the floor. I dressed in my day-old clothes and didn't bother making the bed.

Standing in her bedroom, I stared at the mess of twisted sheets, aware of how deep I'd gotten in with Sarah.

It hurt to think she'd finally opened up last night, had been willing to tell me what was really going on, only to realize she was keeping something else hidden. Just when I was figuring out how to share more of myself in return, I had to walk away. Because I couldn't watch someone self-destruct again.

I'd seen it happen to Lisa and witnessed Jamie's struggle to bring her back. I'd seen Hayden fall more than once; dragging him out of it had been hell the first time. The second time, when Tenley had left him, I hadn't figured we'd get him back. But we did.

I wouldn't go through that with Sarah. I couldn't. I didn't ever want to be so dependent on someone that I'd allow myself to be dragged down into their destruction. Not again.

I found a scrap of paper and left a note beside the bottle of pills.

TWELVE

SARAH

This morning had started out bright. Chris and I had talked. I'd been as honest as I could with him, and he'd been understanding, and then he'd been amazingly sweet and attentive in bed—so different from the last time. I'd wanted to believe he could handle knowing more about my life, about who I am. Funny how a few hours could shift all that.

I'd gone to my internship feeling lighter. I gave a presentation on guerrilla marketing to the senior team, which had gone over well. I'd been armed with statistics and numbers to support the research, and the higher ups had been impressed.

I'd gone to the break room feeling like I could handle whatever was coming next, and I thought I'd make a coffee since my adrenaline was starting to wane. I'd just gotten started when one of the junior account managers came in after me. He was the same guy rumored to have convinced another intern that a blow job in the copy room was a good idea. It irked me that he'd gotten off with nothing more than a slap on the wrist, and she'd lost her place in the program.

She'd been on a full scholarship, and now she was out of the program and likely on the hook for more than a hundred thousand dollars. It made me hyper aware of how bad things could get if Xander ever decided to bring my current employment situation to light.

His too-thick cologne gave me an instant headache as he

reached around me for a coffee cup. He grazed my breast in the process. It wasn't an accident.

"Sorry about that." His smile was all fake apology.

I gave him a look as I dropped a K-cup into the Keurig.

He leaned against the counter and handed me the mug. "You mind making me one of those?"

I knew this game, and while it annoyed me that I had to play it with a douche like this guy, I wouldn't put my placement in jeopardy over some asshole who wanted to treat me like his lackey. If I played my cards right, I'd be using his face as a step on the ladder up to the top of this company anyway.

"You're Sarah, right?"

"Mmm-hmm." I avoided eye contact, focusing on the coffee.

"Is that your real hair color?" He reached out as if he were about to touch a loose tendril that had escaped my bun.

I jerked away. "Yes, it's real."

His grin was more leer than apology. "You never know whether the drapes match the carpet these days. All sorts of false advertising happening with you ladies."

I struggled not to give him the fake smile I would've offered at the club. I'd come to expect far worse than that from the men who frequented The Sanctuary. Here the men were usually less obvious in their douchebaggery. Far more subversive. And occasionally, I actually encountered someone who was professional. Those were the amazing moments. But most of the time, regardless of where I was, men who thought they had the upper hand continued trying to use it.

He was two or three inches shorter than I was, even though my heels were low. He was thirty at best, but I could see the beginning of baldness creeping over the crown of his head. I'd heard he was related to someone higher up, which accounted for his slap on the wrist—and perhaps his presence here in the first place.

I sighed, and something within me hardened. The same something that had left me yelling at Xander the other night after Dee. I was so sick of people thinking they could mess with me. The crap I had to put up with at The Sanctuary was bad enough. I'd made my own mess there, but I wasn't going to tolerate it here, too.

The coffee finished brewing, and I gripped the handle and held the mug out with a smile I was sure looked as calculating as it was insincere. He reached gingerly to take it.

As he did, I stepped in close and found the toe of his shoe with my heel. They weren't high, but they were pointy. I placed my palm against the back of his hand, flattening it against the hot ceramic.

"Every time I'm in a room with you, I'm going to record our conversations. If you ever ask me a question like that again, I'll be sure to broadcast it through the entire building so everyone here knows exactly what a pig you are."

He tensed as the heat from the mug became less bearable. "I'd like to see you try."

"You don't think I can manage that? You don't think someone would help me out if given the right incentive? Besides, my undergrad's in computer programming. I graduated at the top of my class. Pretty impressive for a stupid blond chick, don't you think?"

I lifted my heel from his toe, looking down to note the dent in the leather. Then I released the mug and took a step back. He dropped it right away, the scalding liquid splattering his pants and his shoes, some of the spray reaching his shirt. Hot drops landed on the top of my foot, soaking through my nylons.

"Oh, no! Are you okay?" I asked, feigning concern. "I'll get someone to come clean that up."

I left him there, red palmed and red faced. I hoped that was his whack-off hand.

Though my immediate thought was to share my giddy victory with Chris, I couldn't decide whether I should tell him or not. I wanted him to be proud of how I'd handled the situation, but I worried he'd be upset that it had happened in the first place, especially after Dee.

And she remained on my mind, while my texts to her remained unanswered. I'd seen her physical and emotional undoing firsthand, and I knew now that it wasn't going to be as simple as serving the assholes on left stage when Xander decided to collect his favor from me. He was going to break me if I couldn't get out of there. And if he did, I might never be the same.

I wished I'd never followed my mother's advice and taken that job at The Dollhouse in the first place, or trusted Dee's assurance that The Sanctuary would be better. I should've listened to Chris and focused less on my finances. I could see now that no amount of money was worth this.

I was tired by the end of the day, with all of my worries bogging me down. I wondered if Chris had some time between clients before I had to go to The Sanctuary again. I only had about an hour before I had to leave for my shift at The Sanctuary. I checked my messages on the way up the stairs to my apartment, hoping for a message from him or Dee. I had neither, so I sent Chris another text as I unlocked the door, asking if his day had been busy.

My apartment was as I'd left it last night, except my duffle bag was lying on the hardwood, half the contents spilled out. My cash tips had rolled across the floor, and my black lace bra and panties from last shift's outfit were visible as well.

But that wasn't what made my heart sink. The bottle of pills Dee had given me the other night sat on the kitchen table. Beside them was a note from Chris.

> Sarah,
> We need to cool it for a while.
>
> Chris

Of all the notes he'd left me over the last several months, this was the one I'd never wanted to see.

I knew I shouldn't have kept the pills. But I hadn't wanted Dee to get in trouble. If I'd left them in my locker, though, I wouldn't be dealing with this on top of everything else. Everything had been such a mess that night. But even worse, there'd been a moment when I'd considered how they might make it easier to get to the end of my internship.

I grabbed the note and the pills, stuffing both in my purse, and bolted down the stairs. Running across the street, heedless of the traffic, I burst into Inked Armor.

Lisa wasn't at her usual post behind the glass-front jewelry case. Hayden worked at the first station, adding color to a sleeve. He graced me with an icy, accusing glare and went back to working on the art. Clearly, Chris had talked to him.

Jamie, who was across the room putting an intricate flower on a woman's shoulder, inclined his head to the back of the shop. "He's setting up for a session in the private room."

"Thanks."

The door was ajar, the bass line of hardcore metal shaking the floor. Chris was more of a mellow music kind of guy, unless he was in a bad mood. I slipped inside and closed the door. He didn't look up from the tray of vibrantly colored inks.

"You been home yet?" he asked.

"Yes."

His eyes lifted, flat, cold. "Then what're you doing here?"

"I can explain the pills. They were Dee's."

"So what? You were holding them for her? Real fucking high school of you there, Sarah."

"She threw them to me when I was getting changed for my shift, and Grant came to get her, so I couldn't give them back. Then she did that private party, and well, you know how that went."

He regarded me with cold speculation. "So you brought them home with you? Why'd she give them to you in the first place?"

"She thought she was doing me a favor because I was tired.

It was a hectic night. I'd forgotten about them until I saw them on the counter. I never even meant to bring them home." I crossed the room to stand in front of him.

He swiveled in his chair, moving away from me. "I've got a client coming in ten. You should go."

"I could come by your place after my shift tonight. We can talk then?"

"I'm not really feeling the talking right now, Sarah. It doesn't seem to get us anywhere."

"I haven't taken them. I wasn't planning to."

He laughed, but it was dark and humorless. He spun to face me. Under the harsh expression and the lines of anger, there was sadness. "Why should I believe you?"

"Because I'm telling you the truth."

"What version of it, Sarah?"

"The only version that matters." I skimmed his jawline with my fingertips.

He shot up out of the chair. "You'd think after seeing what Tee's been through—how hard it was for her with all the pain meds after that plane crash and the bullshit and the omissions and how it screwed up Hayden—that you'd get what the issue is here."

"I'm not going to develop an addiction to pain medication. This isn't even close to the same."

He crossed his arms over his chest, the black tribal bands on his forearm cutting across the cityscape on his other arm. "You're right. But it's not just about the pills, is it? What you and I have going on here, it's not remotely like what Hayden and Tee have either. I know that. I get it, Sarah. I really do. But that doesn't mean I have to watch you fuck your life up."

I was shocked and confused by his comparisons. Neither Chris nor I came from particularly stable backgrounds, but we hadn't lost our families to tragedy. And as for what Tenley and Hayden had, I'd thought we were making progress, maybe working toward that kind of connection. I guess I was wrong.

"It's just a prescription for ADHD meds, not coke."

"Not yet. But if you don't see where this is headed, you're not nearly as smart as I thought."

"Just because someone gave me some pills doesn't mean I'm going to turn into a drug addict. That's ridiculous."

"Really? You think so?" He took a step toward me. "What about Destiny? She didn't use to be the mess she is now. You're sliding into the same dark hole they all do. You're no more immune to the pressure than the rest of those girls. You keep looking for an out, but then you make excuses to stay when you get one. It's like you want to be dragged down into that pit so you can wallow there."

"That's not why I'm staying."

"Then why, Sarah? That shithole is starting to seem normal to you. It wasn't that long ago that you were ready to leave The Dollhouse, and you weren't putting up with half the shit you are now. You let Xander walk all over you, and you moan about how much you hate him, but you're still there, taking it."

"You don't understand—" It was on the tip of my tongue to finally tell him why I hadn't walked. That it wasn't because I wanted to be there, but because I was scared of what would happen if I tried to leave.

Chris cut me off before I could. "It won't be long before you're like the rest of those girls—too numb to give a shit about anyone but yourself. Then you'll be snorting coke off some guy's dick because it's gonna put another five hundred bucks in your pocket."

It felt as if I'd been punched in the stomach. This was a whole other kind of assholery—not like the office, not like the club, but personal. Chris was playing dirty and cutting deep.

I drew in a slow breath. "You can be angry at me for having those pills in my bag, but you don't get to pigeonhole me into the same category as Candy or any of the other girls you banged along the way. Just because they made those kinds of mistakes doesn't mean I will."

"Looks like you're already on your way there."

"Screw you, Chris."

"You ever question what you're doing with me? 'Cause I do,

all the fucking time." His smile was hateful. "It's like you can't get enough of the bottom feeders, Sarah. You have all this potential, and you're willing to throw it away for what? A little more time at the bottom before you head to the top? A few orgasms?"

My heart bruised with every verbal punch.

His eyes dropped to my hand, which twitched at my side. "Wanna hit me? Go ahead. Right here." He stepped in close, invading my space, and tapped his cheek. "I bet it'll feel real good."

The coldness in his gaze broke my heart. His jaw clenched in anticipation. He was pushing me on purpose, goading me into doing something that would end this because I'd hurt him, and now he wanted to hurt me back.

A knock on the door prevented me from reacting.

"One second," he called out and looked to me. "Last chance."

I lifted my hand and pressed it gently to his cheek. "Don't ever try to make me into that person. Hurting you physically wouldn't even the score for what you've just said to me. And even if it did..." I shook my head.

He blinked and stepped back, away from my touch, his conflict clear.

"Come in," I said, dropping my hand to my side.

Jamie opened the door, glancing between us. "Your six-thirty is here early. You need a few minutes?"

"Nope. We're all set. Sarah was just taking off."

"Okay. I'll let her know you'll be out in a couple."

"I'm right behind you." Chris brushed past me.

I had no choice but to follow him. A stunning smile broke across his face when a petite redhead with cinnamon brown eyes bounced to her feet.

"You ready, girl?" he asked, sweeping a hand out toward the back room.

"For you? I sure am."

The overt flirtation was yet another backhand. I should've been used to it. It was his way, but it hurt because it was intentional, yet again.

"It's gonna be sensitive, so we'll take breaks whenever you need them." Chris put a gentle hand on her shoulder, ignoring me as he guided her into the private room.

Lisa still wasn't at the jewelry counter. Jamie sat at his desk, ignoring me now, and Hayden was working on a design. There was nothing left to do but go back to my apartment. I turned toward the door.

"Sarah." Hayden's voice stopped me. "You keep going the way you are, you're gonna break him."

I'd never tell Hayden, but part of me thought I already had. And probably myself as well.

THIRTEEN

CHRIS

I tried to distract myself with TV when I got home. It wasn't working. I was considering taking a walk down the street to grab a six-pack of beer when there was a knock at my door. It was too early for Sarah to be off from The Sanctuary, and I doubted she'd stop by anyway after the shit I said to her earlier today.

I felt bad about it, but watching her go down wasn't something I wanted to witness. More than that, I felt responsible for whatever was happening with her right now. Somehow I was all tangled up in that mess as well.

The knock came again, more insistent this time. "Hold on! I'm coming."

Sometimes my neighbor down the hall—the cougar who smoked so much her teeth had turned mottled yellow-black and were rotting out of her head—stopped by for milk. Mostly I think she wanted to scope out my apartment, or find out if I was a pot dealer, based on the odor that followed her down the hall. Or maybe she wanted to get her fuck on with me, which would never happen in a million years. Still, I tried to be nice to her, because people judged the shit out of me all the time because of how I looked.

I checked the peephole. It wasn't my cougar neighbor, though, it was Ivy. I slipped off the chain lock, turned the deadbolt, and opened the door.

She stood in the hall with her ratty-looking backpack stuffed to bursting.

"Hey, little sis, what's going on?"

She practically threw herself at me. I couldn't understand a word through her sudden onslaught of sobbing. I carry-dragged her across the threshold and closed the door, keeping the noise inside my apartment. I didn't need people coming out in the hall to witness her breakdown. Worse, someone could think it was a domestic and call the police. That happened a lot in this building.

Ivy buried her face in my chest, snotting all over me. Not that I cared. She was upset, and she'd come to me, so that was saying something. I'd made some progress with her.

I patted Ivy's back. "You're all right. You're safe. I've got you."

It took a long time and almost an entire box of tissues before she was calm enough to explain what had happened. Even then, some of the details didn't make a whole lot of sense. But it seemed to come down to John and her money again.

"How did John manage to get access to your new bank account?"

The only way was if she'd added him on to it, and I couldn't see her doing that, not unless something, or someone, had forced her hand.

"Not my bank account." She hiccupped. "My tips. I'd been hiding some of them."

"In the house?" Surely Ivy was smart enough to know if she was hiding money in the house, John would eventually find it.

"At first yes, but Dad's always going through paperwork and stuff, and I worried he'd come into my room and find it, so I started dividing up my tips. I always made sure I passed over around fifty or sixty dollars every shift. Sometimes I'd give him a little more or a little less, just depending. Then I'd keep some out for Mom and me, so she could have a bit to spend, right? She doesn't ever get anything for herself, so I thought if I gave her some money she might."

I could see exactly where this was going and what had likely happened. The commiseration between daughter and mother, and the supposed loyalty they should've shared would always be compromised as long as John was around. As much as I hated how he manipulated my mom, I could now see that she allowed it to happen.

"So this had been going on for a few months. Mom had been squirreling it away, I guess, except she didn't put it in a very good hiding spot, and Dad found it. He was so mad, Chris. She'd put it an empty coffee tin and kept it in her nightstand. I'd never seen him that upset before. He broke the kitchen table, and then he went after Mom. She locked herself in the bedroom, and I tried to do the same, but the lock on my door is busted and he, and he, and he—" Ivy broke into a fresh wave of sobs, high-pitched, frantic breaths dragging in as she tried to put a stopper in her emotions.

She made a ball of herself on the couch, knees at her chin, her nails digging into the worn fabric of her jeans. That kind of protective stance indicated much more than being yelled at from time to time. It intimated that she'd had reason to be afraid.

I kept my voice as even as I could. "Did he put his hands on you?"

She shook her head vehemently.

"He didn't touch you at all?"

"N-n-no but—" Another hiccup and a heavy sob cut her off.

"Take a deep breath for me," I said, giving her plenty of space.

She was too jumpy to handle physical comfort. Whatever the trauma had been tonight, it was bad. And Ivy wouldn't tell me the truth—not really. She would censor, because that's what she was used to doing.

It's what we all did. We gave the version of events that hurt the least, resulted in the least shame, were the most socially acceptable:

I'm clumsy.

I fell.

I was playing sports.

I forgot my lunch.

I'm not hungry.

I stayed up too late.

When I'd started coming to school with black eyes, I said I'd gotten into a fight. Then I'd prove it was commonplace by instigating a brawl in the halls or the boy's bathroom. I'd smoke at recess, pick fights with the older kids, swear in class—anything to prove the black eyes and bruises were my fault. Because the other option was to leave my mom and my sister to deal with it, and I couldn't let that happen.

This had worked until I'd gotten kicked out. After that I realized I couldn't protect someone who didn't want to be protected. It had been a painful lesson, and one I still hadn't quite grasped, apparently. I'd told myself I was the problem and all the fights would stop without me around. Everyone would be safer because I wasn't there to cause trouble. But I'd been wrong about that, too.

When Ivy was calm enough to talk again I asked the question I wasn't sure she'd answer. "So if John didn't hit you, what did he do?"

"He wanted to know where I'd hidden the rest of the money. He said he knew I had to be keeping some for myself. I guess he'd had a bad night at poker and didn't have enough to pay the debt. He'd tried to get money from the old account, but there wasn't enough, so he came to get whatever I had.

"There were a couple of guys with him. They'd been waiting on the porch, but then they told him his time was up. They weren't the guys he usually hangs out with. They were huge, bigger than you." Ivy paused to take a breath; it left her on a shudder. "One of them... he, he frisked me."

"What do you mean *frisk*?" There were police pat downs and criminal pat downs. I had a feeling this had been the latter.

"Like they do on the TV when they arrest someone. They had me empty out my pockets, and they checked—" Her eyes were on her feet. She wasn't wearing socks and her nail polish was faded and chipped. She curled her toes under to hide them. "I didn't have the money on me, because I've been hiding it in my locker at work."

It seemed that was as much of an answer as she could bring herself to give me.

"What happened after you were frisked?"

"They left, and Dad went with them. When I was sure they were gone, I tried to get Mom to come out of the bedroom, but she wouldn't. I didn't want to stay in case he came back. I went to work to get the money, and then I thought I'd go to a friend's house, but she was having this party, and it was too much for me right now, so I came here."

"Do you know where John is now?"

"I have no idea. Whatever he's done, I don't think he's getting out of it easily this time."

"Is there a bar he hangs out at? A friend he'd be likely to go see?"

"There's a couple of places, why?"

"Because Ivy, those goons frisked you, and he let it happen. Someone needs to make him understand that's not okay to do to your own fucking kid."

More tears welled. "I don't want to be alone right now. Dad knows where you live. He might assume I'm here. What if he comes looking for me?"

Her panic was real. Now I knew for sure there was more to the story. But she was red-eyed, puffy-faced, and exhausted. Pushing for more information would get me nowhere.

"All right, fine. But tomorrow I'm stopping by the house."

"I don't know if he'll be there."

"Doesn't matter. I'm still stopping by."

I rustled up an extra toothbrush for her and changed my sheets so they didn't smell like Sarah and sex. I put Sarah's pillow and my extra sheets on the couch so it was fit for sleeping.

Ivy came out of the bathroom wearing flannel pajama bottoms with pugs all over them and a Lollapalooza T-shirt with holes in it.

"Thanks for setting that up for me."

"This is for me." I sprawled across the couch, crossing one foot over the other. "You can have my room."

"You don't need to do that. The couch is great. I just needed a place to crash for tonight—"

"And you'll crash in my room until we figure out what to do. I don't care if it's one night or a month. You look beat; you need to get some sleep."

Ivy surprised me when she leaned down and hugged me, planting a swift kiss on my cheek. "Thanks for everything. I don't care what Dad says; you're a really good person."

"I don't know about that, but I'm trying to be a good brother, so it's a start."

She disappeared into my bedroom, and I turned out all the lights except the one in the bathroom. I tried to fall asleep, but my conversation with Ivy kept playing over in my head. There were holes in her story. Big ones. Ones that made me question how safe she'd been all these years—and what exactly she was facing when it came to John.

My mom could only throw her kids under the bus so many times before it backed up and ran over her, too.

FOURTEEN

SARAH

Today had been a shit sundae topped with crap sprinkles. The jerk at my internship had been bad enough, but the note from Chris and the subsequent conversation at Inked Armor had wiped out anything good about my presentation this morning. Now here I was, sitting in my car facing another shift at The Sanctuary. I wished there was something that would make me numb, but wouldn't also ruin my life or make me more of a slave to Xander. The tears I'd been holding back since I left Inked Armor needed to stay where they were. I couldn't afford emotions tonight. I had to get through this shift. Then I could see about trying to work things out with Chris, if that was even a possibility now. I hoped his anger was more a sign that there was something worth saving rather than the alternative, which I couldn't consider at the moment.

I was relieved when Xander wasn't on the floor. That meant I'd deal with Grant instead. This was usually better, but tonight he was in a foul mood.

"Center, back side tonight," he told me as I approached. That was the section closest to left, again. "And don't ask to change, because it's not gonna happen. We're short staffed. You're lucky to be where you are."

"Okay." I was about to walk away, but I paused. "How's Dee?"

His head lifted, eyes dark. "The fuck you know about Dee?"

"She's my friend. I'm worried about her, Grant. Just like you." I stared at him, and he stared back, his eyes narrowed.

"She's been better."

"Will she be in tonight?"

"No." He consulted the clipboard instead of looking at me.

I sighed and shuddered, my relief overwhelming. "That's good."

His eyes flipped back to mine, his typical impassiveness replaced by a haunted expression. "Go serve your tables."

The night dragged on forever. All I wanted was to finish my shift and go to Chris's, see if he'd be willing to hear me out. I was going to have to come clean. No matter how hard it would be, I had to explain why I was choosing to stay at The Sanctuary.

Though my decision to do this gave me some peace, my worries remained. Would Chris feel compelled to take care of the situation for me? Or would he be fed up with dealing with me once and for all? Or had he reached that point already. I didn't think so. The pain he'd worked so hard to inflict on me earlier seemed the work of someone who cared. Still, part of me worried he'd walk, and then where would I be?

About a half-hour after I started my shift, Xander appeared at the bar. He then spent the entire night watching the girls, hyper vigilant. The whole thing was unnerving. At the end of my shift, I headed to the changing room, traded my sluttire for street clothes, and counted my money and receipts, separating out the tips.

It had been a good night tip-wise. I'd had an extra table, so that meant more money. Taking a deep breath, I slung my bag over my shoulder, collected my receipts, and headed for Xander's office.

Grant was stationed outside the door. He gave me a nod and let me into the waiting room. I paced the small space and moved away from the camera that tracked this room. I quickly pulled my phone out of my purse, set it up to record, and shoved it into my bra before I resumed my pacing.

One of the new girls whose name I hadn't learned came out of Xander's office soon after. Her lips were puffy and her eyes red. She shifted her gaze to the floor as she passed, telling me everything

I needed to know about what had gone down in there. At least Xander's *needs* had already been taken care of. I wondered if he'd turned off the security feed to his office, or let it run so he could go back and watch himself degrade the girls after the fact. The idea made me shudder.

I knocked and waited until I was given the okay to go in.

Xander was buttoning his suit jacket when I entered, a tic in his jaw the only marker of emotion. "Close the door, please, Sarah."

I did as he asked, and then set my receipts and cash in front of him. I even took a seat in the chair across from his desk to avoid our usual standoff. Xander said nothing as he methodically counted the bills and tallied the figures.

"You had another good night," he said when he'd finished, fanning out the bills before he put them into an envelope with the receipts. "I'm going to need you to come in tomorrow."

"I didn't think I was scheduled." The extra shift and tips would be good, but I was already exhausted and had been looking forward to a day to focus on my internship, then get some rest.

"You weren't. We're short staffed, so you'll have to pick up the shift."

"Is this because of Dee?" I baited him, hoping he wouldn't see through it.

His hard eyes locked on me. "What about Dee?"

I shrugged and tried to contain my heavy swallow. "She's not here tonight, and this is one of the days she usually works."

He watched me for a few long seconds. "She has a couple of days off. And since you know so much, you'll be picking up the party she was supposed to host tomorrow night."

"Party?" A trickle of sweat worked its way down my spine.

"Yes." He tented his fingers under his chin. Now it felt like *he* was baiting *me*.

"What kind of party is it?"

"An expensive one. They've asked for you specifically since Dee won't be available. You can consider this the favor you owe me."

My stomach turned. "What will I have to do?"

His smile was malevolent. "Entertain them, Sarah."

"Entertain them how?"

"Do I need to get you an instruction manual? Would you like a detailed explanation of what's expected of you?"

I expelled a deep breath. "I can't—"

Xander pushed out of his chair and rounded his desk. He grabbed the arms of my chair and shoved it back to make room for himself. I pressed my knees tight together so he couldn't edge his way between them. I didn't want to think about what would happen if he found the phone on me. He leaned in until his face was an inch from mine. His jaw was tight, the rage I'd seen him throw at other people suddenly directed at me.

"You can and you will, Sarah, because you *owe* me."

"There has to be something else. I've paid you back the money. What if I, I—" I scrambled for an alternative. "—paid the interest too? What would that be? A few hundred dollars more? I could give that to you now."

"A few hundred?" His laugh was humorless. "What the fuck do you think this is, a goddamn bank? I've got plenty of money. That's why your interest is a favor. That's what we agreed to, and that's what you're going to do. Tomorrow night you will take your clothes off, and you will do whatever those men decide they want you to. Do you understand?"

"But I didn't—"

"This is what you owe me, Sarah. I was there when you needed me. Now it's your turn."

"I, I, I—"

The words wouldn't come. Dee had been sitting in this exact same chair, in the exact same position the last time I saw her. But it hadn't been Xander standing over her. It had been Grant kneeling in front of her, consoling her because something had gone terribly wrong.

I felt the hardness within me return, along with my voice. "I know what happened last night with Dee."

Xander's smile was razorblade malice. "Oh you do, do you?"

"I know the video feed was tampered with, and those men tried to hurt her. It's your job to keep her safe."

"Are you trying to blackmail me? If so, it's a pretty weak attempt. I think you're forgetting that you have an awful lot to lose. I have an incredible amount of footage to choose from when it comes to you in skimpy clothes, being manhandled by patrons with a smile on your face. In fact, it looks to me like you rather enjoy your job here." He ran a single finger down the side of my neck. "I guess it doesn't always pay to be a good actress, does it?"

I turned my head away from his face and the unwanted contact. The tears I'd been fighting finally broke free, sliding down my cheeks.

Xander caught one with a fingertip. "Look at you. Where's the fierceness now?"

A knock on the door made me jump, and Xander's jaw clicked with tension. "Not now," he barked.

The door opened, and Xander straightened. Grant glanced from me in the chair to Xander, that hard, haunted look returning. I wiped the back of my hand under my eyes to clear away the tears and ducked behind my hair to avoid looking at him.

"We've got an issue to deal with," he said.

"Well, then go deal with it."

Grant sucked his teeth. "It's not my issue. Girls have some questions you need to answer if you want things calm around here."

Xander exhaled a hard breath, knuckles cracking as he clenched his fists. "I'll be right out."

Grant just stood there, and Xander made no move to leave the office.

"Close the fucking door! I said I'd be right out. Whatever it is it can wait two goddamn minutes."

Grant didn't bother to acknowledge Xander again; instead he looked at me. "You okay, Sarah?"

"She's fine. Now get the fuck out of my office, and get back to your post."

Grant ignored the directive. "Sarah?"

"I'm fine," I croaked.

"Two minutes, boss." Grant tapped his watch and pulled the door closed. It sounded more like a threat than a warning.

I pushed up out of the chair and tried to get around Xander to avoid being trapped again, but he grabbed my arm, pulling me close.

"There is only one option that will keep you safe." His voice was low, and shaking with rage, maybe because of the interruption, or maybe because Grant had very clearly disobeyed him. Xander didn't appreciate insolence. "Do you want to know what it is?"

I made a sound—more of a whimper than a confirmation.

"You want to avoid the party tomorrow night?" He was so close, his grip on my arm far too tight to allow for movement.

"Yes." I shifted my gaze to his, locking it there as satisfaction crept into his smile.

"Then you have to make a trade. That's how this works, Sarah."

"What kind of trade?" I shook now, fear having won out over anger.

"An hour with a roomful of strangers or an hour with me. It's your choice, but I will tell you, I'm the better deal. No one in that room is going to care if you scream, or cry, or come, whereas I'll guarantee that you do all three."

I shuddered as he stroked my cheek again, his gentle touch a macabre counterpart to the new, even more horrifying deal he offered.

"You don't have to answer now. You sleep on it, take some time to decide." He smiled again.

The hard rap on the door made him let go of my arm. I stumbled away and yanked on the handle, fumbling before I finally managed to make it turn. Grant stepped back as I rushed out of Xander's office, about to throw up.

Clutching my bag, I rushed through the dressing room, the girls' chatter a fuzzy hum, their faces a blur through my tears.

I waved at Max as I headed for my car. As soon as I was inside, I slammed down all the locks and shoved the key into the ignition. The engine sputtered instead of revving to life. I tried not to panic.

My car had just been fixed. It had to start. I took a deep breath and tried again. This time the engine turned over.

With shaking hands I pulled my phone out of my bra and stopped recording. Then I hit play, praying my shirt hadn't muffled it to the point of being unintelligible. I clamped a hand over my mouth to stop the sob when I heard Xander's voice clearly outlining my choices. Then I cranked the stereo and dropped my face into my palms, letting the sob I'd been holding back finally burst free.

I had no idea how I'd use this, but I knew I had to. Otherwise I'd never escape, never get free. Maybe it was already too late for me, but I could still bring Xander down. This was my fault. I should've realized a job like this would put my scholarship at risk.

Now I was in so deep, I had no idea how I was going to get out. It was one thing to tell Chris about the car and the debt I'd owed Xander, but this favor was something else. I was ashamed to have gotten myself into this situation, and I couldn't bear to see that shame echoed in Chris. And after seeing what had gone down with Dee and Trixie, I knew if I went through with it, the emotional repercussions would far outlast the physical.

I must've sat there a long time, because a knock on my window startled me. It was Grant. I turned down the music and swiped my eyes with the sleeve of my shirt while he tried to open my door without success. Shoving my phone into my purse, I rolled my window down a few inches.

He took one look at my tear-streaked face and gritted his teeth. "Jesus. This place is about to implode. You wanna tell me what the hell was going on back there?"

"Nothing."

"Oh yeah? Well, Xander just laid into me about you knowing shit you shouldn't, so maybe you wanna come clean with someone."

I suddenly found the choice of words ironic. There was no coming clean after this. "I owe Xander a favor, and he's decided to collect."

"For what?"

"Does it even matter?"

"What kind of favor are you into him for? It's not drugs, is it?" He glanced down at my arms.

"He loaned me money to have my car fixed. The favor is the interest."

Grant tapped the hood of the car in agitation. "So he wants you on the stage?"

I shook my head. "He wants me to work a party."

"For getting your car fixed?" He shook his head. "This isn't right. He's—look, I'm going to help you out on this, but I need you to do something for me."

"I don't want to owe anyone any more favors," I snapped.

"Yeah. I don't need that kind of favor, Sarah. You and Dee, you talk, yeah?"

"Sometimes. I mean, I talk to her more than the other girls."

"I see your number on her phone sometimes. I know you've been texting her."

At my confused expression he continued, "I'm keeping an eye on her right now, but she hasn't answered my messages for the last hour, and we've been checking in regularly. I can't get out of here for a while. If I give you directions, will you check on her for me?"

"You're in Xander's pocket all the time. How do I know this isn't some kind of trap?"

He regarded me carefully. "I guess you don't. But I can tell you that things aren't always the way they look."

"Why should I believe you?"

Grant pulled his phone out and did some clicking before he passed me the device. A picture of Dee reclined on a pale gray leather couch was displayed on the small screen.

"Scroll to the right," he said softly.

So I did. After a few photos it wasn't just Dee anymore. It was Dee with Grant—selfie after selfie chronicling the progression of their relationship. The smile she wore with him was one I hadn't ever seen in the club.

I stopped at a picture of him kissing her on the cheek. "How long?"

"Long enough that we got careless."

"Does Xander know?"

"He does now." His expression turned grim.

"That party—"

"—was a message. Will you check on her for me?"

I had so many questions that couldn't be answered. "I can do that. Of course."

"Can you stay until I get there?"

"Definitely."

While I put the directions in my phone, Grant passed over a key. If what he was saying was true, Xander had set Dee up. Had he been the one to cut the feed? And for what? To make a point? I didn't even really understand who Grant was to him, other than head of security.

"Call me as soon as you get to her."

"I will."

"And I'm going to help you find a way outta this mess."

"Thanks." I wasn't sure how he thought he was going to fix this for me, but anything I could do to secure his help was worth it. Especially with Dee being involved.

I followed the GPS north, away from The Sanctuary and into the Loop. It took a while for me to find the correct building and secure legal street parking. Dee lived right downtown, as if she were a cog in the corporate machine, not their entertainment.

I made my way up to her floor and knocked at her apartment, but I didn't expect Dee to open the door for me, since Grant said he'd told her not to go anywhere or answer for anyone. After a moment I used the key he'd given me to get in and closed the door behind me, locking it again.

Lined up on the mat to the right were Dee's heels and a pair of men's running shoes, which I imagined were Grant's. A baseball cap and a jacket hung next to her hoodie. Whatever they had was real.

I crossed through the open kitchen to the living room. The TV was on silent, a movie trailer looping. A pale gray blanket had been discarded on the equally pale gray couch—the one in the pictures

Grant had shown me, further proof of his presence in her life. A half-empty glass sat on the end table, but it was the tipped-over pill bottles, the powdery residue, the rolled up twenty, and the square of mirror that shot panic through my veins. Dee's phone was there, and the screen flashed with a text from Grant. It was one of ten.

"Dee?" I crossed over to the table and picked up the bottles: oxycodone, some kind of morphine, prescription-strength Tylenol, and anti-anxiety meds, all prescribed to different people.

Any one of these could mess a person up, but all together, they could be lethal. I pulled my phone out of my purse and snapped a few pictures of the table. Grant seemed like one of the good guys, but I had no real way of knowing he wasn't as crooked and heartless as Xander, so I wasn't taking any chances with more blackmail opportunities. I wanted the leverage I'd been missing all these months.

My phone rang, startling me. It was Grant. I swallowed my guilt and answered the call.

"Are you in? Is Dee okay?" he barked.

"I haven't found her yet."

"What'd you mean you haven't found her?"

"I just got here. She's not answering when I call for her. Her phone is in the living room, though; she can't be far. Look, Grant, there are a lot of pill bottles here, and it looks like she's been snorting whatever she's taking."

"Fuck. *Fuck*. What kind of pills? Never mind—check the bathroom. She likes baths. It's in the master bedroom, through the living room, second door on the right."

"I'm going now." I made my way through the living room and found the second door on the right open. I went inside, calling Dee's name again. The king-size bed was unmade. "I can hear the water running. You're right—she must've decided to take a bath."

I called her name again, louder this time, and knocked on the bathroom door, which was also ajar. My knocking caused it to open a little more. What I found wasn't Dee in the bath, though. The tub had overflowed and water now cascaded over the edge, inching it's way closer to where I stood. But that wasn't what made me scream.

In that instant, I understood what it meant to be marked by someone else's torment in an irrevocable way. I would never forget, for as long as I lived, how Dee looked, unconscious and naked, lying beside the tub. It wasn't her nakedness that would stay with me, but the gray pallor of her usually tanned skin, marred by the words written in black marker covering her body. Under the scrawl bloomed countless bruises. Block letters spelled out her trauma: *whore, slut, bitch* repeated over and over, across her stomach, her arms, her legs.

"Sarah? *Sarah?* Fucking answer me. What the hell is going on?"

"I think she OD'd." I rushed to the tub and turned off the faucet, then dropped to the floor beside her, the water soaking through my jeans. It was so cold. Her lips were blue.

Grant's voice was terrifyingly even. "Does she have a pulse?"

I took a deep breath, trying not to let my absolute horror take over. "I'm checking."

I felt sick as I flipped to camera mode, recording the scene in front of me. In my head I apologized to Dee for wanting more leverage to save myself, if I needed it. Because I wouldn't be this. I put my fingers at the side of her throat. There were bruises there too, like someone had tried to strangle her. I made sure to get close-ups of those; someone needed to be responsible for what had happened to her.

It was hard to stay calm, seeing what Xander had allowed to happen to her the other night. I kept searching for a pulse, but there wasn't anything normal—just an occasional flutter under cool skin. "I'm not getting anything, Grant."

"Are you sure? Check again."

I took another deep breath. "Okay, okay. There are words written on her body, they're everywhere."

Grant cleared his throat. "Yeah. We've been trying to get those off, but the permanent marker's a problem."

I tried not to think what that must've been like for Dee when it happened. I pressed my shaking fingers against her throat and closed my eyes so I didn't have to look at her bruises or the words. "I still can't feel much of anything."

"But there's something?"

"It's not regular.

"Okay. I need you to stay calm, Sarah. Can you do that for me?" There was a waver in his voice.

"Yes."

"Good girl. Do you know CPR?"

I reached out and moved Dee's wet hair away from her face. There was even a bruise on her cheek, faint purple standing out against the gray.

"Um… I took a course in high school. It's been a long time."

"I'll walk you through it. I need you to do this for me. I need you to stay calm and help me take care of Dee. Can you do that, Sarah?"

"What if it doesn't work?"

"Let's not think like that. I've already called 9-1-1, and I'm on my way. It won't take me long to get there."

"Okay."

I hit speaker, put my phone on a towel, and followed Grant's instructions—the chest compressions, the breathing. I was horrified by how cold Dee was, and by her lack of response.

It seemed like an eternity passed while I pushed and breathed and waited for Grant to arrive. Suddenly I could hear him in stereo, the heavy sound of footfalls echoing down the hall until the sounds merged.

"Motherfucker." He dropped to his knees, landing in the water that had covered the floor. "I'll ruin him."

He put his fingers to Dee's throat, checking her pulse. "You're not allowed to leave me. He's not allowed to win."

FIFTEEN

CHRIS

Thanks to my shit sleep, I was wide awake at five in the morning. My couch was a great location to pass out watching *Cops* reruns, but not the best place to spend the entire night. My bed was a king, and the couch wasn't even quite a single. But Ivy was asleep, which was good. I'd heard her tossing and turning for a while before she finally settled around one.

Since going back to sleep wasn't an option, I decided an early morning stop at my mom's might shed more light on what had happened there last night. I was lucky to have left a basket of clean laundry by the couch, so I didn't have to wear the same clothes I'd slept in.

I tried to peek in on Ivy to make sure she was okay before I left, but the door got stuck about two inches in. She'd propped a chair under the knob. I could see her through the narrow slit. She was curled up in a tiny little ball in the center of my bed. Her head was tucked up between two pillows and the sheets and comforter were wrapped around her, cocoon style. She had to be roasting under all that covering, but she was completely cashed, soft snores coming from beneath the blankets.

I shut the door as gently as possible, hoping not to disturb the chair too much. It pained me that she'd done that. Actions like that were borne out of habit, and that brought to mind a lot of rage-inducing questions.

I left a set of keys for her on the counter and a note telling her I'd be back before I had to leave for work. I stuck directions to Inked Armor to the fridge with a magnet in case she slept late or wanted to go there. I set out towels in the bathroom, glad Sarah's shampoo and conditioner were still there for her to use.

I paused for a second when I saw them, considering how I'd jumped the gun yesterday with the way I'd freaked out over the pills. She'd told me they weren't hers, and I should've believed her. Instead, I'd pushed her on purpose, looking for some kind of retaliation that would make the things I'd said okay. But she hadn't snapped, and even if she had, I was in the wrong.

I needed to call her, or better yet, see her, but first I needed to deal with this. Besides, it was too early to stop by her place.

Nabbing my helmet, I checked for my wallet and keys, and headed out the door. I wished the chain lock was in place, but Ivy would be safe enough in my apartment for now.

I arrived at my mom's house just after six. If I was lucky, she'd be home for a while before her shift at the deli. It took her half an hour to get to work by bus. John's rig wasn't parked outside, so maybe he was off on another one of his runs. If he did happen to be around, I would happily interrogate the fuckwad as well—with my fist.

The grass had been partially cut since the last time I was here. The right side was mostly done, but the turned-over mower sat abandoned in the weedy garden bed. Ivy had probably managed to get it running only to have it crap out on her again. Much like everything else in her life.

I knocked on the door and waited. After a second round of knocking produced no response, I went around the back. The lock on that door had always been sticky, and sometimes it didn't catch. It opened with a loud creak. The house was quiet apart from all the noise I was making.

"Mom? You here?" I left my boots on since the floor was dirty again.

Her bedroom door was shut tight. There were fresh holes in

the wall. This time the frustration that ruled my emotions whenever I came here was replaced by a deep-seated hatred I could barely contain. It wasn't just for John, either. It extended to my mother.

Reining it in and tamping it down, I knocked on her bedroom door. "You in there, Moms?"

I put my ear to the panel, listening for sounds of occupancy. I heard the bed creak.

"Are you alone?" she called meekly.

"Yeah. It's just me."

Silence stretched out as I waited for her to open the door so I didn't have to talk to her through a barrier. I took a couple of steps down the hall and peeked inside Ivy's room. It was an absolute wreck. Worse than the last time. All of her clothes were ripped from their hangers and strewn across the floor. Her desk was turned upside down, the ancient computer smashed.

The single mattress had been sliced down the middle and gutted, her dresser drawers pulled out, with girly underwear scattered all over the place. Most of it was simple stuff, the same kind Sarah usually wore, but a few pairs stood out. I looked away, not wanting to see that my baby sister wasn't a baby anymore.

Fury took hold, adrenaline ripping through my veins, making my heart feel like it was about to explode in my chest. "Mom, you need to come out here and take a look at this."

The sound of furniture scraping across the floor was followed by the turn of the doorknob. Her face appeared in the narrow opening, her wide, fearful eyes scanning the space beyond me.

I raised my hands to show her I wasn't here to do any more damage. It took a few more long seconds before she opened the door wider and stepped out into the hall. She wore her work uniform. It was huge on her, and there were buttons missing at the very bottom and the top. She crossed her arms over her chest and hunched over like she was looking to protect herself from a blow— verbal or physical, I wasn't sure.

"What happened last night?"

"Is Ivy here? She can tell you better than me."

"Ivy's at my place. She'll be staying with me for a while." As long as I could convince her that was best.

"I don't think John will like that. He doesn't think you're a good influence on Ivy."

There was no room left in me for patience or tolerance, and that's not what came out when I opened my mouth.

"Do you even hear yourself? Look around you." I gestured to the holes in the wall beside her. "You think you're a better role model? You think this is a better place for her to be?"

"Of course I do; I'm her mother." There was no conviction in her words.

"And what does that mean exactly? How are you taking care of her? What are you doing to ensure her safety here?"

"D-don't yell at me." Cowering, she took a step back, toward her bedroom.

I hadn't even realized I'd raised my voice. My hands went up in a show of contrition, however semi-authentic it was. I understood that she would run if she felt I was a danger to her. "I'm sorry. I didn't mean to yell." She was like a beaten dog. Her terror was a real, living, breathing thing, threatening to choke the life out of her.

If she locked herself in her bedroom again, I'd never get anything out of her, and Ivy had already said as much as she was going to.

"John was in a bad way last night."

"Yeah. I got that much." I pointed at the fresh holes in the drywall. "These from his fists?"

"He was upset about the money Ivy's been hiding from him."

"You mean the money she gave you?"

"She shouldn't have been holding it back."

"Have you seen her room, or have you been locked in yours all night?" I already knew the answer.

"He was angrier than I'd ever seen him 'afore, and he had these men with him. I didn't know who they were. I think John may have gotten himself into a situation."

I closed my eyes for a moment. She'd been in there for a long time—too afraid to leave in case John was sitting out here, waiting for her.

He would kill her eventually. Whether with his own hands or because she was so neglected was the only question. She'd surely get sick again, and it could turn into pneumonia and finally take her down. I knew now I likely couldn't save her from herself, but I wouldn't let the same thing happen to my sister.

"You need to look at this." I took her by the elbow, gently but firmly, and steered her to Ivy's room.

She brought her fist to her mouth, knuckles pressing hard against her chapped lips. "I don't know why she didn't tell them where the money was. They wouldn't have done this if she'd just told them—"

"She gave the money to you," I said pointedly.

"But if she was giving some to me, John said she was surely holding some back for herself, too. He needed it."

"For fucking what? His gambling problem? His cigarettes? A case of beer? Look at what he did! Look!" I swept my hand over the destroyed room. Everything was ruined. The bedframe had completely crumpled.

"It's bad enough she's gotten herself a private bank account, thanks to you, but then she was holding back the money, and with John having issues—"

"Stop." I put up a hand. "I can't hear this shit anymore. Let me tell you something you might not know: as a mother it's your goddamn duty to protect your children. Locking yourself in your room while John and his goons ripped apart hers doesn't fucking qualify."

"She put herself in that position—"

"Are you kidding me with this? Do you hear the crap you spew? She's a nineteen-year old girl, for Christ's sake. She should be going to college, having fun with her friends, not working full time to support her asshole, abusive father."

"John's not—"

I cut her off. "Did you know they frisked her? Checked her over to make sure she didn't have the money on her?"

She blinked.

"They put their hands on her. While you were hiding, those goons put their damn hands on my sister, and that dickhead father of hers stood by and let it happen. So I gotta ask you, is there anything else I should know?"

"I-I don't know—"

"Did they hurt her?"

"I'm n-not sure."

I wasn't going to get anything out of her this way. I'd seen it a million times—watched her pull into herself like this on countless occasions when I was a kid and John would come after me. At first she'd tried to fight him for me, but he'd always pushed her off and dragged me to my room so he could smack me around in peace. Ivy had been a baby. After a while, when it had become part of the routine, Mom had scooped her up and whisked her out the front door as soon as it started, so neither of them had to witness anything. Just before she walked out, her eyes would always go dead, like she was shutting out the memories. It had been survival for her. I'd been the sacrifice.

"I'm going to ask you one more question, and I need you to answer it honestly. Is John's fist connecting with anything other than the walls?"

"I talked to him about that—"

"It's a yes-or-no question."

Her silence was a scream.

"Is it just you, or is he putting his hands on Ivy, too?"

"Everything was fine until you came around again."

"You're welcome to blame me for your problems, but I need an answer to my question." I tried not to let it hurt, but her next statement was a sledgehammer to the chest.

"If I hadn't had you, my life would've been different. It would've been better."

"Wow." I took a deep breath, letting the sharp ache settle. "Pretty sure it would've been better for me, too."

"I was doing my best!"

"Bullshit!"

She was everything that was wrong with me. This woman who should've kept me safe had offered me up as a punching bag so she wouldn't have to be. I'd been her shield, and now I worried Ivy had been, too. My mother was more of a manipulator than John.

I pointed at her, my fury uncontained. "You made me like this. How I turned out? That's on you. You're the one who let that fucker beat the shit out of me. You're the one who let him walk all over you, and then you did it all over again with your goddamn daughter. You pretend to be the martyr, but what you did was sacrifice both of your kids."

She wrapped her arms tighter around herself, as if they could protect her from the truth.

"I'm going to do everything in my power to keep Ivy out of this house. It's toxic. You're toxic. If you call her and try to guilt her into coming back to this hell, I will tell her everything you let John do to me."

Her eyes widened with a fear I'd never seen before. "But I'll be alone."

"No, you won't. You'll have John."

I turned to walk away, but she grabbed my arm. "I'm sorry. I didn't mean—"

I shook her off. "Yes, you did. And if I find out you let him do the same things to Ivy, I will end him."

I walked out the front door, wondering if I'd just signed my own mother's death certificate.

SIXTEEN

CHRIS

The knot in my stomach tightened further as I got on my bike and started the engine. A huge part of me wanted to go back in that house and find a way to make my mother see that she needed to get out. But it never worked. I knew how hard it was to walk away from abuse, because that's what I had chosen to do now. And it was shredding up my insides.

All these years I'd been blaming myself for the way things had turned out for her. But she'd been the one to make a mess of her own life—and she'd had a pretty big part in making a mess of mine. I didn't want her to have that kind of power over me anymore, and that meant owning the choices I'd been making recently, as hard as that might be.

Having already had one difficult conversation this morning, I figured it'd be a good idea to stop in at Sarah's and see if she was awake and up for hearing an apology.

Before I went to Sarah's, though, I decided to check on Ivy. I picked up some bagels, pastries, and a couple of coffees from a bakery not too far away, uncertain what kind of fresh food I had in my apartment these days. I was already feeling the effects of too little sleep and a morning full of stress, so the coffee was a necessity.

Ivy was in the shower when I returned. She came out of the bathroom, fully dressed, with a towel wrapped around her head and an armload of dirty clothes. She screamed when she saw me hanging out on the couch.

"I didn't mean to scare you." I held out a coffee as a peace offering, but her arms were full. I nodded to the laundry basket beside the coffee table. "Just drop it on the floor. I'll do a couple loads tomorrow or something."

"When'd you get back?" She took the coffee cup and curled up on the right side of the couch. She wore a short-sleeved shirt, showcasing the fresh bruises dotting her arms.

"About five minutes ago. I have to head out again in a few, but I wanted to check in with you first, see how you're doing." I glanced at the purple marks on her biceps that looked like fingers.

"I'm okay." She followed my gaze and self-consciously covered the bruises with her palm.

"Are those from last night?"

She shrugged. "I don't know."

I sighed. "I went to Mom's."

She sat up straighter. "Is she okay?"

"As okay as she ever is. We need to talk about you not going back there."

Ivy took a sip of coffee. "Leaving her there alone—"

"—isn't going to be easy, but she can't keep using you as a shield against John."

I let that sit for a minute while she took another sip of her coffee, and I rooted through the bag of carbs for a Danish.

"I never thought about it like that," she said eventually. "For so long it was us against him, and then she hung me out to dry. Or maybe she's been doing that all along, and I'm just seeing it now."

Her last comment came out a question. I scrubbed my hand over my face. It was hard to watch her come to that realization. The woman who'd shared her misery and uncertainty had been the driving force behind it.

My mom had kept Ivy bound to her by guilt. And she'd done the same with me. I got that now. The occasional phone calls that came a few weeks before a birthday or around a holiday—as if she were checking up on me—always circled back to her needing something. There was no unconditional love with my mother. The price of her attention was steep.

"People do bad things when they feel unsafe," I told her. "They make sacrifices they shouldn't."

"What do I do when she calls and asks me to come home? How do I say no?"

"You don't answer, and you give me the phone so I can talk to her."

"I can't stay here forever."

"You can stay here as long as you need to, and we can figure something out for after that."

She propped her cheek on her fist. "You can't keep sleeping on the couch."

"Sure I can. Look, I spent a lot of years not being a very good brother. Now I get to make it up to you."

She gave me a weak smile.

"What're you doing today?"

"I don't have to work, so I can do your laundry if you want."

"Why don't you come to the shop? You can hang out and just take it easy for once."

"Are you sure that'd be okay? I won't be in the way?"

"Not even a little bit."

"Okay. That'd be nice. I like Lisa."

She'd only been in the shop once before, but Lisa was easy to like. I'd had a few ideas about how I could manage this situation with Ivy, and a decent plan was forming. She'd always been into art, just like me. We'd spent a lot of hours drawing pictures when we were kids.

Over the years I'd gotten the occasional hand-drawn card from her for my birthday, and the walls of her bedroom had been covered in art projects done in pastels and charcoal. She had clear vision and an eye for color and depth. I might not be able to afford to send her to college, but I could help get her a steady, reasonable paycheck so she could make decisions for her future.

If Hayden agreed to it and she was game, she might even be able to rent the apartment across the street. That would give her some stability, and an opportunity to get away from the neighborhood we grew up in.

One thing at a time, though. First I needed to see if Inked Armor was something Ivy was even interested in. Then I needed to see if they were interested in her. And before any of that, I needed to talk to Sarah.

"I was thinking about leaving soon. I need to stop at a friend's place first."

"I can ride my bike over in a while. That way I can take off if it gets too busy or whatever."

A knock on the door stopped me from arguing. Ivy's eyes went wide. "Do you think it's Dad?"

I lifted a placating hand, even though I shared some of her anxiety. If John wasn't alone, it could be a problem. "It could be my neighbor. Let me check."

I was quiet about going to the door and checking the peephole to see if I wanted to answer or not. Like last time, it wasn't my neighbor, but it wasn't John either, thankfully. Sarah stood in the hall, her face obscured because she was looking at the floor. I guess I didn't need to leave early after all.

I glanced over my shoulder before I took off the chain latch. "It's not John; it's my friend."

Ivy breathed a relieved sigh and relaxed.

Sarah's head came up in slow motion as I opened the door, and she blinked at the same speed. Her eyes were red rimmed, with the mascara and liner from last night half smeared in lines down her cheeks, like she'd been crying. A lot. Her gaze flitted from me to my sister sitting on the couch. Ivy had just taken the towel out of her hair and was finger-combing it.

Sarah let out a noise of disbelief. Her teeth cut a line across her bottom lip as her eyes shifted back to me, hurt and distress the primary emotions behind them.

I couldn't understand what that was all about until I realized she'd never met Ivy, and she was looking at the back of her freshly showered head. It probably looked like I'd brought some girl home.

"Ivy stayed here last night," I said by way of greeting and explanation.

"Ivy?" She adjusted the strap of her bag.

"My sister." Jesus. She was totally out of it.

At her name, Ivy turned around and raised a hand in greeting. Her face froze mid-smile, making it look more like a grimace. Probably because of Sarah's appearance.

"Oh. I should go then." Sarah turned to leave.

I grabbed her arm. "Whoa. Wait! What's going on?"

She stumbled into me and grabbed my shirt. A broken sob escaped as she pressed her face against my chest and mumbled something.

My sister gave me a questioning look. I mouthed the word *girlfriend* and shrugged, because I had no idea what the hell was going on, and Sarah's lack of actual response, as well as her appearance, unnerved me. Also, the fact that she was hugging me after the shit I'd said to her yesterday was a concern.

I took a few steps back into my apartment with her still clinging to me and shut the door. "Sarah, baby, wanna talk to me?"

She let go and swiped under her eyes with shaking hands. "Dee OD'd last night."

The shock was like a backhand with brass knuckles. "You mean, like, she's dead?"

Sarah shook her head. "N-no. She's in the hospital. I found her."

"Jesus. Where? What happened?"

I didn't know who to focus on. My sister was busy quietly gathering her things. She nabbed the directions to Inked Armor from the fridge and motioned to the door, making the I'll-call-you-later gesture before she left. I didn't like that she was going without me, but she'd be safe once she got there, and she was way out of her usual 'hood.

My apartment had become Crisis Central Station.

FRACTURES IN INK

"In her apartment. I found her in her apartment," Sarah said, bringing my attention back to her.

"Why were you at her apartment?"

"I should've told you, but I didn't, and now I don't know… I've ruined everything, and Dee… I was so scared. Her lips were blue, and she was covered in these awful words."

Nothing she said made a lot of sense, and I was cooking up worst-case scenarios, but this time I willed myself to hear her out and really listen—not like yesterday. Sarah rarely lost her composure, and right now she was unraveling.

"Come here." I led her to the couch and put my hands on her shoulders, guiding her to sit.

She dropped down, and a shuddering breath left her as she rubbed between her eyes. Tears tracked down her cheeks as quickly as she wiped them away. "I wasn't going to take those pills, Chris. I mean, I thought about it, but I wouldn't have taken them."

She was all over the place with her thoughts. "I'm not worried about the pills, Sarah. I'm sorry about the things I said yesterday. But right now tell me what happened with Dee. Start at the beginning."

She nodded and steeled herself with another deep breath. Keeping her head down, she whispered, "I made a mistake."

The words hit me like bullets. Her tone told me they came with a side of pain that was more emotional than physical.

She lifted our connected hands and rubbed my knuckles across her cheek. They came away damp. "I made a really big mistake."

She unfurled my fingers and clambered into my lap. I felt the warm press of her lips against my neck, along with a wild tremor that ran through her body.

I could feel her words against my skin, but they were too muffled to hear. At least they were until her mouth started traveling across my neck. Then their clarity made the hairs on the back of my neck prickle.

"I'm sorry. I made a mistake. I'm sorry. I didn't know what else to do. I didn't have a choice."

A heaviness settled in my gut as ideas formed about what she was likely sorry for. But again, I tried to stop myself. Instead of pigeonholing Sarah into the same box as Candy, I allowed myself, for a brief moment, to appreciate the way she felt all curled up in my lap. She had come to me, finally, and in spite of all the ways I'd tried to screw things up between us. She was warm and safe; a version of home I'd never thought I'd experience, even if she was breaking down.

I stroked her back with a soft palm. "What kind of mistake did you make?"

When she made no attempt to respond, I held her shoulders and tried to get her to look at me. She resisted at first, but eventually she gave in and leaned back. She used her palms to swipe away more tears.

"Sarah, you gotta talk to me. That's why you're here, right? I know we're not good at this, and in the past I've shut you down, but I want to know. Whatever's happened, I want you to tell me."

She released an uneven breath, her expression pained. "You won't forgive me."

The heavy feeling became a lead weight. "You don't know that."

She looked so sad and resigned. "I didn't have a choice. Xander didn't give me one."

I took her hands in mine, because her touching me created a whole lot of conflict I wasn't sure I could handle if this conversation was going where I thought it might. It was bad enough that she was still in my lap when I asked the next question.

"Did you end up in the same kind of situation as Dee?"

This time she finally looked up as she shook her head.

My relief was short-lived as I thought about the pill bottle I'd found. "Did you screw somebody for money?"

"No." It came out a whisper, followed by more tears.

I lifted her off my lap and set her on the couch. I needed perspective and some breathing room. "Did you fuck someone for drugs?"

All I got was more vigorous head shaking and even more tears. I doubted my tactless questions were much help.

"Then what could be so bad that you think I won't forgive you for it?"

My getting angry wouldn't make this better, considering how fast the tears had started to fall, and I forced myself to take a deep, steadying breath. This wasn't like the conversation with my mother earlier. The only person Sarah put in danger was herself. And she seemed to do it repeatedly, even if it might be unintentional. So I needed to keep my cool. She wasn't here blaming someone else; she was likely owning something that wasn't her fault, just like I'd been doing all my life.

Maybe that was why I didn't want to let her go. Maybe that was the real reason we worked together, despite all our flaws.

Sarah wiped her face with the hem of her shirt and crossed her legs, settling her hands in her lap. "I didn't cheat on you."

"So that means what? You got on the stage? How did you end up at Dee's?"

"I'm not dancing, but that would be better than what Xander wants. I ended up at Dee's because Grant wanted me to check in on her."

"She wasn't at the club?"

"She hasn't been at the club since the party, and she hasn't been answering my messages. I know why now. I was worried about her, and I was right to be, because whatever happened to her at that party was bad. She was covered in bruises—and writing. Someone tried to choke her."

"What the fuck? Did Grant try to choke her?"

"No, no. Grant's trying to help her—they're together, that's how it looks, anyway—but I don't know if she's going to be okay. It's all bad things, Chris. She was breathing but still unconscious when I left the hospital. She was hooked up to all these machines. It was so scary. Grant stayed with her. The police were there; they were guarding her room."

Her voice picked up speed as her fear took over. "I came right here after. I don't know what to do. I have pictures. I documented everything. I don't want to end up like Dee, and Xander, he wants me to do this party tonight because I owe him a favor—"

My head was spinning. There was so much information to sift through, and with her panic, she didn't seem to be able to unload things in a linear fashion. "Whoa, whoa. Back up, baby. What do you mean he wants you to do a party? Like the kind Dee did?"

She nodded, her hand pressed to her mouth to keep in the quiet sob.

"That's the favor you owe him?"

"That's what he wants."

"Why would you owe him that kind of favor?"

"I didn't think it was going to be that kind. I don't know what I thought it was going to be, but I didn't expect—" She hiccupped through another sob.

I rubbed my temples. "Okay. I need you to take a few deep breaths, and then I think maybe you start *all the way* at the beginning."

I stroked her cheek, mostly to try to calm her down. She turned into the touch, pressing my palm against her face. After a couple more minutes, she seemed to get herself under control.

"You remember when I first started working at The Sanctuary?"

I hadn't meant start at the beginning of time, but if that was where she needed to go, so be it. "Dee lined up an interview for you, and you were pretty much handed the job on the spot."

"She told me I'd make a lot more money there than I would at the bar."

"And she was right," I said.

"She was. And Xander was good at talking the talk. He made it sound like it would be… better than The Dollhouse." Sarah sighed. "And for the first couple of weeks it was, but then things started to change, and I had second thoughts."

"So why didn't you quit?"

"I'm getting to that." Sarah nodded, as if she'd expected the question. "I wanted to. I even talked to Tenley about Elbo. She was going to find out whether they were hiring or not. But then it ended up not mattering, because I couldn't quit."

She wiped away another tear and took a couple of deep breaths before she continued. "I never told Xander where I went to school. I just told him I was working on business courses at a local college. But he did some digging, because that's what he does." Her smile was cold. "He found out I was on a scholarship at Northwestern. Tuition to my program is over a hundred thousand dollars, Chris. My scholarship covers half, and I have grants to cover another chunk, but the rest is student loans that I'll have to start paying back once I graduate. Plus I'll have my undergrad loans as well."

"I don't understand what that has to do with quitting."

"There's a propriety clause associated with my scholarship, which makes sense, of course. The donors want to invest their money wisely. The school has a reputation to uphold. I should've known better."

The pieces were starting to fall into place. "What does Xander have to do with your scholarship?"

"He read the fine print where I didn't, or he made phone calls, or whatever. I assumed the propriety clause just covered things like acting like an idiot, stealing, cheating, fraternizing with supervisors, the usual stuff. One of the girls at my internship was fired early on for blowing a staff member in the copy room. She was on scholarship, too. She's been expelled from the program and has to pay restitution to the college. She's not getting a degree."

"Shit. That's a lot of money to owe." I could see how a propriety clause would come in handy to weed out students interested in partying their way through college, or using blow jobs to get what and where they wanted.

"It is. Especially when she's not even going to finish the program now. Anyway, when I mentioned to Xander the possibility of me quitting, he suggested I reconsider my options. I thought he was just being a jerk until he mentioned that any image from the cameras could be turned into a photograph, and wouldn't it be too bad if one ended up on my dean's desk."

"But you're not giving lap dances or getting naked." That's what she'd led me to believe all this time, and I prayed she'd been telling the truth.

"No, but anything can be misconstrued. You've seen what I wear to work. Xander could find the worst possible image and make it look like something it wasn't. I'd lose my internship and my scholarship and my degree."

"So he's been blackmailing you?" At least at The Dollhouse management had been fairly transparent in their manipulations.

Sarah rubbed her lips with her fingertips. "I don't think his threats are ever idle. You can see how I couldn't risk leaving after that."

"How long ago did he threaten you with this?"

"A couple of months."

"Christ, Sarah, why didn't you say anything before now?"

"What would you have done? I'm not in the clear until I graduate. They can't revoke my scholarship after I get my diploma. All I can do is wait it out."

"But you could've told me. Why keep it a secret?"

"I was afraid of what you'd think of me for one. And you already had so much to deal with. You'd just put that new furnace in at your mom's, the trial was going on, and I knew that was hard on you even though you didn't want to talk about it. I didn't want to burden you with my crap, too, especially when there wasn't anything you could do. More than that, I didn't want to lose this." She motioned between us.

"Why'd you think telling me you're being blackmailed by an asshole who deals in illegal sex trade would make me leave?"

"Because I know how much you hate my job and how you've wanted me out of there from day one. I worried you would blame me for the situation, because I sure blame myself. You were right about everything—about how I'm not immune, how it starts to become normal even though it isn't. But I can't backtrack out of the mistake."

"Sarah—"

She held up her hand. "Wait. There's more."

Of course there was. We hadn't even gotten to the part about Dee.

"Remember how my car broke down and I ended up serving left stage a while back?"

I nodded, bracing for whatever the hell was going to be next.

"Rent was due, and so was my loan payment. I couldn't cover all of that and get my car fixed. I was already so stressed. My internship was about to start, so when Xander threatened to send me home for being late, I was beside myself. I didn't know how I was going to manage. I lost it."

"Lost it how?"

"I just couldn't keep it together. I started crying in Xander's office. And right then I knew I'd screwed myself. Showing weakness in front of Xander is a huge mistake, but it was just too much. And then it was like… he flipped a switch. It was so… off-putting." She shuddered. "He went from being pissed off to being totally understanding. He was so nice about it, saying it must be hard to be under so much pressure all the time. I was frazzled by everything and freaked out that when he made his offer, I couldn't come up with any other options."

"What was the offer?"

"He told me I needed to serve left stage. That I'd only have to do it this one time, and in return he'd loan me the money to get my car fixed. Plus I'd owe him a favor. He called it interest on the loan."

"You gotta be shitting me. Come on, Sarah, you're smarter than that."

"I know." She dropped her head. "But I didn't know what else to do. All my loans are capped. I couldn't ask you for money. I don't have that kind of space on a credit card. I didn't want to be another person in your life taking from you. Xander said it wouldn't be a big deal, and then he reminded me I wasn't in much of a position to argue, what with my internship being at stake."

"So he blackmailed you again?" This guy was so much worse than Sienna, and all this time Sarah had been dealing with him on her own.

"I guess. That was the night I panicked and decided to break it off with you because I'd made a horrible mistake. I had no idea what kind of favor he was going to ask for, but I knew I'd made a bad deal. I started paying him immediately to get that part over with, and we're square now, except he didn't collect on the favor right away. And then there was the stuff with Candy—the idea of you with her threw me." Sarah huffed and shook her head. "I wanted to tell you, but I didn't know how, and I knew you'd be mad."

As much as I didn't like it, I could see where she was coming from. Particularly considering how I'd dealt with things recently where she was concerned—projecting my past experiences on her, and us, I guessed. "Why would you let him control you like this?"

"What choice do I have? I couldn't risk ruining everything by losing my scholarship and getting kicked out of the program. With no degree, I'd never dig myself out of the debt I've piled up. The last thing I ever wanted was to become my mother, and I could very clearly see that path being the only one left for me if I didn't do things his way."

I didn't know much about Sarah's relationship with her mother, just that they rarely talked and she avoided going home during the holidays, opting to stay in Chicago and spend them working. Or with me, if time allowed.

"I kept waiting for Xander to call in the favor, but he didn't. Then that party with Dee happened, and I started to get scared, because I knew it was going to be a lot worse than I'd ever anticipated. And I was right."

"Why can't you just pay him the interest? Why's it gotta be a favor?"

It was a pointless question. I already had the answer: it kept Sarah under his thumb and would get her exactly where he wanted her, making him more money.

"I tried that. Xander gave me two options." Her laugh was dark and derisive. She pulled out her phone and hit a couple of buttons, then passed it to me. "Press play."

"What is it?"

216

"I recorded my conversation with Xander. He's not the one with all the leverage anymore."

I nodded, impressed. After a moment Xander's voice came through—slightly muffled, but definitely audible—as he offered her a room of strangers or himself. I could hear Sarah's soft whimper of fear, and it echoed in front of me as she pressed her palm against her mouth, likely reliving the entire conversation.

"Motherfucker."

"I'd like to say that's the worst part, but then Dee happened." Her breath hitched as she paused. "I'd just left Xander's office, and I was going to come directly to you and tell you everything, but Grant asked if I could check on Dee, so I went and—"

She sucked in another one of those gasping breaths.

"That's when you found her?"

She nodded and handed me her phone, looking unsure.

I scrolled through images of a very disturbing OD.

"I felt bad taking those, but I don't know much about Grant other than he works closely with Xander. He seems to care about Dee, and he was willing to take her to the hospital, so that has to mean something, right?"

"I don't know, Sarah." This was all too familiar and too fucked up. So much of it reminded me of what had happened with Lisa so many years ago. Fortunately there hadn't been any kind of blackmail in the mix there, and we'd extracted her, and ourselves, from The Dollhouse before things could get to the point that they had with Dee. Lisa had still had a hell of a time going through withdrawal, not to mention the psychological damage that place had done to her.

"He sent me to check on her, and it wasn't some kind of trap, which I was half expecting." Sarah picked at her jeans, pulling threads free and rolling them into tiny balls.

I was silent for a while, trying to figure out how I was going to help her get out of this shit without making more of a mess of her life. My help seemed to do that sometimes. I flipped through the pictures again, thinking about how different Destiny had been just a couple of years ago. How she'd had plans—maybe not the same kind as Sarah, but she'd wanted a life that didn't include stripping.

"You can't do that party tonight, Sarah. I won't let you become this." I stared at the image of Dee lying on the wet floor, her skin gray and bruised, scrawled with hateful words.

"I know. But if I don't..."

"You can't."

She closed her eyes and nodded. Tears that seemed to have no end tracked down her cheeks again.

I had no idea how to save her from the problems this had caused. Doubling her debt and losing her master's was a downward spiral that scared me. It could break her.

"I wish it had never come to this," she breathed.

Her hair was in her face, her head bowed. I tipped her chin up. She was slow to lift her eyes, and they never met mine.

"Look at me, baby," I urged.

"I don't want to see how ashamed of me you are."

Fat tears pooled on my finger, running down the side of my hand. I wondered if she'd cried this hard in front of Xander. He'd made her humanity a weakness, one he'd manipulated and made bigger. But to me her cracks meant a way in. A way to share her vulnerability.

I sighed. "I'm not ashamed of you."

"You should be. I am."

She finally lifted her gaze, and I saw it—the hopelessness, the fear, her shame. It was all so clear now.

"I ruined everything," she said.

"You didn't ruin anything."

"Yes, I did. I kept this from you, and you'll never forgive me for it."

"What exactly do you need me to forgive?"

"Me. For making a mistake. I should've listened."

"Then you're forgiven."

"It can't be that simple, Chris."

"Sure it can. Forgiveness is the easy part."

She brushed her fingers across the back of my hand, keeping it pressed against her cheek. "What's the hard part?"

"Forgetting. Knowing you felt like there weren't any other options, and that you didn't even consider coming to me for help."

A tiny flicker of hope bloomed behind Sarah's eyes. "But I'm here now."

"I know." I pulled her toward me, and she came willingly. She clung to me as if I could keep her from drowning.

And she was. We both were. Ivy's situation—which I was determined to help manage—wasn't quite so dire, but in a lot of ways it was just as bad.

Separately, these struggles could break us down. But maybe if we could hold on to each other and figure them out together... we could stop the fractures from becoming too big and keep the cracks from forming fissures we couldn't repair.

SEVENTEEN

SARAH

I had no idea if things were going to be okay or not... between Chris and me, with Dee, at The Sanctuary, with school.

I let my mind go blank for as long as Chris held me. For those fleeting seconds, I allowed myself to believe that this good thing I had wasn't going to disappear again, that I was done making these kinds of mistakes. As much as I'd fought not to be like my mother, I'd also allowed her to push me in directions that had sabotaged my efforts to escape a life I didn't want. If I could get out of this, I swore I'd do things differently.

I was still amazed that I'd ended up with someone like Chris. He was the exact opposite of every man I'd ever seen my mother with. All their suits, their clean-cut looks, and well-spoken manners had given the illusion of goodness, and my mother was always searching for something better than she had. But none of it was ever real. Hers was false luxury born from deceit, and often depravity. In my experience—as a child, at the club, and hell, even at the marketing firm—a careful, well-crafted façade often housed the most disturbing men.

I'd fallen for it with Xander. His glossy exterior had blinded me, and I'd taken that job thinking maybe he wouldn't be as bad as management at The Dollhouse. In a way I'd been right. He wasn't *as bad*; he was far, far worse.

If I lost everything now, it would be the worst kind of karmic retribution. It would be the universe telling me I could never claw my way out of the hole I'd been raised in. I'd be permanently bound to an existence I could never quite break free of, because I'd allowed it to happen. I'd walked into it and stayed, because it was what I knew. And with my mother always in the back of my mind, I'd thought I could handle it. Only now, faced with the possibility of losing everything I'd worked for, could I finally see my error.

What was a little more debt in exchange for my dignity? My safety? A shot at a real relationship? I should've turned my back on this life so much sooner.

Chris stroked my hair, murmuring something into my neck. I turned my head and caught his soft lament. "I just want to keep my girls safe."

My heart broke for him, because it beat for him. I had no idea what was coming for me, but I knew with certainty that he was the one steady, loyal person I could rely on right now, despite everything.

But when I pressed my lips to his skin and kissed my way up the side of his neck, Chris pulled away. He cupped my face and brushed his lips across my forehead.

"I can't right now, Sarah. You need to give me some time to deal with this."

I tried to drop my chin, but he held me firmly.

"This isn't me saying no to you. This is me needing time to sort through all of this and find a way forward. I need to get my head around you keeping something this important to yourself, even though I understand why you did."

I nodded my understanding, but it still hurt.

"Do you have to work today?"

"Oh, God!" I checked the clock on his stove. It was already eight. "I'm supposed to leave in twenty minutes."

"Just call in and say you need the day."

"And tell them what?" I couldn't imagine telling anyone my stripper friend had OD'd and I'd spent the night in the hospital.

"That you've had an emergency, that a close friend is in the hospital, and you need the time. They're not going to say no, Sarah, and they're not going to ask for more details unless they're assholes."

I was such a mess right now. Simple thought processes were nearly impossible to manage. All I wanted was to stay wrapped up in Chris's arms and forget everything that had happened in the past twenty-four hours—maybe even the last two months.

I called my supervisor at work first, then my program mentor at Northwestern. Both were extremely understanding.

Chris's phone chimed with a message as I ended the second call, and while he thumb-typed a response, I looked around his apartment. His sister had been here when I first arrived. Unless I'd hallucinated that.

"Wasn't Ivy here?" I asked.

Chris slid his phone back in his pocket. "She went over to Inked Armor right after you showed up. That was her, saying she's there and Lisa's trying to talk her into a nose ring."

"I didn't make the best first impression," I said, embarrassed at the state I'd shown up in, and how I'd pretty much thrown myself at Chris.

"She's not judgy; she understands shitty situations."

"Is she okay? You said she stayed here last night?" It finally registered that there was a pile of crumpled sheets and a pillow stacked on the coffee table.

"Yeah. Some shit went down at my mom's last night, so Ivy came here, which is good, 'cause she needs out of there. I stopped by my mom's early this morning; it was a bad scene."

"Bad how?" I could see, now that I wasn't focused only on myself, that Chris looked as exhausted as I felt.

"John has a gambling problem, and he's gotten himself into some trouble, which he brought to the house last night in the form of a couple of goons. They ripped Ivy's room apart and fucking frisked her like a goddamn criminal. She's got bruises all over her arms—and I'm guessing it's from that—and John just let it happen."

"Oh my God."

Chris nodded somberly. "It was pretty fucked up."

"What about your mom? Is she okay?"

He laughed, but it was mirthless. "She barricaded herself in her bedroom and left Ivy to deal with it on her own."

"What?"

"Yeah." He twirled a lock of my hair between his fingers. "She puts herself before her kids every single time. I have no idea how bad it's been for Ivy all these years, but I know what it was like for me when I lived there."

"What do you mean?" I didn't want to push too much, but I longed to better understand him.

"When Ivy was little and I did something that pissed John off, which was often, he'd use his fists to keep me in line. When that happened, my mom used to take Ivy for a walk, partly so Ivy wouldn't have to see it, but mostly because she didn't want to be the one subjected to the violence. Afterwards, she'd come back and tell me I'd brought it on myself, and if I could do what I was told, it wouldn't keep happening. It wasn't a great way to grow up."

My heart ached for the man in front of me. He was imposing based on size alone, but as a child—he must've been helpless in those situations. I could understand now why Chris was so closed off, why he kept me at a distance. We were equally broken inside, just in different ways—a lot like Hayden and Tenley, actually, despite what we'd thought the other day. It gave me hope that maybe we could find our own way through all of this. Finally finding a way to talk to each other seemed a great first step.

"I'm so sorry."

"Better me than Ivy. I took the beatings because I didn't ever want it to be her, you know? She was a good kid—smart in school, followed the rules, didn't push the boundaries. Not like me. Eventually I started to fight back, and when I was bigger than John, I did as much damage to him as he did to me. He'd loved the fights until then. That's when I got kicked out. Then I started working for Damen…and, well… here I am, trying to get Ivy out of the same bad place."

"How is she?" His comment about wanting to keep his girls safe made sense now. Being included was another reason to keep hope.

"I don't know. I think she's put up with a lot more than she'll ever be willing to talk about. I'm trying to get her to stay with me for a while. I'd like to get her out of the house permanently, but it's going to take some convincing."

We were all fighting our conditioning. It wasn't easy to leave behind familiar things, even when they were bad for us. "And all of this happened last night? God, Chris, are *you* okay?"

"None of it happened to me directly."

"That doesn't make it easier to deal with."

"Sometimes I feel like I'm the problem, not part of the solution."

"You didn't create any of this. You know that, right?"

He nodded, but I could see he didn't believe it. Instead of answering, he checked his watch. "We should head over to Inked Armor before my sister ends up with a full sleeve or something."

Now it was my turn to nod. I could have asked him questions all day, but he'd shared more with me this morning than he had in the entire time we'd been together. "Okay."

I used the bathroom to freshen up, horrified by the state of my face and my makeup. I washed it all off, clearing away the smears of day-old mascara. I smoothed my hair with the brush on the vanity— one I assumed belonged to Ivy since Chris kept his hair short.

On the way down to street level, I passed Chris the keys to my car. I wasn't in any state to drive. My phone rang halfway to the shop, and I answered even though I didn't recognize the number. Maybe they needed something from me at my internship after all.

"Sarah?" It was Grant, but he wasn't calling from the same phone he'd used earlier.

"Is Dee okay?"

Chris gave me a questioning look.

"She's fighting, so I hope she's going to pull through." His voice cracked, and he cleared his throat. "But that's not why I'm calling."

"Should I come back to the hospital?" I asked, trying to read between the lines.

"No. Don't do that. We've got her under watch, and they're doing everything they can. Listen, I need you to stay home tonight."

"But what about—"

"I know it's hard to do right now, but you need to trust me on this and not come in to work. Can you do that?"

I hesitated, considering all that had happened. "Do I have much of a choice?"

"There's always a choice. You just need to make the right one, and that's staying with the people who can keep you safe."

A click and dead air followed.

"Who was that?" Chris asked.

"Grant."

"What did he say?"

"He told me stay home tonight."

Chris frowned. "I agree that's a good plan, but why would *he* say that?"

"I have no idea." My absence tonight would push Xander over the edge.

"What exactly did he say?" Chris pressed.

"Well, he updated me on Dee, but then he told me not to come in to work tonight and to stay with the people who can keep me safe."

Chris rubbed the back of his neck. "What the fuck is going on?"

His question seemed rhetorical, but I felt compelled to answer anyway. "I really don't know."

"Do you think you can trust him?"

"I don't know that either. I want to, though."

Chris tapped the wheel in agitation. "What's the worst thing that can happen if you don't go in tonight?"

"Xander uses the leverage he has against me, and I lose my placement in my program and have to pay back the scholarship money."

"But if you go in…" He let it hang.

"I don't want to end up like Dee," I whispered.

"That's not going to happen."

Parking in my spot, he cut the engine and slipped his hand under my hair, his thumb stroking a soothing line down my neck. "Want me to walk you up?"

I thought about that for a moment, about being alone in my apartment. It didn't matter that Chris would be right across the street, that I could literally look out my window and see him through the Inked Armor storefront.

"Is it okay if I hang out at the shop? I don't want to be by myself right now."

He rubbed my neck in slow, tight circles. "Yeah, baby, of course. Ivy's there too, so you'll have company if you want. But you gotta be beat. Have you even slept?"

"I don't know that I could fall asleep right now anyway."

He regarded me for a long while. "When I have a break between clients we can come to your apartment, and I'll hang out while you catch a nap."

"Okay." Though it made me feel needy, I agreed. I was serious about not being alone. I didn't think I could close my eyes without seeing Dee's body on that cold tile floor, or the look on Grant's face when he'd realized how weak her pulse was.

When we entered the shop, Chris's sister was behind the front desk, clearly fascinated as Lisa reviewed the various piercings and the gauges for each one.

They both looked up, and Lisa's eyes went wide. "Heeey." The *are you okay* was implied by the way she looked me over.

I looked to Chris, to see his reaction. He caressed my cheek with his fingertips.

"Rough night," he said to Lisa. "Can you see about rescheduling my afternoon appointment? If I can free up a couple hours that'd be great."

"I can do that." Lisa picked up the phone, glancing between us.

"You don't have to rearrange your appointments for me," I murmured.

"I want to. Why don't you spend some time with the girls while I get set up?"

"Okay." This was what I needed—someone to tell me what I should do. I didn't feel capable of making my own decisions at the moment.

He kissed me on the cheek. At my small, unintentional plaintive sound, he took my chin between his thumb and forefinger and brushed his lips over mine.

Lisa was quick about rescheduling Chris's afternoon client, and when she hung up, she avoided asking all the personal questions I was certain she wanted to. Instead, she asked whether I thought a hoop or a stud would look better in Ivy's nose. The normalcy was needed. I couldn't get into anything heavy with Ivy here. I'd embarrassed myself enough this morning, and now I knew she was going through her own stuff. Sometimes pretending everything was okay was simpler.

"Should we get coffee? We could run across the street and grab one before clients start showing up," Lisa suggested, alleviating some of the awkwardness.

"That'd be great," I agreed. Anything to keep me awake and my mind off The Sanctuary.

After taking orders from the guys, the three of us headed over to Serendipity, the bookstore/coffee shop beneath my apartment. We stopped to say hi to Hayden's Aunt Cassie before we crossed through to the café.

I was surprised when she came out from behind the cash register to hug Chris's sister.

"Ivy, it's so nice to see you again! I was just asking Chris about you last week. How're you doing?"

Ivy seemed shocked by the affection. It might not have been something she was used to. She tentatively patted Cassie's back in return. "I'm okay. I mean, I'm good."

Cassie held her at arm's length, tilting her head to the side. "And your mom? She's good, too?" She sure knew how to cut right to the chase.

Ivy dropped her head and shifted awkwardly. "Uh… she's okay. Sort of. I've been thinking it might be time to get my own place soon. Chris is letting me stay with him for a while until I get things figured out."

"He's a good brother, isn't he?"

Ivy nodded, and a small smile appeared. "He really is. He slept on his couch last night so I could have his bed. I'm gonna have to figure things out quick since he only has that one bedroom, but maybe things'll calm down at home…" She faded out at the end, clearly not believing that last part.

"You know, Tenley's old apartment hasn't been rented yet, and Nate just finished having the floors refinished and air put in." Cassie pointed to the ceiling, indicating the apartments above us. "Maybe you'd consider moving in there. Then you could have Sarah for a neighbor." She turned her somewhat-concerned smile my way.

"That's actually a great idea!" Lisa clapped her hands.

"It'd be super convenient," I agreed.

"That's real nice of you to offer, but I work down by Midway, so it's a bit far."

"Oh. I thought Chris mentioned maybe you'd be interested in working at Inked Armor. Aren't you looking to hire someone, Lisa? Or is Hayden being difficult again?"

Ivy looked confused, probably like I did, but Lisa's smile was all devious excitement. "We hadn't gotten that far yet, but I was planning on sweet-talking Ivy today." She winked.

"Oops. Well, I guess that secret is out."

"Does someone want to tell me what's going on?" Ivy suddenly sounded a whole lot like her brother.

Lisa and Cassie exchanged a look. "It's just an idea Chris was tossing around. No pressure. Something to think about," Lisa said.

"Why don't I show you the apartment, at the very least. There's no rush, and you don't have to make any immediate decisions," Cassie suggested.

"Sure. Okay. That'd be nice." There was a waver to Ivy's voice as Cassie threaded her arm through hers.

She locked up the store, putting up a *Be Back Soon* sign on the front door, and we followed her upstairs to the vacant apartment.

Ivy got emotional over how nice it was. "I don't think I can afford this place."

"The rent is always negotiable," Cassie said. "Especially when we're talking about family." She gave Ivy's shoulder a squeeze and winked at me.

Chris really was an amazing person. All this time he'd been planning how to help his sister find her way to a better shot at life. He would've done the same for me if I'd let him, but I'd stupidly shut him out, instead.

When we came back to the shop almost an hour later, Lisa had a few things to take care of, so Ivy and I sat on the couch and leafed through one of the custom albums while we chatted.

"Chris is really talented," Ivy remarked, running her fingers across a photo of a Celtic design on someone's back.

"He really is. I keep trying to convince him to put some of his art on me." I tried not to sound sad about it.

"Do you have any tattoos?"

"Not yet, but I know what I want. I just have to convince Chris. What about you? Do you have any ink?"

"I have one on my lower back, but it's pretty bad. I got it for cheap from a friend." Ivy surveyed the shop before she lifted her shirt to show me the poorly done cartoon character. "Chris would probably be pissed if he knew about it, so don't tell him, 'kay?"

"I'm sure he'd be happy to cover it with something nice for you. He's done it for Hayden before."

"You don't think he'd be mad?"

"At you? No. At himself for not being the one to put it on you in the first place is far more likely."

Ivy chuckled. "You're probably right."

She flipped through the album and stopped at a tattoo of a stack of books. "When I was little, Chris used to come and get me from school. I was in maybe first or second grade, I guess? Anyway, he'd come get me and ride me home on his handle bars 'cause it was a long walk. Sometimes we'd stop and get ice cream on the way, or he'd bring me half a sandwich. They were so good, those sandwiches. I don't know why I remember them, but I do. Maybe because we never had that kind of food in the house.

"He used to read me stories before bed when my mom worked nights and my dad would be out. Sometimes I had a hard time sleeping, especially when my dad was in one of his moods. Anyway, Chris would lay on the floor beside my bed until I fell asleep." She was silent for a few seconds, maybe lost in the memory. "And then one day he wasn't there anymore. I thought maybe I'd done something wrong… for a long time I was mad at him for leaving, but then he started coming around again, and well… I don't know where I'd be right now if it wasn't for him."

I returned her sad smile. "I know exactly what you mean."

"Do you love him?"

The boldness of her question shocked me, which my face must've indicated.

"Sorry. Maybe I shouldn't have asked that. It just seems like you do."

"No. It's okay. And the answer is yes."

Ivy nodded. "That's good. I hope one day somebody will love me."

It was such an honest statement. And I understood in so many ways what she meant. People like us always had to fight to feel worthy of the things we weren't sure we deserved. I reached over and squeezed her hand.

She looked at me oddly for a moment, and then smiled.

At some point we must've stopped talking, because gentle shaking pulled me out of sleep. Lisa stood over me. "Hey, why don't we go over to your apartment?"

"I don't wanna be alone," I mumbled through the fog.

"I'll stay with you. Ivy'll watch the front desk for me." She gestured to the jewelry counter where Ivy sat.

"Oh, okay." We gathered my things, and Lisa took me back to my apartment.

"Chris said you had a rough night. He told me about Dee. Are you okay?" she asked as she slipped the key into the lock and let me into my own apartment.

"I don't know. I don't think so."

That's what it boiled down to. I wasn't okay with this anymore. As humiliating and devastating as it would be, I knew losing a scholarship and my degree was better than losing my dignity or even myself. I needed to follow Grant's instructions to stay home tonight. He'd proved himself a better person than Xander. I had to trust he wasn't out to do more damage.

I kicked off my shoes and followed her to my bedroom, flopping down on the mattress.

"I made some pretty bad choices. I let Xander drag me into things I never wanted to be a part of. I just want Chris to be able to forgive me for that."

Lisa lay down beside me and tucked her hand under her cheek. I knew she understood only too well where I was coming from. "We all make bad choices, Sarah. I don't think it's about Chris forgiving you for whatever mistakes you have or haven't made; it's about you forgiving yourself."

"You make it sound so easy."

"It isn't, but it's necessary if you want to accept that what you and Chris have is more than some temporary thing." She was quiet for a few seconds before she asked, "Do you think Dee will be okay?"

"Honestly, I don't know. The doctors were talking about liver and brain damage. Grant is with her, and he said she's hanging in there. I guess we just have to wait and see."

"I hope she gets through this."

"Me, too. I don't know what Grant's plan is, but I hope he can keep her out of the club. I mean, you got free, right? She and I should be able to, too."

Lisa was quiet for a long while before she finally answered. "When I started working at The Dollhouse, Chris used to come and sit in my section. I think he must've spent half his paychecks on me. He never came to watch the girls; he just made sure I was okay.

Or as okay as I could be with all the shit Damen and Sienna were feeding me. Every night I worked, he was there—especially when Jamie couldn't be."

"Jamie loves you."

"He does. But sometimes it was hard to watch me spiral down. Chris was there when it was too much for him to handle."

"What was Chris like back then?" Now that I'd begun to understand his past, I wanted to fill in all the information I could.

"Chris was always charming, but you have to understand, he's spent his entire life trying to protect the people he loves from being hurt, and he lived in that house with Damen and all those girls. It was a messed-up situation. I know; I lived there for a while, too."

"Messed up how?"

"There weren't a lot of rules, but Chris wasn't the kind of guy to take advantage of anyone. He was so young when Damen gave him a job, so talented, and he had no idea. The girls in that house wanted to take care of him the same way he wanted to protect them. He was like everyone's teddy bear. He was safe."

I could see him as a boy, verging on man, with softer features and a less ominous presence, baby-faced and broken. He would've been something to covet. He still was.

"Did you ever—" I hesitated, unsure whether I wanted to know.

Lisa shook her head. "I always belonged to Jamie, even when I didn't."

Lisa never talked willingly about her time at The Dollhouse, so I appreciated her sharing this with me.

"The sacrifices Chris makes are always to keep people safe. He tried with Candy, but she couldn't see past the drugs."

"So what does that make me? Another girl he wants to save?"

"It's not about saving you; it's about keeping you safe. Chris wants what we all want—to be loved."

"I couldn't seem to get past the armor with him until today."

"He doesn't really let people in, so you have to be patient. Give him time. How Chris sees himself and the reality of who he is are two different things. He has a hard time believing he deserves you."

"Funny, I feel the same way about him."

"We're all broken, Sarah. It's not always about fixing the parts that don't work; it's about making the most of the ones that do."

I considered the accuracy of that statement.

"If you need to talk about what happened at The Sanctuary, you can, but I understand if you don't want to."

I tucked my hand under my cheek. "Xander got the upper hand on me, and I didn't think I had any options."

"People like him are good at making you think that's the case. It was the same at The Dollhouse."

"I wish I could take it back. I just want out."

"I know. We'll find a way."

I closed my eyes and took a few deep breaths. I wasn't sure if the racing in my head would slow enough to let me go to sleep, but after a while, I fell back into darkness.

The next time I woke, Lisa wasn't lying beside me anymore. Instead, a strong arm decorated with beautiful ink was wrapped around my waist. Chris's broad chest pressed against my back, and his breath caressed my shoulder. I brushed my fingers along the grayscale patterns on his forearm and checked the clock on the nightstand. It was well into the evening. I'd slept for ages. I should've been at The Sanctuary three hours ago.

Anxiety ripped through me like an electric current as my phone buzzed from somewhere inside my purse on the floor. I tried to lift Chris's arm, but it tightened around me.

"Let me up. I need—" I didn't know what I needed. Before I'd fallen asleep I'd decided to trust Grant. Going to The Sanctuary wouldn't do me any good now regardless, but I couldn't stop the panic.

"Everything's going to be okay," Chris whispered.

I wanted that to be the truth, but missing this shift could change the entire trajectory of my life. Another buzz from my phone told me more messages were coming in.

"I need to check that."

He sighed. "I'll get it."

Chris lifted his arm and turned away. I shivered. When he rolled back, he had my purse in his hand. He dropped it on the bed beside me and wrapped me up again. I rummaged around until I found my phone, then pulled up the messages.

The first was from an unknown number. It was a link to a video. I clicked on it, my stomach flipping, all my worst nights at The Sanctuary replaying in my head. I was fully prepared for the bottom to fall out, and it definitely did. But not in the way I'd expected.

On the small screen played a Breaking News report no more than fifteen minutes old. I had to watch it twice to understand fully what I was seeing, because it was so much the opposite of what I'd anticipated. There'd been a takedown, and The Sanctuary was one of four area clubs that had been targeted.

A total of fifteen arrests had been made on a variety of charges, predominantly related to sex trafficking, as well as distribution of illegal narcotics, and Xander was among those in custody.

The investigation had begun shortly after The Dollhouse had shut down last winter as the dangerous link between the sex trade industry and strip clubs in the city came to light. Several undercover agents had infiltrated the clubs, compiling a mountain of evidence to take down four local operations on more than seventy-five violations.

"Oh my God." I looked at Chris. "Does this mean what I think it does?"

Now the cryptic call from Grant made sense. He must've been one of the agents involved in the takedown. He'd been trying to protect me, in a way he hadn't been able to do with Dee—not until it was too late. I had to wonder if she'd be okay after this, and if she and Grant would be able to make things work. I hoped so, because Dee deserved to have something good.

I both saw and felt Chris's relief as he pulled me into his arms. "I think it means you don't have to keep hiding in the dark spaces."

I held on to him, still shocked by the sudden turn of events. He was right; that was exactly what I'd been doing—finding the darkest spaces in my life and clinging to them. Except with Chris.

He was the opposite of all the things from a past I didn't know how to shake.

I sat up and scrolled through more videos, most of them giving a version of the same information. The clubs were being shut down, and at the center of the plot was Xander. He was facing deportation, and several others were looking at serious jail time. Apparently they'd been following a trail he'd worked hard to cover up for years—changing aliases, moving around the country—until someone opened the doors and let out all the secrets.

"How could he have gotten away with this for so long?"

Chris trailed a single finger along my jaw. "It's hard to see in the dark. But everyone trips up eventually."

It scared me that I'd been trapped there for months, unable to find a way out. And now, just like Xander's closet full of secrets had been opened, so had the door to my cage. That burden of anxiety and fear had been with me so long, I hardly knew what to do without it. But this wasn't a second chance I would waste.

"I'm going to talk to Tenley about Elbo again."

"Maybe you shouldn't get another job."

"Ha ha! We're having an above-average day for sure, but let's not get crazy. How am I going to afford rent without one?"

"You have what, less than a month left at your internship? Don't you think it'd be kind of nice to do that one thing, focus your energy on the life you want?"

"Elbo wouldn't be like The Sanctuary."

"Maybe not, but it's still a bar. The hours aren't going to be much better, and you're already exhausted all the time. Do you even remember what real sleep is?" He skimmed the hollow beneath my eye.

I didn't have any room left on my line of credit, but I'd managed to squirrel away about a thousand in emergency funds so I'd never have to repeat that situation with Xander. If I could make that last a couple of months, it could work. "What if I only had to pay half the rent?"

"I'm sure Cassie would go for that."

"I don't mean asking Cassie to do that." Although she'd suggested she would for Ivy.

"I'm pretty sure she'd rather give you a break than watch you work yourself into a hole, or put yourself in another dangerous position."

I sat cross-legged beside him, smoothing out the comforter because I couldn't seem to stop fidgeting. "Probably, but that isn't really what I meant."

"Oh. I can help you pick up the slack."

"I don't mean borrowing money from you, either." God, I hadn't expected this to be such a hard question to ask. "I thought maybe you'd want to move in here."

Chris's eyebrows climbed his forehead. "Like, into your apartment?"

"It makes sense, right? You work across the street. We could cut a lot of costs." I searched his face, but he wasn't saying anything. "It was just a thought," I added. "Maybe it's stupid."

"No, no…" He nodded seriously. "I'm not tied to my lease. I could stay with you for a couple of months—longer if it's better for you financially."

I didn't like his focus on the financial benefit. "We'd get to see each other a lot more, too—especially if I don't have to work two jobs."

"We would."

"And it wouldn't have to be temporary. I mean, unless you want it to be."

Chris tucked an arm behind his head, his thick biceps flexing with the movement. "I can stay as long as you want me to."

"Maybe I'll never want you to leave."

He looked away for a moment. "You never know what kind of opportunities you're going to have in the future. Someone could offer you a job halfway around the world that you can't turn down. Or you'll meet someone out in the business world and realize you can do a whole lot better than this." He motioned to himself.

I dragged my finger down his arm. "There is no better than this."

He laughed. "I think working in that club has messed with your idea of what constitutes good. I don't even own a suit, and you're going to be living in a world of high-rises and educated people. What happens when there's some kind of company party and you have to bring your boyfriend or whatever? What're you going to tell people I do?"

"The truth."

"How's that going to go over in a room full of corporates? I don't even have a high school diploma, Sarah."

"So what? Hayden didn't go to college either, and Tenley doesn't care. Why should you? Why should I? Wearing a suit and having an education doesn't make a person good, Chris."

"Hayden's a genius, though. And he makes good financial decisions. Together they'll have a good, stable life, which is what they both need, and it's what you should have."

"What about what you should have? Don't you deserve that, too?"

"I don't ever want to hold you back."

"How would you hold me back?"

"By not fitting into your life once you start a job you'll be proud of. I'll move in here, but I don't want you to end up stuck, Sarah."

"Stuck?"

"With me."

"You're a choice, Chris."

"And I keep wondering if you're gonna realize there are much better ones out there."

EIGHTEEN

CHRIS

I wished I knew how to keep my damn mouth shut. Here Sarah was, inviting me to move into her apartment, and I was spouting off points to dissuade her. I wanted this, didn't I? Candy hadn't worked out so well, but I was different now, and Sarah was sure as hell different. Sarah was unlike any other woman I'd been with ever, which was part of the reason I felt like I should give her an opportunity to change her mind.

She propped her chin on her fist. "I think my idea of better and your idea of better differ fairly significantly."

"I think you go to school with a bunch of guys who fit right into the category I'm talking about, not to mention the ones you're working with at your internship."

"Those guys are self-righteous assholes who think they're God's gift to women." She dropped her hand and her head, focusing on her fingers. "When I was a kid, my mom went out with the kind of guys you're talking about. They showed up in suits, drove expensive cars, bought her all sorts of gifts and clothes. The money they'd give her was insane. I had such nice things as a kid—for a while, anyway. All the good things we had disappeared as quickly as they came."

I'd had very brief glimpses into Sarah's life before she moved to Chicago, and details about her mother were limited to tongue-in-cheek comments about her being busy with her latest boyfriend.

She'd never mentioned her father. I'd assumed she was like so many other kids who grew up with one parent absent from their lives.

"We'd live in these nice apartments for a while, and then all of a sudden we'd be back in some crappy one-bedroom, and she'd be pawning the jewelry the last guy gave her. For the longest time I didn't understand why it was so extreme."

Sarah followed the seam of her jeans with a finger as she got lost in a memory.

"Then one day we were at the grocery store, and some woman came up to her and started screaming. She called her a home wrecker and a whore. She said she'd ruined her marriage and slapped her across the face. I was horrified—at first because this woman had slapped my mother and called her such horrible names, but later because I realized the woman was right, and what she'd said was true."

"Jesus Christ. How old were you?"

"Old enough to understand what it meant to be a mistress. It was our normal for so long, and my mom always had excuses. He said he was going to leave his wife. He said he was filing for divorce and they were going to start a life together. She never really worked, other than some part-time thing at a country club, and in between the boyfriends, she'd go on these dates. She always looked so glamorous, and for a long time I thought she had the most amazing life... But it wasn't. It was empty and dangerous and sad, and she wanted me to be just like her.

"For a while I believed the lies she fed me about what she was doing, but things changed when I got older. She set me up with a waitressing job at the country club she sometimes worked at. Occasionally I was invited to hostess at private parties in big houses, like mansions. At first it all seemed very innocent—until it wasn't anymore."

"What happened?"

"One of the parties was different than I thought it was going to be. That's when I realized my mother was a glorified prostitute, and she was grooming me to be the same."

My stomach turned. It wasn't that far from what had happened at The Sanctuary, just with a different clientele.

"I didn't want the life she had, so I worked hard at school. College was expensive, so I kept waitressing. I didn't date. I didn't go out. I worked and went to school. My mom couldn't understand my motivation; she was far too focused on maintaining the life she'd set up for herself.

"She learned the hard way that beauty is fleeting. The older I got, and she got, the longer the spans of time between the excess and the poverty and the more time we spent living in unfortunate circumstances. It was... difficult."

Based on the way she couldn't seem to look at me, I had to assume unfortunate circumstances meant more than just below the poverty line. I chose my next words carefully.

"I don't get how you ended up at a place like The Dollhouse. It seems counterintuitive."

Sarah huffed out a laugh. "I didn't ever want to rely on someone else to take care of me. When I told my mom I was coming to Chicago, she was upset, but then I guess she realized I'd be in a program with a bunch of wealthy assholes. I don't know if she thought I was going to scope out her next bank account to leech off of, or find one of my own, but she's the one who gave me the name of the club and made the initial contact."

"She sent you there? Why?"

"Because I was making choices she didn't agree with? To sabotage my efforts to become something she couldn't? To show me how easily men will pay for something pretty to play with? I really don't know. I think she honestly believed I would eventually do it her way. What a legacy, right? Anyway, I didn't fully realize what I was signing on for at first, but then it was too late."

"What do you mean? Why didn't you quit and go somewhere else? Do something different?"

"The money was stupid, and I needed it to pay the debt I already had from undergrad. I don't know. Maybe part of me still believes I don't deserve what I'm working for, like you believe you're responsible for everyone else's bad choices. Plus, then you started sitting in my section all the time. After that it wasn't so bad anymore."

"Don't tell me you stayed because of me."

"I stayed because the money was better than it would've been anywhere else, and waitressing there was still a preferable alternative to what my mother wanted me to do. It was kind of like a middle finger to her. And it's a helpful reminder of what my life could look like if I don't make better choices than she did."

"That's a shitty lesson to torture yourself with."

"It was stupid. I see that now, especially with how much I put myself and my potential future at risk. But I met you, so that's something good out of something bad."

"I'm the best of the worst."

"That's not true. You've never pretended to be anything you're not, Chris." She gestured to the ink on my arm. "You aren't hiding behind a false exterior. Those men my mother dated looked so nice, but they were all screwing someone over, lying all the time. They promised my mother the world, and then they left her behind. I'm not saying she didn't deserve it, but they were complicit in the decision to be unfaithful. They spent money on someone they didn't love, had sex with someone they weren't married to because she'd do things—or let them do things—their wives wouldn't. And probably because they could get away with it. I never want to end up with someone like that."

"That's not every suit-wearing guy, though."

"It's more of them than you'd think." She traced a line of ink on my arm. "I could put you in a suit, but it wouldn't change what I know about you. You work hard to take care of the people you love. You're loyal, and you're as beautiful on the inside as you are on the outside. That's why I want to be with you, and that won't change, no matter what else about my life does."

I caught her hand and brought it to my lips. "If there's anything I've learned, it's to appreciate the good things I have while I have them, and that includes you."

Sarah dragged the hand I was holding to my chest and pressed her palm there. "Then let me in, and let me stay there."

"If you're sure that's what you want…"

"It is. You are."

I placed my hand over hers. "You've been in there for a long time already; you just didn't realize it."

NINETEEN

CHRIS

Like Sarah said, sometimes good things came out of bad circumstances. At the moment, one of my good things was rushing up the stairs to the apartment so she could drop an armload of my crap and hold the door open for Hayden and me. The other good thing was bringing up the rear of our mattress parade.

"Why the fuck is this thing so goddamn heavy?" Hayden adjusted his grip on the mattress as we continued to climb.

"Maybe you're just weak," I huffed.

"Can you two stop arguing and keep moving? This thing is freaking awkward!" Ivy called from behind Hayden, who was at the back end of the mattress. She carried a box that was definitely too big for her, but she'd insisted on it.

Hayden looked over his shoulder. "We can switch if you want."

"Less bitching and more moving," she shot back.

I imagined he was giving her a look, but I couldn't see past the mattress to know. I was just happy I'd soon be sleeping on this mattress with Sarah, rather than hers. I felt a little bad for Ivy, who'd inherit Sarah's rock of a mattress, but it was still a huge step up for her.

A lot of things could change in a short period of time. The current happenings were a good indicator of that. Today I was moving into Sarah's place, and Ivy was taking the apartment across the hall. She'd decided to train under Lisa at Inked Armor, and she'd worked her final shift at the sports bar a few days ago. Hayden had been surprisingly cool about the whole thing, probably because Lisa was so excited.

Moving in with Sarah halved the rent for both of us, and allowed her some breathing room for the final weeks of her internship. But it wasn't just about smart financial decisions. Not for either of us. Although that might've been the way I'd framed it initially, that was for my own comfort. The truth was that Sarah and I were finally moving forward. Sometimes it took almost losing the things you needed the most to recognize their importance—and to see your own worth. Somehow, Sarah and I had become that thing for each other. And I was done fighting against it.

Sarah had the door propped open when we finally managed to get the mattress around the corner. We'd already moved her bed over to Ivy's apartment, along with half of her furniture.

Telling Mom her plan hadn't been easy for Ivy, and neither had the subsequent guilt trip. For now Mom wasn't talking to either of us. It was hard on Ivy, but I knew it was only a matter of time before Mom needed something from me. And sad or not, Ivy told me she was done being someone else's shield. I hoped I could help keep it that way.

We spent the morning moving my stuff in to Sarah's, and relocating the last of Sarah's extra stuff to Ivy's apartment. There were a few tears from Ivy, partly because it was a big step for her to take, and partly because she wasn't used to having anyone actually take care of her. Once everything was in its new homes, we helped Ivy set up. It didn't take long since she didn't have much. I'd given her most of my kitchen stuff since Sarah already had her own. The pots and pans were a huge step up from what she was used to.

"This is so nice," Ivy said, adjusting the comforter on her new, much bigger bed. "I don't know how I'm going to deal with all the space."

"You'll get used to it." I moved a box of clothes over to the dresser. "You need me to unpack anything else, or are you good for now?"

"I think I'm good. I'm going to put away some clothes, and then I'll head over to the shop to see if Lisa needs me for anything."

Ivy had taken to Lisa, and she was showing a lot of promise beyond setting up appointments and bookkeeping. When she wasn't helping Lisa, sometimes she'd hang out and watch one of us work on a tattoo. I had a feeling she was going to fit in well over the long term, particularly since she didn't take crap from anyone. In the short time she'd been at Inked Armor, she'd quickly become part of the family.

"You can take the day, you know. No one expects you to go in."

"I know, but Jamie's got a big piece scheduled this afternoon, and I wouldn't mind watching for a while. Do you think that'd be okay?"

"He'll be fine with it."

We were still facing some bumps in the road outside of work, but all in all, things were good in Ivy's life. Better than they had been in a long time.

Leaving Ivy to her clothing, I went back to Sarah's to help her unpack the last of my things. The living room was already set up; we'd rearranged my couch until it worked with the rest of Sarah's furniture. She'd refused to part with her ugly armchair, but I could live with that if it meant I got to live with her.

The kitchen was empty when I came in, but low music filtered from down the hall, so I had to assume she was in the bedroom. I stopped in the kitchen to grab a glass of water and noticed a note card propped up, with a selfie of Sarah and Dee lying on the counter beside it. I flipped open the note card; it was from Grant. Dee was out of the hospital, but she wasn't recovering as quickly as he'd hoped. The OD had been hard on her body, compromising her liver function and leaving behind some holes in her memory. I wasn't sure that was so bad, considering how things had gone down for her. Grant had moved her out of the city, hoping the tranquility would help. I resolved to talk to Sarah about planning a visit, once she was through with her internship.

I left the note card where it was and headed to her bedroom, which was now ours. We'd set up the frame of my king bed and put on the mattress, but it was covered in bags of my clothes, and we needed to find the sheets.

I kissed the back of Sarah's neck as she opened a box and looked inside. "I vote as soon as the bed's made we have a naked wrestling match."

She tilted her head, encouraging me to keep up the kissing. "I think that's a fantastic idea, except I'd like to shower first."

I sniffed loudly and wrapped an arm around her waist so she couldn't get away from me. "You smell good to me. We can shower after."

"I've been running up and down the stairs all morning, I'm gross."

"You want to get cleaned up so I can make you dirty again?"

"When you say it like that..." Her sarcasm made me smile.

She wore a pair of cut-off jean shorts and an oversized shirt that slipped conveniently off her shoulder, exposing pale skin now dotted with freckles, thanks to time spent in the sun. I kissed the bare expanse and sucked lightly. "You taste good, too."

"Probably not where it counts," she muttered.

I chuckled. "You looking for full service today, huh?"

"Full service is my favorite."

I pressed my hard-on against her. "Better hurry up then, or you're not gonna make it to the shower before I get you naked." This time I nibbled my way from her shoulder to her ear.

Sarah reached up to hold on to the back of my neck, clearly not interested in stopping. I took advantage and slipped my hand under her shirt, tracing her taut stomach. A tiny moan passed her lips, and she pressed her ass against my hips. But before I could get my hand under her bra, she twisted away and sprinted out of the room.

"Where are you going?"

"To shower!" she called back. "You should come too if you're looking for full service!"

I left all the bags on the bed and pulled my shirt over my head. My basketball shorts hit the living room floor. The shower was already running and Sarah was in the process of getting naked when I entered. I closed the door as she slid her shorts down her legs.

I let out a groan, taking in the toned, curvy expanse of skin. "I get to see this every damn day now."

Sarah's eyes dropped to my cock, which was sticking straight out. "You seem pretty happy about that."

"We both are." I gave my dick a pat.

She opened the curtain and stepped over the rim of the tub, making room for me by backing into the spray. The pipes groaned, the sad stream petering out to a trickle as it ran over her hair and down her chest.

"I'm making it a priority to get this fixed. I don't know why you haven't said anything to Cassie. She'll get it taken care of no problem." I tapped the showerhead. The gentle rainfall picked up for half a second.

"It's not that bad. At least it doesn't feel like my nipples are being pelted with pebbles." Sarah reached around me for the shampoo, grazing my erection with her hip.

"That sounds unpleasant."

"That's how your shower felt. Like machine gun water pellets."

"Now it's just a little tickle." I cupped one of her breasts and circled the tight peak with a finger.

Sarah fumbled the shampoo, and it dropped with a thud, skidding toward the drain.

"I'll get that." I shifted her around so I could retrieve it and ended up level with her crotch. I couldn't pass up the location. I handed her the bottle and grabbed her hips, looking up as I pressed my lips below her navel.

Her lids lowered as she watched me kiss my way down.

"I need to get clean," she murmured, like a warning, but the fingers she ran through my hair didn't pull me away.

I found the bar of soap and ran my palm across it, then slid my fingers between her thighs, rubbing her clit a few times. "Clean enough for me." I cupped my other hand under the spray, then splashed her before I licked her.

This time she pulled on my hair, dragging my head up. "So dirty."

"So tasty," I countered, sucking on the skin above her pelvis. I didn't push it though. I knew Sarah wouldn't enjoy herself nearly as much if she was self-conscious. So while she washed her hair, I washed her body, which proved to be quite distracting to her, likely because I spent a long time on very specific body parts—ones that elicited orgasms. She was pretty well boneless by the time I finished. I gave myself little more than a quick rinse, mostly because there was a good chance I'd need another shower by the time we were done.

I turned off the water and grabbed a towel, drying Sarah while I kissed along her neck to her mouth. "Ready to get sweaty again?"

"Only you get sweaty; I get dewy."

I backed us out of the bathroom, bumping the doorjamb with my shoulder. "Is that right? So does that mean I smell bad, and you smell like a delicate flower?"

"Pretty much. You're about to walk into the wall."

I angled us to the right to correct our course. "You do realize how unnecessary the shower was, right?"

"I feel better about full service when I'm fresh."

"You mean dewy?"

I went for her mouth, and she turned her head away, covering my face with her palm. "Ew!"

"Not ew. I fucking love going down on you. Wanna know what I love the most?"

"Not if you keep calling it dewy."

"You're the one who started that." I walked us sideways into the bedroom. I didn't let go of Sarah as I shoved my bags of clothes on the floor and knocked some boxes off along with them. I spotted the black garbage bag that contained my comforter.

Still kissing her, I snagged it with two fingers. I tore it open and did a half-assed job of tossing it over the mattress before I laid Sarah on top.

"If you weren't so impatient, we could be doing this on a fully made bed," Sarah said.

"Yeah, but then I'd have to wait to do this." I shouldered my way between her legs and dipped down, gliding along her slit with my tongue.

I was rewarded with one of her breathy gasps, so I did it again. Sarah's hand went into my hair, and she lifted her hips, seeking exactly what I wanted to give her. I kept licking at her, soft strokes of tongue that pushed her higher, making her gasps louder and her sweet moans more frequent.

I wasn't in a rush, so I settled in, taking her close to the edge, then backing off enough to keep her there without pushing her over.

"Chris," she groaned my name on my next feather-light stroke.

I lifted my head. "Yeah, baby?"

Her cheeks were flushed a deep pink, along with her lips, because she'd been biting the bottom one, as was typical when she held back the little noises she made when she was close to coming.

"Please," she whispered.

"Please what? Aren't I giving you what you want?" I flicked her clit with my tongue.

Her mouth dropped open, and she propped herself up on an elbow, watching as I did it again.

"Feel good?" I asked.

She nodded and another quiet groan escaped as I kissed her clit, a barely there brush of lips. She flopped back on the bed and huffed, lifting her hips at the same time. I almost laughed, except I knew better than to piss her off.

Sarah could be super serious during sex, and quiet. While I didn't have a problem with either, if we were going to be doing this on a much more regular basis, I figured we could throw in some fun.

"You know, if I'm not doing it right, you can tell me. It won't hurt my feelings."

She tried to give me a look, but I went ahead and gave her a nice long tongue stroke, and her eyes rolled up. Then I slipped in two fingers, because I was pretty much done with foreplay. But not until Sarah came, which happened on the next finger curl combined with a nice, firm lick.

Her legs almost closed on my head, but I brought up my free

arm and held the left one open, just in time to catch the sweetest and probably the loudest moan I'd ever heard from her as it tumbled out of her pretty, sexy mouth. A violent shudder surged through her, and she bucked against my mouth and fingers.

I let her ride it out before I licked a line up the center of her stomach, pausing to suck on each delicate nipple.

"Did I do it right?" I nipped at her chin. "It sounded like maybe I did it right."

Sarah pursed her lips. "Don't make fun of me."

"I'm not making fun." I kissed her softly. "My favorite part about going down on you is watching you come. Just before it happens, you always bite your lip and try to hide in your shoulder, like you're keeping all that sexy to yourself. It's okay to let me know you like what I do to you, for you."

"I know."

"Then you should just let it out."

I traced the contour of her bottom lip, and she opened her mouth, letting me slip my finger inside. She bit down gently, her warm tongue swirling.

Sarah hooked a leg around my waist and released my finger. A small, devilish smile tipped her mouth. "Maybe you need to give me a reason to."

"I thought I just did."

"Here I thought that was a warm up."

"Warm up, huh? That sounds a lot like a challenge."

She was slick and hot, and I groaned at the feel as I settled between her thighs. I rolled my hips, once, twice, a third time. Sarah pulled her leg up until I felt her knee pressing against my ribs.

"You should definitely keep doing that," she breathed.

"What's gonna happen if I don't?"

"Nothing good. Kittens will cry, a unicorn will expire."

"That sounds awful." On the next hip roll I slid down and Sarah let out one of her breathy gasps. Before my brain could catch up with my dick, she put a hand on my lower back and pushed down as she lifted her hips.

The sound that came out of her was half whimper, half sigh. She stared up at me with wide eyes that were anything but innocent as she clamped her legs around my waist and locked her feet. "Stay."

For a second I didn't understand what she meant. Clearly I wasn't going anywhere since all my stuff was now in her apartment. And now didn't seem like the best time to have that conversation anyway, considering our current position. Intense, amazing sensation made my brain slow to process why it felt so damn good.

"Shit." I wasn't wearing a condom.

"Please stay." She held on to my shoulders, and her lips connected with my chin before she sucked my bottom lip.

I closed my eyes, unable to focus the way I needed to because I really didn't want to say no. "Just let me get a condom."

"We don't need a condom. I'm safe. You're safe. Just stay with me. Love me."

It was those last two words that broke me. We'd been circling emotions for a while now. The feelings were there, the walls had come down, but the words were unspoken. I wasn't sure if she was waiting for me to say them or I was waiting for her.

"Isn't that what I always do?" A shiver ran through her as I slid an arm under her. I considered for a few long seconds the ramifications of going without a condom. My first instinct was to panic, but then, we were adults, not kids with no concept of the repercussions. And she was right, we were safe in all the ways that counted. We were each other's and no one else's.

Tilting her hips up farther, I started a slow grind. Sarah matched my rhythm, her nails digging into my back as I picked up speed. Those sweet, sexy moans of hers grew louder the faster I went.

When she came, her eyes stayed on mine and my name was a raspy cry. I didn't falter, just kept going until my own orgasm punched me in the spine. After I came, I rolled us over and pulled Sarah on top of me so I wouldn't crush her.

Her wet hair was a wild, tangled mess in the back, compliments of all the thrusting. Getting a brush through it wasn't going to be easy without another round of conditioner to loosen up the nest.

"Chris."

"Yeah, baby?" I smoothed a hand over the back of her head, to see if that helped.

She rested her chin on my chest. "Thank you."

"For what?"

"For loving me."

"Are we still talking about the sex now?"

She bit her lip. "We don't have to be."

"You telling me how I feel about you?"

"Is that how you feel about me?"

God, the look on her face. I couldn't understand how she could still be so uncertain. Now that I'd come around to her way of seeing things, I was looking to stay as long as I could. "You don't already know the answer to that? Or are you waiting for me to say it so you can?"

She dipped her head and kissed my chest before peeking back up at me. "Tell me why you stayed." It was barely a whisper.

I laughed. Anything to get it out of me first. "Because you asked me to."

She tried to hide her smile. "Why else?"

"Because you love me." Her tiny grin faltered for a second until I continued. "And I love you."

The smile that lit up her face was totally worth backing down for. "I knew that."

I locked my arms around her waist. "You're not gonna say it?"

She pushed up on her arms and took my face between her palms. "I love you."

And then she kissed me so I could feel her love as much as I could hear it and see it.

EPILOGUE

CHRIS

I finished with my last scheduled client early, which meant I had extra time to prepare for my session with Sarah.

Tonight I would give her the present she'd asked for as soon as I moved into her place and we finally owned how we felt about each other. Sarah had also finished her internship today, and her supervisor had offered her a full-time position before she could even walk out the door. The guy she'd be replacing was some douche who kept screwing the interns and secretarial staff. He'd left a lot of half-finished, half-assed projects for her to manage. Finally, with Xander facing deportation and Sarah completing the last of the requirements for her degree, she was clear of the propriety clause.

We had a lot to celebrate, but instead of doing what normal couples did—dinner, or a night out—Sarah wanted a tattoo. The one I'd designed, and redesigned five times since then, was laid out in the private room, along with the ink. It would likely go on her ribs, but we'd decide that together, like we did most things these days.

The small key was symbolic of a lot of things—the unlocking of her future, the doors she had yet to open, the ones she'd already closed—but also a reminder of how we'd shared and unshared the keys to our separate apartments before we'd finally been honest about how we felt and grown brave enough to do life together.

I still had another forty-five minutes before she was due at the shop, so I texted to let her know she could come now if she wanted. When I didn't get a message back right away, I figured I'd go home—I loved that I could call it that now. In the short time we'd been living together, it already felt more that way than any other place I'd ever kept my stuff.

If I was lucky, she'd be in the process of getting ready for the session. Based on the wood I'd been sporting on and off all day—it sprung up quite literally every time I thought about our session—I had a feeling the tattoo was going to be followed by some intense loving. Or preceded, depending on whether or not I could wait until after the session to get my girl naked.

On the way up to the apartment, I stopped to check the mail, mostly because Sarah only did it once a week, and our box kept getting jammed up with flyers and junk mail. Today there were a couple of letters: one from the bank, another from her school, and one that looked like a card.

I'd already bought a suit for her commencement next week. I'd suggested she let her mom know, which she reluctantly had, but then her mom was off on some month-long holiday in Europe with her newest boyfriend, so it hadn't mattered anyway. It made me sad that someone who should be there celebrating with Sarah was too busy with her own bullshit. But sometimes that's how it is. We don't choose our family, but we choose the people we love and let love us back. I finally got that.

In the weeks since Ivy had moved, my mom had finally found the backbone she'd been missing—maybe because she didn't have a shield anymore, or maybe she realized she'd lost all the people who cared about her because she hadn't returned that care without conditions.

Whatever the reason, she'd called me last week to tell me she wanted to make some changes, starting with leaving John, not that there was much to leave at this point. He'd been gone more and more since he'd run into whatever trouble that was. But this made Mom's decision simpler to execute. She could get out while he was away on one of his trips, as long as she didn't back out.

I'd hooked her up with a free lawyer, and we were working on a plan. Life would never be easy for my mother, but if she could stay away from the chaos and the abuse, maybe she and Ivy would have a chance at rebuilding their relationship. So far Ivy had talked to her a couple of times on the phone, with my prompting and supervision, but she wasn't ready to see her. When she was, I'd be there, if she wanted me to.

I let myself into the apartment, half expecting to find Sarah stretched out on the couch, or at the kitchen table working on some project. Papers covered the coffee table in organized piles, but she wasn't in the living room.

I kicked off my shoes and passed the open door to the bathroom. She wasn't there either, so I headed for the bedroom, which was exactly where I found her—with her ass in the air and half her body under the bed. She wore a pair of shorts that did a phenomenal job of hugging her curves.

"This looks like a really awkward new sex position."

A box came shooting out from under the bed. I cringed at the loud bang followed by a shriek. Sarah backed up on all fours and shot me a glare, rubbing the top of her head.

"I didn't mean to startle you." I bent down to pick up the box, and she launched herself at me.

Sarah was pretty graceful most of the time—a side effect of having served drinks while wearing murder heels for so long—but this was no smooth move on her part. She ended up swatting the box out of my hand, and the contents scattered across the floor.

"What's this?" I gestured to the scraps of paper.

"It's nothing!" She scrambled around, trying to collect them.

I dropped into a crouch and picked one up. I recognized the printing as my own, the words BITE ME scrawled on the Post-it. She plucked it from my fingers. Her face was beet red, which meant I now needed to know exactly what else was in that box.

I grabbed a handful of the papers.

"Don't crumple them!" she yelled.

I held them over my head. "Don't try to take them, and I won't."

Sarah plunked down on the floor and gave me a dirty look,

apparently resigned to the fact that I was going to get what I wanted. Which I'd discovered was typically the case since I'd moved in. Sarah was kind of a pushover, but only when it came to me, thankfully.

I sifted through the handful. They were all notes from me. I remembered writing some of them. A few were basic instructions, like EAT ME, or BLEND ME for those times when she'd showed up at my place in the middle of the night, likely to be unfed. Others were a couple of sentences about how she looked when she slept, or how I wished the night had more hours in it.

"Is that whole box full of these?"

She cradled it to her chest protectively. "Yes."

"Are all of those notes from me?"

She nodded. "I usually keep them in the closet, but they got shifted around when you moved in. I thought maybe they'd accidentally gotten thrown out." Her eyes went the kind of glassy I associated with tears as she cuddled the box. "But I found them, so it's okay now."

"So you're hoarding old Post-its? How long have you been doing this?"

"I'm not hoarding." She sifted through the box until she found an old, tattered napkin. It had my cell number on it. I'd left it for her at The Dollhouse the first night I'd met her.

"You kept this?"

She lifted a shoulder. "I kept all of them."

"Why?"

"They were sweet, and you have pretty handwriting." She unfolded a short note. "They made me feel like you cared."

"That's because I did." I stroked her cheek with my thumb. "And I always will."

Sarah climbed into my lap.

"What's going on, sugar?"

She pulled her shirt over her head, revealing a lack of bra. "What does it look like?"

"You don't want to wait until after the tattoo session?"

"I've been waiting for you all day. I think you should love me now so we're not distracted when you're putting that pretty tattoo on me."

"This is why you're the brains behind this operation. So smart." I ran a finger down her side considering how good that tattoo would look beside her left breast, where no one but me would get to appreciate it. "You know, if I put the key right here it might be tough to wear a bra for a few days."

"You sound broken up about that."

"I am. Totally broken up." I cupped her breasts and dipped my head to kiss her nipple.

She arched and sighed. "So that's your motivation for the location? My not being able to wear a bra? And here I thought it was because it would be close to my heart."

"That, too."

"Mmm-hmm." Sarah pulled my shirt over my head. "And maybe because you're the only one who gets to see it?"

"I'm pretty transparent, aren't I?"

"I like you transparent." She picked up a handful of Post-its and sifted through them until she found a few she liked. She stuck a BITE ME to her neck and a KISS ME to her chin, grinning cheekily.

"These are quite useful, aren't they?" I peeled off the paper, letting it flutter to the floor, and followed the directions.

We made love among the reminders of our beginning as we created another new memory that would build our future.

THE END

ABOUT THE AUTHOR

HELENA HUNTING

NYT and USA Today bestselling author of the PUCKED Series, Helena Hunting lives on the outskirts of Toronto with her incredibly tolerant family and two moderately intolerant cats. She's writes contemporary romance ranging from new adult angst to romantic sports comedy.

KEEP READING FOR A PREVIEW OF

CLIPPED WINGS

AVAILABLE NOW!

1

HAYDEN

My head ached. A night of piss-poor sleep had turned the mildly irritating into infuriating. Between the droves of freshmen who had been passing through the shop recently and the naïve girl currently in my chair, I'd had it.

I rubbed my temple to ease the dull throb that had developed over the course of the day. Ten more minutes and I'd be done with the design *if* I could stay focused. I was having difficulty winning the battle, because I was preoccupied. Once I completed the unicorn tattoo, there were no more appointments scheduled and more than an hour before closing. If I was unlucky, I would get stuck with another college brat walk-in who wanted a cartoon character slapped on their skin.

The preferred option was to finish with my client so I could duck across the street to my aunt Cassie's used bookstore and café. Coffee runs to Serendipity had become my new favorite pastime over the last four weeks, ever since Cassie hired the new girl. She was the reason I was so distractible. I hadn't seen her lately even with my increase in caffeine consumption, and I was looking to rectify that, stat.

I swiped a damp cloth over the fresh ink. The girl in my chair had been relatively quiet since I started shading in the outline, which was fine. I wasn't in the mood for idle chitchat. Instead I focused on the hum of the tattoo machines. The sound never bothered me. It soothed, like good music.

It was the superfluous stuff that irked: the inane chatter of teenagers, the nervous tapping of a shoe on the polished hardwood, and on the flat-screen, the loud drone of a newscaster as he spouted off the devastation of the day. The nasal timbre of his voice annoyed the hell out of me. Yet I couldn't stop listening, drawn in by the desire to know that other people's lives sucked more than mine.

"Can you turn that down?" I called to Lisa, our resident bookkeeper and piercer.

"Just a minute." She waved me off but palmed the remote.

The other artists in the shop were also working fixedly on clients. I seemed to be the only one with attention issues. The bell over the door tinkled, saving me from further irritation. Lisa changed the station and heavy rock beats filled the air, the bass vibrating the floor. She turned the volume down to a reasonable level.

Pausing, I glanced over, praying it wasn't another insipid college girl looking to flirt with deviance. The next client would be mine. Then I'd never get to Serendipity before it closed.

Any potential aggravation evaporated the moment I saw Cassie's new employee. She clutched a pile of books to her chest like a shield, her long hair windblown around her face. Her eyes darted away when she caught me looking at her.

Her name was Tenley. I didn't know this because we'd been formally introduced—even though I had spoken to her a few times—but because Cassie imparted the information upon my request. Cassie, fountain of information that she was, also informed me that Tenley came from Arden Hills, Minnesota, and was in a master's program at Northwestern. She didn't act like one of those typical Ivy League type snobs, though. She seemed pretty down to earth based on what little she'd said to me. Which, admittedly, wasn't a whole hell of a lot.

The first time I saw her was almost a month ago. I went over to Serendipity to visit my aunt and buy coffee, which wasn't unusual. However, the new addition to Cassie's store was. She was tucked behind the counter with a textbook on deviant behaviors propped in front of her, so only her eyes showed. She was so immersed in what she was reading that she didn't hear the door chime, signaling my entrance.

I scared her when I asked if Cassie was around as an excuse to get a closer look. Her textbook toppled over and her half-full coffee went down with it, dousing the page in beige liquid. When I offered to help clean it up, she stammered a bunch of nonsense and almost fell off the stool she was sitting on. She was gorgeous, even though her face had turned a vibrant shade of red. Cassie appeared from the back of the store to see what all the commotion was. That put an end to interaction number one.

The next couple of times I went in she was either holed up in the basement sorting through the endless boxes of acquisitions or hidden in the stacks shelving books. Cassie didn't dissuade me when I went to the philosophy section to see if there was anything of interest there, besides this Tenley girl. I found her sitting cross-legged on the floor with a pile of books at her knee, arranging the volumes alphabetically before she shelved them. I was in love with her organizational skills already.

I made a point of clearing my throat to avoid surprising her this time. It didn't help. She gasped, her hand fluttering to her throat as she looked up at me. She was stunning; her dark hair al- most brushed the floor it was so long, her features were delicate, eyes gray-green, framed with thick lashes. Her nose was perfectly straight, her lips full and pink. It didn't look like she was wearing makeup.

"I didn't mean to startle you," I said, because it was true. I was also staring. "I'm Cassie's nephew, Hayden."

Her eyes moved from my feet up, pausing at the ink on my arms, taking it in before lifting higher. She unfolded her long, lean legs and used the shelf for support to pull herself up. She flinched as she did so, like she'd been sitting for a long time and had gotten stiff. She was far shorter than me, all soft curves and slight build.

"You own the tattoo shop across the street," she replied.

"That's right." I nodded to the shelves. "I'm looking for *The Birth of Tragedy.*"

She gave me a curious look and trailed a finger along the spines as she scanned them. "I haven't seen any Nietzsche lately, but if I find a copy I could bring it to you… to Inked Armor, I mean."

I smiled, liking the idea of her in my shop. "Sure. You could stop by even if you don't come across a copy."

"Um… I don't… maybe." Her eyes dropped and she bent to pick up the remaining books on the floor. "I should put these away." Her hair fanned out as she turned away. The scent of vanilla wafted out as she disappeared around the corner, reminding me of cupcakes. Interaction number two was moderately better than interaction number one. I was intrigued, which was unusual for me. Not a lot held my attention.

It was a while before I ran into Tenley again. This time, when I walked into the store, she heard the chime. She was sitting behind the register. There was a sketchbook flipped open in front of her.

Beside her was a stack of books with a plate of cupcakes perched on top. In one hand she held a black Pitt pen. In the other was a cupcake. I had a penchant for that particular dessert item.

I caught her mid-bite; lips parted, teeth sinking into creamy icing. She let out a little moan of appreciation, a sound I might attribute to a particularly satisfying orgasm. At least that was what my imagination did with the noise. Her eyes, which had been closed in a familiar expression of bliss, popped open at the sound of the door. She hastily set the cupcake down, her hand coming up to shield her mouth as she chewed.

"Sounds like it's good."

I grinned as her face went a telling shade of red. Her throat bobbed with a nervous swallow, and she swiped her hand across her mouth, eyes on the counter. I glanced at the open sketchbook. A single feather, rendered in striking detail, covered the page. Fire licked up the side, consuming it, tendrils of smoke drifting up as it floated in the air.

"You're an artist?"

She flipped the book shut, pulling it closer to her. "They're just doodles."

"Pretty detailed doodles if you ask me."

She stored the sketchbook in a drawer under the counter. Her shoulders curled in and she peeked up at me, the hint of a smile appearing.

"Tenley, can I get a hand?" Cassie called from the back of the store.

"Coming!" Her eyes shifted away. "I still haven't found your Nietzsche, but I'm keeping a lookout."

"Thanks for thinking of me."

"It's nothing, really. Feel free to help yourself." She motioned to the plate of cupcakes, then disappeared into the back of the store with a wave.

There was no way I would say no to cupcakes, so I took one and devoured the frosted dessert in three huge bites. It was incredible. I nabbed a Post-it, scribbled a note, and stuck it to the plate.

When it was obvious she wouldn't be back anytime soon, I cut through Serendipity to get coffees from the adjoining café. I came through the store on my way out, but Cassie was at the desk instead of Tenley. I took another cupcake because they were that good.

That was five days ago; hence my impatience with the client under my needle. It looked like I didn't need to worry anymore now that the distraction in question was standing in my shop looking anything but comfortable.

Her nervousness gave me ample opportunity to check her out again. She wore a long-sleeved black shirt and dark jeans. Lean lines gave way to the soft curve of her hips and slender legs, which stopped at a pair of ratty purple Chucks, like she couldn't be bothered to care by the time she got to her shoes. As usual, she was untouched by artifice. I wanted to know if she was hiding anything noteworthy under her clothes. If the way she hovered near the door was any indication of her unease with the environment, she was probably an ink virgin.

"Tenley!" Lisa's excited greeting captured her attention, giving her somewhere safe to look. "Did Cassie tell you I ordered in new jewelry?"

A genuine smile lit Tenley's features as she approached the desk where Lisa sat. It bothered me that she could hardly look my way but she was all cheer and pleasantries with Lisa.

Ironically, every time Lisa went over to Serendipity to get coffees, Tenley always seemed to be available, based on Lisa's recent reports. The two of them appeared to have struck up a friendship. It was easy to understand how that might happen.

Lisa's cotton-candy pink hair and '50s attire never failed to make an impression. She was like sunshine in human form, with a nose ring, a Monroe piercing, and a half-sleeve. June Cleaver fused with a Suicide Girl. Lisa tended to keep a tight circle, which meant it was difficult for her to escape some of the girls from her past. They weren't the best influence. Most of them were still immersed in the world of drugs she'd managed to get free from. A new friend couldn't hurt, and Tenley seemed normal enough, if a little edgy.

Tenley set the books on the counter, the spines facing me. It looked like she found my Nietzsche. I was in for some heavy reading.

"I'm just dropping these off for Hayden."

Tenley didn't look at me when she said my name. I wanted her to. Her sultry voice paired with her smokin' body resulted in immediate discomfort below the waist. It was inconvenient, but unsurprising, considering how attractive I found her, not to mention captivating.

This wasn't the first time she'd stopped by the shop. Cassie had sent her over the day following the cupcake interaction with a couple of books for me. Unfortunately, I'd been busy with a client in the private tattoo room, so I'd missed her. Now that she was here, in my space, I wanted to talk to her. Maybe get her to throw me one of those smiles she had for Lisa. That was probably asking a bit much, though; I didn't exactly exude warmth.

"I'll be done in five if you want to wait," I told her, hoping she'd take the bait.

Tenley's eyes settled on my arms, pausing at the exposed ink.

She never made it above my mouth. Yup, I still made her nervous. She thumbed over her shoulder. "Cassie's expecting me back."

"I'm sure she can live without you for a few minutes."

Tenley looked across the street. Through the windows I could see Cassie sitting behind the register, bent over what was likely end-of-day paperwork. As if to drive my point home, the neon closed sign blinked on. She turned back to Lisa. "I guess I could have a look at the jewelry."

The answer might not have been directed at me, but I would take it. Lisa linked arms with Tenley and guided her to the piercing room before she could change her mind. I watched them disappear through the doorway and resumed my work.

After Tenley's last visit I'd gone over to Serendipity to thank her, but she'd already left for the night. Cassie had promised to relay the message. She'd also told me when Tenley worked next. Not that she'd needed to. I'd memorized Tenley's schedule. I couldn't fathom Cassie setting the poor girl up with someone like me; I'd eat her for breakfast. At that, I imagined what she might look like naked, spread out on my kitchen table. I liked the idea.

Despite the distractions, I finally finished the design for the girl in my chair. It looked as good as it could for what it was. Once complete, I explained the aftercare process, strongly suggesting she stay out of tanning beds for the next few months. She hadn't arrived at the artificial shade of Oompa Loompa orange by simply hanging out in Chicago in late September.

As we chatted, I confirmed my original hypothesis; she was a freshman at the University of Chicago, and it was her first time living away from home. She'd even managed to score a fake ID, which she proudly showed me, like she thought I'd be impressed. I didn't bother to tell her she'd been ripped off, since the card looked like crap. She would find out when she tried to use it.   For the past several weeks my client base had been primarily composed of varying versions of the same girl. It was becoming tedious.

College kids tended to be the most deviant at the beginning of the school year, when their freedom was freshest. Nothing screamed nonconformity more than a rose strategically placed on a tit. I rarely turned anyone away, but it crushed my artistic soul a little every time one of those kids picked a design off the wall and asked me to put it on their body.

Chris, one of my partners, managed to finish with his client before I did. He was already at the register checking out the schedule as I rang up my client and sent her on her way. I waited for the ribbing to start. If nothing else, Chris was predictable in his enjoyment of my irritation.

"That one seemed like a load of fun. She flip you her number?" I didn't respond. Her number was already in the system, and I would never use it for personal purposes. Beyond her unappealing fakeness, we had one rule in the shop that couldn't be broken: Don't fuck clients. Both Chris and I had learned the hard way why it was in poor taste, particularly when we got involved with the same client. Not at the same time, but still.

"We hitting the bar tonight? Or maybe The Dollhouse? I can't remember the last time you came with me," Chris said as he flipped the page in the appointment book to check tomorrow's lineup.

"Depends. You and Lisa coming out?" I called to Jamie, the third partner in our trifecta. Jamie and Lisa had been together since we opened the shop. Where she went, he went.

"Maybe? Ask her when she's done with Tenley," Jamie responded as he worked on his client.

If Lisa was in, The Dollhouse wasn't an option. Lisa wouldn't be interested in watching strung-out, mostly naked women humping poles. Particularly since many of them were her former col- leagues.

But I hated The Dollhouse for other reasons, not the least of which was the people Chris associated with. Damen, the guy we apprenticed under before we opened Inked Armor, hung out there on the regular.

He'd been a colossal prick back then, and nothing had changed since. Ever the entrepreneur, Damen ran a side business, dealing illegal substances. He took advantage of The Dollhouse's close proximity to his tattoo shop to facilitate his second income. The real kicker was that the manager of The Dollhouse, Sienna, encouraged her dancers to indulge in whatever drugs he had available and happily took a cut of the profits. Aside from my disdain for their moral low ground, I had a long history with Sienna, and she liked to remind me of that every time I ran into her. I hadn't seen her in more than a year, and I wanted to keep it that way.

"You all right, man?" Chris asked.

I shrugged him off. "Yeah. I'm fine. Just done with freshman season."

The influx of college kids might have been part of the issue, but they certainly didn't encompass the whole of my problem. Every time Chris suggested a trip to The Dollhouse, I declined. I didn't feel like I owed him an explanation, but it was clear he wanted one. I had no desire to get into it, though, with him or anyone else. Further discussions about where to go were thwarted when the door to the piercing room opened and Lisa stepped out, Tenley following close behind.

"What's the damage?" Chris asked as they approached the counter.

"I'd hardly call it damage." Lisa stepped to the side, bringing Tenley into view.

Chris let out a low whistle. "Very sexy."

I wanted to punch him. Which made no sense. Chris flirted with everything that had boobs. It didn't mean a damn thing, but I still had the irrational urge to lay the beats on him. I slid between Chris and Tenley, cutting off his view to get one of my own. "Let's have a look."

Tenley appeared startled by my interest, so I gave her my best nonthreatening smile. She inhaled sharply as I put a finger under her chin. Sliding my thumb along the edge of her jaw, I turned her head to the side. It felt like there was a current buzzing just beneath the surface of her skin. An electric jolt zipped through my veins and headed south, ending right behind my fly. It took all my reserve to block out the barrage of perverse images invading my mind.

While reveling in the intensity of benign contact, I studied the contours of her face. The tiny diamond stud was artfully placed on the right side of her nose. Her full lips were slightly parted, eyes downcast, making her look particularly subdued. The rapid thud of her pulse told me otherwise.

I was being a dick. She was uncomfortable and I was the cause, but I didn't want to stop touching her. It was fucking weird.

"She picked the one you liked," Lisa said, elbowing me in the ribs.

It was a not-so-covert way of telling me to back off. I ignored her. I swept Tenley's hair over her shoulder. It was as soft as her skin and silky as it slipped through my fingers. The kind of hair I'd like to bury my face in or wrap around my hand. I tucked it behind her ear, exposing a ladder of rings traveling the shell. A minor show of rebellion, which denoted a hidden predilection. Interesting. Maybe she was a closet deviant.

She met my curious stare with a timid one. The uncertainty there flared to life and she took a step back, severing our contact. A slight tremor passed through her. If I hadn't been paying such close attention, I never would have caught it. Tenley brought her fingers to the place mine had been, confusion marring her other- wise flawless features. I'd made an impact. It made her all the more intriguing.

"I should probably get back."

"Already?" That was a disappointment. I tapped the books sitting in a neat pile on the counter. "Tell Cassie I appreciate her letting you bring these by for me."

I would personally thank Cassie the next time I saw her and dig for more information on this girl. There was something about her I liked, beyond the fact that she was gorgeous and clearly into steel.

"It's not a problem." Tenley edged toward the door and away from me. "What do I owe you?" she asked Lisa.

Before Lisa could reply, I cut in, "Don't worry about it. This one's on the house as long as you promise to come by again."

Chris coughed.

"But it wasn't just the—"

Lisa cut her off. "It's cool. We can work it out next time. I'll stop by Serendipity tomorrow."

"Okay." Tenley nodded, her face fiery as she looked anywhere but at me.

That sucked. Apparently I'd overstepped my boundaries more than usual. She said a hasty good-bye and rushed out of the shop, almost tripping on the curb when she crossed the street. We all stood there, staring at the door after she left. Well, I stood there staring at the door while everyone else stared at me.

Lisa was the first one to break the silence. She punched me in the shoulder.

"Ow. What was that for?"

"Are you serious? What the hell is wrong with you?"

I gave her my best bewildered look. I probably came off a little too... me. But Tenley was hot and I found her intriguing. Maybe it was because she seemed so damn uncomfortable around me and completely at ease with Chris and Lisa. Maybe it was the hint of rebellion hidden beneath that hair. I still planned to corner her again and attempt a real conversation. One that consisted of more than a couple of sentences.

"Dude. You have a problem." Chris scoffed and hid a grin with his fist. I wanted to knock it off his face.

"What's the deal?" I asked, looking back and forth between him and Lisa. I understood I might have breached the whole personal space continuum, but other than that I couldn't see a horrific social faux pas.

Chris pointed at my crotch and snickered. I looked down. Huh. My brain wasn't the only part of me that found Tenley enthralling. I seriously hoped she hadn't noticed, because my shirt didn't come close to camouflaging the issue.

"That's just disturbing." Lisa covered her eyes with her hands. "You need to get a handle on yourself."

"It's probably better if I wait until I get home." The masturbation joke wasn't appropriate, but I was deflecting.

Lisa ignored my attempt at juvenile humor. "She wants a tattoo, you know."

"Oh? Where? What kind of design?" Chris was way too interested.

I pointed a finger right in his face. "You're not touching her. So don't even think about it."

My territorialism was unwarranted. We took clients based on our skill sets. Chris specialized in lettering and tribal art, Jamie had a talent for portrait pieces, and I ran the gamut from dark and sinister to light and feminine. Whatever body art Tenley wanted could fit any one of our strengths.

"Have you seen the design?" I asked.

"No. But I almost convinced her to bring it by so you could have a look. Then you ruined it when you got all up in her space and tried to dry hump her."

"I didn't try to dry hump her."

"You would have if there hadn't been witnesses present."

It was hard to argue, given my current issue. "I wasn't intentionally a dick."

"I'll see Tenley tomorrow and do damage control. If I can get her to agree to bring the design over, you have to promise you'll keep your hands to yourself."

"You do realize that won't be possible if I'm putting ink on her, right?"

"I'm serious."

"So am I."

Lisa shook her head. "I don't know why I even bother with you. It's like herding a cat."

I laughed. She wasn't wrong. When it came to walking the line, I didn't have much patience. People stuck to social codes because they worried about what other people might think. I didn't give a shit. Mostly. There were a select few whose opinions impacted my decisions. Aunt Cassie's was one, and Lisa's was another. For that reason I would try to be on my best behavior where Tenley was concerned, but I couldn't guarantee I'd be successful.